THE
ARTHUR RACKHAM
FAIRY BOOK

THE ARTHUR RACKHAM FAIRY BOOK

A· BOOK· OF· OLD· FAVOURITES
WITH· NEW· ILLUSTRATIONS

CHANCELLOR PRESS

First published in Great Britain in 1933 by
George G. Harrap & Co. Ltd

This new arrangement published in 1986 by
Chancellor Press
59 Grosvenor Street
London W1

ISBN 1 85152 019 8

Printed in Czechoslovakia
50609

ILLUSTRATOR'S PREFACE

For this book I have gone to those old favourites of the nursery that have such a hold on our affections that their incidents, characters, and even phrases have become part of our everyday thought and expression, and help to shape our lives. There's no doubt that we should be behaving ourselves very differently if Beauty had never been united to her Beast, or Sir Richard Whittington listened to the bells. Or if Sister Anne hadn't seen anybody coming; or if "Open Sesame!" hadn't cleared the way, or Sindbad sailed.

It is convenient to call them all fairy-tales, though some have very little of the magical or even fantastic about them. Most of them had a long and eventful life of oral tradition before somebody who could write caught them as they flew and consigned them to cold print. And even then they have often since been embroidered or trimmed to suit the special circumstances of their telling. Others have been so beautifully told and so mingled with the story-teller's own creations that no one yet has wished to improve or edit a single word. Of such are Andersen's. The traditional English tales, like Jack the Giant-killer, too often unfortunately fared rather badly, falling into uninspired hands when first written down, yet in other respects they compare well with the best. Now and then some one-time famous story drops out. It is true, for instance, that the purse of Fortunatus is still a household word; but his own history is no longer current, and I felt that he and his "old gentleman called Loch-Fitty, who was a native of Scotland," might be left out of my list. How different from Shacabac's generous but eccentric "old gentleman" named Barmecide! If descendants of that honoured family no longer survive, so much the worse for Bagdad.

And now, in our own day, inspired story-tellers go on adding original characters to the stock—an Alice, a Peter Pan, and a Mr Toad. It is impossible not to believe that in time even these exalted personages will gather legends round their beloved heads, for surely they are too full of life not to grow. Yet another sort of story is still coming to perfection in the development of the not unfamiliar kind of folk-tale, often of mainly antiquarian or ethnological interest, but so glorified in the very manner of its retelling as to rank as great literary creation. One can hardly conceive of Brer Rabbit's adventures in any other words than those of our revered Uncle Remus.

In the Contents the main source of each story is given when possible, though some came to us from more countries than one, and the versions that we are most attached to are ' varieties,' as a gardener would call them, produced by our own soil and climate.

The illustrations are new and have never been published before, though in the case of several of the stories this is not the first time that it has fallen to my lot to illustrate them, in the thirty years and more that my work has led me through enchanted lands.

A. R.

CONTENTS

ILLUSTRATIONS

ILLUSTRATIONS IN COLOUR

ILLUSTRATIONS IN THE TEXT

ILLUSTRATIONS

DICK WHITTINGTON

IN the reign of King Edward III there lived in Somersetshire a boy called Dick Whittington, whose father and mother had died when he was very young. The people where he lived were very poor, and he had very little to eat, but he heard talk about the great city of London, which they said was so rich and fine that all the folks there were great ladies and gentlemen, and that the streets were all paved with gold. And as he grew older he made up his mind that he would somehow manage to go to London, where he could make his fortune. One day there drove through the village a large wagon with a team of horses on its way to London. So he took courage and begged the wagoner to let him come too. The wagoner was moved to pity when he heard how badly off poor Dick was, so he told him he might come if he liked, and they set off together.

When he reached London he said good-bye to the wagoner, who gave him a groat on parting, and with this as his sole possession Dick wandered here and there, wondering what he should try to do next, and bitterly disappointed to find that in the streets that he had expected to be paved with gold he found nothing but mud and dirt.

After he had spent the little he had and had gone hungry for two days he sat down to rest on the doorstep of a merchant's house in Leadenhall Street. Soon the cook, who was exceedingly bad-tempered, saw him, and threatened to kick him from the door.

Just then the master of the house, Mr Fitzwarren, came home from the Royal Exchange. When he noticed the boy there he asked him what he wanted, and then told him that he must go away at once. Dick tried to do so, but was so faint from want of food that he fell down again when he tried to stand. Then he told Mr Fitzwarren that he was a poor boy from the country, and that he would do any work that was given him, if only to get some food. The merchant

felt sorry for him, and as he happened to want a boy to help in the kitchen he ordered one of his servants to take him in, saying what work he should be given to do. Then a good meal was set before Dick, and you may be sure that he was very glad to see it.

But all was not by any means easy and pleasant for him. The servants made him a laughing-stock, and the bad-tempered cook ordered him to do innumerable jobs in the kitchen, threatening to break his head with her ladle if he did not do them quickly enough.

Still, he got enough to eat now, and that was a change. And Miss Alice, his master's daughter, seeing him in the kitchen, found some old clothes for him that were better than

his poor rags, and gave orders to the cook and the other servants that he was to be treated kindly.

So it was decided that he should stay, and a bed was made up for him in the garret.

But he found that the rats and mice in the garret were almost as troublesome by night as the cook was by day. They ran over Dick Whittington's face, and disturbed him so with their squeaking and scratching that he was almost tempted to run away once more.

Soon after a merchant came to dinner, and as it came on to rain very hard he was invited to stay the night. In the

morning Dick cleaned his shoes, and when he took them to
the merchant he was given a penny for his trouble. A little
later, as he was going on an errand, he saw a woman with a
cat under her arm. He asked her if she would sell it. She
said that as it was a fine mouser she would not take less than

sixpence. But when Dick replied that a penny was all he had
the woman let him have the cat.

He took the cat home, and hid her in his garret all day, for
he was afraid that the cook would kill her if she was found in
the kitchen. He always saved scraps from his dinner to take
up to her, and at night she worked so well for her living that
Whittington was troubled no more with rats and mice.

Now whenever the merchant, Mr Fitzwarren, sent out a
ship it was his custom to call all his servants and ask them to

venture something of their own in it. As he was now sending out a ship everybody but Whittington came, and brought what they could for it. Miss Alice noticed his absence, and ordered him to be called, but he tried to excuse himself, saying that all he could call his own was a poor cat which he had bought for a penny that had been given him for cleaning shoes. When Miss Alice heard this she offered to put something in the ship for him, but her father told her that it was the custom for everybody to venture something of his own. He therefore told Whittington to bring his cat. This he did very unwillingly, for he was parting with his best friend. He had tears in his eyes as he gave it to the master of the ship, the *Unicorn*, which immediately started off down the river on her voyage.

After this the cook often made fun of Whittington's venture, and altogether she scolded and harassed him so much that at last he made up his mind to run away rather than be so tormented any longer. He packed up his bundle, and early the next morning got up with the idea of going away into the country. He went through Moorfields, and in time he reached Holloway, where he sat down at the top of the hill to rest on a stone, which to this day is called "Whittington's Stone." As he sat there he could hear Bow Bells ringing merrily. It seemed that they were speaking to him, and saying:

"Turn again, Whittington,
Thrice Lord Mayor of London."

That seemed to him to be such a grand idea that he decided that he had better not run away after all. As it was yet early he thought that he might reach home before his absence was noticed. And so it happened. And he was able to creep quickly in and start doing his usual work without being seen by anybody.

While all this was going on the ship in which Whittington's cat had been taken, after having been buffeted by contrary winds, had sought shelter on the coast of Barbary. The inhabitants of this region were Moors, and they were quite unknown to the English. As they seemed disposed to be friendly, however, the ship's captain determined to trade with them. He brought all his wares on deck and displayed them

so that the Moors could see what he had. They were so pleased with the goods that news was carried to the King, who sent for samples, and afterwards invited the master to come to the palace.

As was the custom in that country, everybody sat on the floor, which was covered with rich carpets. Upon these various dishes were laid, and the appetizing odour soon attracted a great number of rats and mice, who quickly ate all that they could see. The captain, in great astonishment, asked some of the people if they did not object to the presence of such vermin.

"Yes," was the answer, "we dislike them extremely. His Majesty would willingly give half of what he possesses to get rid of them." The captain then thought of Whittington's cat, and he lost no time in telling the King that he had in his ship an animal which would quickly destroy these pests.

This was welcome news to the King, and he desired to see this wonderful animal at once, saying, "If this is so and you will let me have it I will fill your ship with precious gems."

The master replied, "She is indeed the most wonderful creature in the world, but I cannot spare her, for she keeps the ship clear of rats and mice, and so prevents my goods from being destroyed."

The King, however, would not hear of any objection, saying that he was willing to pay any price for such a precious animal.

Accordingly the cat was brought, and when the dishes were spread on the floor the rats and mice scurried in as before. The cat, however, made short work of them, and came purring to the King, as if asking for a reward. Naturally he admired her greatly, and gave ten times more for her than for all the freight besides.

The ship then set sail with a fair wind for England, and arrived safely at Blackwall. Taking the casket of jewels with him, the master presented his bill of lading to Mr Fitzwarren, who naturally rejoiced in so prosperous a voyage.

When he assembled all his servants to give each the portion that belonged to him the master showed him the casket of gems, and told him that this was all for Whittington's cat. Mr Fitzwarren immediately sent for Whittington, who was in the kitchen washing pots and pans. When, after some hesitation, he came in the merchant ordered a chair to be

placed for him. Poor Dick, thinking that they were all laughing at him, knelt before his master, and with tears in his eyes asked him not to make a game of a poor fellow who meant nobody any harm.

Mr Fitzwarren, helping him to his feet, addressed him as "Mr Whittington," and said, "We are very much in earnest.

At the present moment you are a richer man than I am." Then he gave him the casket, the value of which amounted to three hundred thousand pounds.

When he could be induced to believe that all this was really true Whittington turned to his master, and laid his wealth at his feet, but Mr Fitzwarren said, "No, Mr Whittington, I could not dream of taking even the smallest portion from you. May it bring you much happiness!"

Whittington then turned to Miss Alice, but she would not

take anything either, so he gave shares to his fellow-servants, not even forgetting his old enemy the cook, and he rewarded handsomely all the ship's crew.

Then he was given clothes in keeping with his new position, and as he was now dressed he was seen to be a very presentable young man; so much so that Miss Alice began to look at him with favour. Her father, seeing this, thought that it would be a good idea to arrange a match between them.

This was soon settled, and the Lord Mayor and Aldermen were invited to the wedding.

At the conclusion of the honeymoon Mr Fitzwarren asked his son-in-law what occupation he would wish to choose. Whittington replied without hesitation that he would like to be a merchant. As a result they entered into partnership, and both became extremely wealthy.

All this good fortune did not make Richard Whittington proud or overbearing. Indeed, he was such good company that all took delight in being with him, and he was particularly kind to the poor. In the year 1393 he was made Sheriff of the City of London, during the time that Sir John Hadley was Lord Mayor.

Four years later he was chosen as Lord Mayor himself, and received the honour of knighthood from the King. And he filled the duties of that office with such prudence and distinction that on two later occasions he was chosen for the same office.

In the last year it fell to his lot to entertain King Henry V after he had returned from his conquests in France. The King and Queen were feasted at the Guildhall so splendidly that the King said, "Never had prince such a subject!" To which Whittington replied, "Never had subject such a prince!"

Till the year 1780 the figure of Sir Richard Whittington with his cat in his arms might be seen carved in stone over the archway that spanned the street by the old prison of Newgate.

HOP-O'-MY-THUMB

THERE once lived in a village a faggot-maker and his wife, who had seven children, all boys, the eldest no more than ten years old, and the youngest only seven. It was odd enough, to be sure, that they should have so many children in such a short time; but the truth is the wife usually brought him two or three at a time. This made him very poor, for not one of these boys was old enough to get a living; and, what was still worse, the youngest was a puny little fellow who hardly ever spoke a word. Now this, indeed, was a mark of his good sense, but it made his father and mother suppose him to be silly, and they thought that at last he would turn out quite a fool. This boy was the smallest ever seen; for when he was born he was no bigger than a man's thumb, which made him be christened by the name of Hop-o'-my-thumb. The poor child was the drudge of the whole house, and always bore the blame of everything that was done wrong. For all this, Hop-o'-my-thumb was far more clever than any of his brothers; and though he spoke but little he heard and knew more than people thought. It happened just at this time that for want of rain the fields had grown but

24

half as much corn and potatoes as they used to grow, so that the faggot-maker and his wife could not give the boys the food they had before, which was always either bread or potatoes.

After the father and mother had grieved some time they thought that as they could contrive no other way to live they must somehow get rid of their children. One night, when the boys were gone to bed and the faggot-maker and his wife were sitting over a few lighted sticks to warm themselves, the husband sighed deeply, and said, "You see, my dear, we cannot maintain our children any longer, and to see them die of hunger before my eyes I cannot bear. Therefore to-morrow morning I will take them to the forest, and leave them in the thickest part of it, so that they will not be able to find their way back. This will be very easy; for while they amuse themselves with tying up the faggots we need only slip away when they are looking some other way."

"Ah, husband," cried the poor wife, "you surely can never consent to be the death of your own children."

The husband in vain told her to think how very poor they were.

The wife replied that if she was poor she was still their mother; and then she cried as if her heart would break. At last she thought how shocking it would be to see them starved to death before their eyes; so she agreed to what her husband had said, and then went sobbing to bed.

Hop-o'-my-thumb had been awake all the time; and when he heard his father talk very seriously he slipped away from his brothers' side, and crept under his father's bed, to hear all that was said without being seen.

When his father and mother had left off talking he got back to his own place, and passed the night in thinking what he should do the next morning.

He rose early and ran to the river's side, where he filled his pockets with small white pebbles, and then went back home.

In the morning they all set out, as their father and mother had arranged; and Hop-o'-my-thumb did not say a word to any of his brothers about what he had heard. They came to a forest that was so very thick that they could not see each other a few yards off. The faggot-maker set to work cutting down wood; and the children began to gather the twigs, to make faggots of them.

When the father and mother saw that the young ones were all very busy they slipped away without being seen. The children soon found themselves alone, and began to cry as loud as they could. Hop-o'-my-thumb let them cry on, for he knew well enough how to lead them safe home, as he had taken care to drop the white pebbles he had in his pocket along all the way he had come. He only said to them, "Never mind, my lads. Father and Mother have left us here by ourselves, but follow me, and I will lead you back again."

When they heard this they left off crying, and followed Hop-o'-my-thumb, who soon brought them to their father's house by the very same path which they had come along. At first they had not the courage to go in; but stood at the door to hear what their parents were talking about. Just as the faggot-maker and his wife had come home without their children a great gentleman of the village sent to pay them two guineas for work they had done for him, which he had owed them so long that they had given up all hopes of ever getting a farthing of it. This money made them quite happy; for the poor creatures were very hungry, and had no other way of getting anything to eat.

The faggot-maker sent his wife out immediately to buy some meat; and as it was a long time since she had made a hearty meal she bought as much meat as would have been enough for six or eight persons. The truth was when she was thinking what would be enough for dinner she forgot that her children were not at home; but as soon as she and her husband had done eating she cried out, "Alas, where are

our poor children? How they would feast on what we have left! It was all your fault, husband! I told you we should repent leaving them to starve in the forest! Perhaps they have already been eaten by the hungry wolves!" The poor woman shed plenty of tears: "Alas! alas!" said she, over and over again, "what is become of my dear children?"

The children, who were all at the door, cried out together, "Here we are, Mother, here we are!"

She flew like lightning to let them in, and kissed every one of them.

The faggot-maker and his wife were charmed at having their children once more with them, and their joy lasted till their money was all spent, when they found themselves quite as badly off as before. So by degrees they again thought of leaving them in the forest; and that the young ones might not come back a second time they said they would take them a great deal farther than they did at first. They could not talk about this matter so secretly but Hop-o'-my-thumb found means to hear all that passed between them; but he cared very little about it, for he thought it would be easy for him to do just the same as he had done before. But though he got up very early the next morning to go to the river's side to get the pebbles, a thing which he had not thought of hindered him, for he found that the house door was double-locked. Hop-o'-my-thumb was now quite at a loss what to do; but soon after this his mother gave each of the children a piece of bread for breakfast. Then it came into his head that he could make his share do as well as the pebbles, by dropping crumbs of it all the way he went. So he did not eat his piece, but put it into his pocket.

It was not long before they all set out, and their parents took care to lead them into the very thickest and darkest part of the forest. They then slipped away by a by-path as before, and left the children by themselves again. All this did not give Hop-o'-my-thumb any concern, for he thought himself

quite sure of getting back by means of the crumbs that he had dropped by the way; but when he came to look for them he found that not a crumb was left, for the birds had eaten them all up.

The poor children were now sadly off, for the farther they went the harder it was for them to get out of the forest. At last night came on, and the noise of the wind among the trees seemed to them like the howling of wolves, so that every moment they thought they would be eaten up. They hardly dared to speak a word, or to move a limb, for fear. Soon after there came a heavy rain, which wetted them to the very skin, and made the ground so slippery that they fell down almost at every step, and got dirty all over.

Before it was quite dark Hop-o'-my-thumb climbed up to the top of a tree, and looked round on all sides to see if he could find any way of getting help. He saw a small light, like that of a candle, but it was a very great way off, and beyond the forest. He then came down from the tree, to try to find the way to it; but he could not see it when he was on the ground, and he was in the utmost trouble what to do next. They walked on towards the place where he had seen the light, and at last reached the end of the forest, and got sight of it again. They now walked faster; and after being much tired and vexed (for every time they got into lower ground they lost sight of the light) came to the house it was in. They knocked at the door, which was opened by a very good-natured-looking lady, who asked what brought them there. Hop-o'-my-thumb told her that they were poor children who had lost their way in the forest, and begged that she would give them a bed till morning. When the lady saw that they had such pretty faces she began to shed tears, and said, "Ah, my poor children, you do not know what you are come to. This is the house of an Ogre, who eats up little boys and girls."

"Alas, madam," replied Hop-o'-my-thumb, who trembled

from head to foot, "what shall we do? If we go back to the forest we are sure of being torn to pieces by the wolves; we would rather, therefore, be eaten by the gentleman: besides, when he sees us perhaps he may take pity on us and spare our lives."

The Ogre's wife thought she could contrive to hide them from her husband till morning, so she let them go in and warm themselves by a good fire, before which there was a whole sheep roasting for the Ogre's supper. When they had stood a short time by the fire there came a loud knocking at the door: this was the Ogre come home. His wife hurried the children under the bed, and told them to lie still, and she then let her husband in.

The Ogre asked if supper were ready, and if the wine were fetched from the cellar; and then he sat down at the table. The sheep was not quite done, but he liked it much better half raw. In a minute or two the Ogre began to sniff, saying that he smelt child's flesh.

"It must be this calf which has just been killed," said his wife.

"I smell child's flesh, I tell thee once more," cried the Ogre, looking all about the room. "I smell child's flesh; there is something going on that I do not know of."

As soon as he had spoken these words he rose from his chair and went towards the bed.

"Ah, madam," said he, "you thought to cheat me, did you? Wretch! Thou art old and tough thyself, or else I would eat thee up too! But come, come, this is lucky enough, for the brats will make a nice dish for three friends who are to dine with me to-morrow."

He then drew the children out one by one from under the bed. They fell on their knees, and begged his pardon as humbly as they could; but this Ogre was the most cruel of all Ogres, and, instead of feeling any pity, he only began to think how sweet and tender their flesh would be; so he told his wife they would be nice morsels, if she served them up with plenty of sauce. He then fetched a large knife, and began to sharpen it on a long whetstone that he held in his left hand; and all the while he came nearer and nearer to the bed. The Ogre took up one of the children, and was going to set about cutting him to pieces; but his wife said to him, "What in the world makes you take the trouble of killing them to-night? Will it not be time enough to-morrow morning?"

"Hold your prating!" replied the Ogre. "They will grow tender by being kept a little while after they are killed."

"But," said his wife, "you have got so much meat in the house already; here is a calf, two sheep, and half a pig."

"True," said the Ogre; "so give them all a good supper, that they may not get lean, and then send them to bed."

The good creature was quite glad of this. She gave them plenty for their supper, but the poor children were so terrified that they could not eat a bit.

The Ogre sat down to his wine, very much pleased with the thought of giving his friends such a dainty dish: this made him drink rather more than common, and he was soon obliged to go to bed himself. Now the Ogre had seven daughters, who were all very young like Hop-o'-my-thumb and his brothers. These young Ogresses had fair skins, because they fed on raw meat like their father; but they had small grey eyes, quite round, and sunk in their heads, hooked noses, wide mouths, and very long, sharp teeth standing a great way off each other. They were too young as yet to do much mischief; but they showed that if they lived to be as old as their father they would grow quite as cruel as he was, for they took pleasure already in biting young children, and sucking their blood. The Ogresses had been put to bed very early that night: they were all in one bed, which was very large, and every one of them had a crown of gold on her head. There was another bed of the same size in the

Hop-o'-my-thumb went up to the Ogre softly and pulled off his seven-league boots

room, and in this the Ogre's wife put the seven little boys, and then went to bed herself, along with her husband.

Now Hop-o'-my-thumb was afraid that the Ogre would wake in the night and kill him and his brothers while they were asleep. So he got out of bed in the middle of the night

as softly as he could, took off all his brothers' nightcaps and his own, and crept with them to the bed that the Ogre's daughters were in: he then took off their crowns, and put the nightcaps on their heads instead. Next he put the crowns on his brothers' heads and his own, and got into bed again. He expected, after this, that if the Ogre should come he would take him and his brothers for his own children. Everything turned out as he wished. The Ogre waked soon after midnight, and began to be very sorry that he had put off killing the boys till the morning: so he jumped out of bed, and took hold of his large knife. "Let us see," said he, "what the young rogues are about, and do the business at once!" He then walked softly to the room where they all slept, and went up to the bed the boys were in, who were

all asleep except Hop-o'-my-thumb. He touched their heads one at a time, and, feeling the crowns of gold, said to himself, "Oh, oh! I nearly made a terrible mistake. I must have drunk too much wine last night."

He went next to the bed that his own little Ogresses were in, and when he felt the nightcaps he said, "Ah, here you are, my lads!" And so in a moment he cut the throats of all his daughters.

He was very much pleased when he had done this, and

then went back to his own bed. As soon as Hop-o'-my-thumb heard him snore he awoke his brothers, and told them to put on their clothes quickly and follow him. They stole down softly into the garden, and then jumped from the wall into the road: they ran as fast as their legs could carry them, but were so much afraid all the while that they hardly knew which way to take. When the Ogre waked in the morning he said to his wife, grinning, "My dear, go and dress the young rogues I saw last night."

The wife was quite surprised at hearing her husband speak so kindly, and did not dream of the real meaning of his words. She supposed he wanted her to help them to put on their clothes; so she went upstairs, and the first thing she saw was the seven daughters with their throats cut, and all over blood. This threw her into a fainting-fit. The Ogre was afraid his wife might be too long in doing what he had set her about, so he went himself to help her; but he was as shocked as she had been at the dreadful sight of his bleeding children. "Ah, what have I done?" he cried. "But the little rascals shall pay for it, I warrant them."

He first threw some water on his wife's face; and as soon as she came to herself he said to her, "Bring me quickly my seven-league boots, that I may go and catch the little vipers."

The Ogre then put on these boots, and set out with all speed. He strode over many parts of the country, and at last turned into the very road in which the poor children were. For they had set off towards the faggot-maker's cottage, which they had almost reached. They watched the Ogre stepping from mountain to mountain at one step, and crossing rivers as if they had been tiny brooks. At this Hop-o'-my-thumb thought a little what was to be done, and, spying a hollow place under a large rock, he made his brothers get into it. He then crept in himself, but kept his eye fixed on the Ogre, to see what he would do next.

Seven-league boots are very tiresome to the person who

wears them; so the Ogre now began to think of resting, and happened to sit down on the very rock where the poor children were hid. As he was so tired, and it was a very hot day, he fell asleep, and soon began to snore so loudly that the little fellows were terrified.

When Hop-o'-my-thumb saw this he said to his brothers, "Courage, my lads! Never fear! You have nothing to do but to steal away and get home while the Ogre is fast asleep, and leave me to shift for myself."

The brothers now were very glad to do whatever he told them, and so they soon came to their father's house. In the meantime Hop-o'-my-thumb went up to the Ogre softly, pulled off his seven-league boots very gently, and put them on his own legs: for though the boots were very large, yet, being fairy boots, they could make themselves small enough to fit any leg they pleased.

He then went off as fast as the boots would take him to the Ogre's house again, where he found his wife crying bitterly for the loss of her murdered daughters. Hop-o'-my-thumb then told the Ogre's wife a long tale which he had invented, that the Ogre had been taken by a gang of thieves who had sworn to kill him if he didn't give them all his gold and silver. The good woman was sadly frightened, and was easily persuaded to hand over to him all she had, so that he might take it and ransom the Ogre: for this Ogre, you must know, was a very good husband, though he used to eat up little children. Hop-o'-my-thumb, having thus got all the Ogre's money, came home to his father's house, where he was received with very great joy.

JACK AND THE BEANSTALK

ONCE upon a time there was a poor widow with an only son named Jack, who was a lazy and careless boy who never could be got to do any work. And all they had to live on was the milk they got from their only cow, which they sold in the market. One morning the cow gave no milk, and they didn't know what to do. The widow reproached her son for his idleness, but he could think of nothing better than to try to sell the cow at the next village, teasing her so much that she at last consented. As he was going along he met an old pedlar, who inquired why he was driving the cow from home. Jack replied that he was going to sell it. The pedlar held some curious beans in his hand; they were of various colours, and attracted Jack's attention. This did not pass unnoticed by the man, who asked what was the price of the cow, offering at the same time all the beans in his hand for her. The silly boy could not conceal the pleasure he felt at what he supposed so great an offer; the bargain was struck instantly, and the cow exchanged for a few paltry beans.

When Jack went home and showed his mother the beans

her patience quite forsook her. "There," she cried, "there go your precious beans out of the window!" And she tossed them into the garden. Then she threw her apron over her head and cried bitterly. Jack tried to console her, but in vain, and they both went supperless to bed. Jack woke early in the morning, and, seeing something uncommon darkening the window of his bedchamber, ran downstairs into the garden, where he found some of the beans had taken root and sprung up surprisingly: the stalks were of an immense thickness and had twined together until they appeared to be lost in the clouds. Jack was an adventurous lad; he determined to climb up to the top, and so he set out immediately. After climbing for some hours he reached the top of the beanstalk, quite exhausted. Looking round, he found himself in a strange country, where not a living creature was to be seen anywhere.

Jack walked on, hoping to see a house where he might beg something to eat and drink. He journeyed on till after sunset, when, to his great joy, he espied a large mansion. A kind-looking woman was at the door; he begged that she would give him a morsel of bread and a night's lodging. She said it was quite unusual to see a human being near their house; for it was well known that her husband was a powerful giant, who would never eat anything but human flesh if he could possibly get it; that he would walk fifty miles to procure it, usually being out the whole day for that purpose.

This greatly terrified Jack, but still he hoped to elude the giant, and therefore he again entreated the woman to take him in for one night only and hide him. She at last suffered herself to be persuaded, for she was of a gentle and generous nature, and took him into the house.

She bade Jack sit down, and gave him plenty to eat and drink; and he, not seeing anything to make him uncomfortable, soon forgot his fear, and was just beginning to enjoy himself, when he was startled by a loud knocking at the outer door, which made the whole house shake.

"Ah, that's the giant; and if he sees you he will kill you and me too!" cried the poor woman, trembling all over. "What shall I do?"

"Hide me in the oven," cried Jack. So he crept into the oven—for the fire was not alight—and listened to the giant's loud voice and heavy step as he went into the house.

"Wife!" he cried in a terrible voice, as soon as he had entered. "Wife, what's this I smell?

" Fee-fi-fo-fum,
I smell the blood of an Englishman.
Let him be alive, or let him be dead,
I'll grind his bones to make my bread."

"Nonsense," cried his wife. "No man has passed by here. You must smell the blood of the two calves you have brought in."

At last he seated himself at table, and Jack, peeping through a crevice in the oven, was amazed to see what a quantity of food he devoured. It seemed as if he never would have done eating and drinking; but he did at last, and, leaning back, called to his wife in a voice like thunder: "Bring me my hen!"

She obeyed, and placed upon the table a very beautiful live hen.

"Lay!" roared the giant, and the hen laid immediately an egg of solid gold.

"Lay another!" And every time the giant said this the hen laid a larger egg than before.

He amused himself a long time with his hen, and then sent his wife to bed, while he fell asleep by the fireside, and snored like the roaring of cannon.

As soon as he was asleep Jack crept out of the oven, seized the hen, and ran off with her. He got safely out of the house, and, finding his way along the road he came, reached the top of the beanstalk, which he descended in safety.

His mother was overjoyed to see him. She had feared that he had come to some bad end.

"Not a bit of it, Mother! Look here!" And he showed her the hen. "Now lay," and the hen obeyed him as readily as the giant, and laid as many golden eggs as he desired.

These eggs being sold, Jack and his mother got plenty of money, and for some months lived very happily together, till Jack had another great longing to climb the beanstalk and carry away some more of the giant's riches. He had told his mother of his adventure. He thought of his journey again and again, but still he could not summon resolution enough to break it to his mother, being sure that she would try to prevent his going. However, one day he told her boldly that he must take another journey up the beanstalk; she begged and prayed him not to think of it, and tried all in her power to dissuade him. She told him that the giant's wife would certainly know him again, and that the giant would desire nothing better than to get him into his power, that he might put him to a cruel death, in order to be revenged for the loss of his hen. Jack, finding that all his arguments were useless, ceased speaking, though resolved to go at all events. He had a dress prepared which would disguise him, and something to colour his skin; he thought it impossible for anyone to recollect him in this disguise.

A few mornings after he rose very early, and, unperceived by anyone, climbed the beanstalk a second time. He was greatly fatigued when he reached the top, but pursued his journey to the giant's mansion, which he reached late in the evening; the woman was at the door as before. Jack addressed her, and begged that she would give him food and a night's lodging.

She told him (what he knew before very well) about her husband's being a powerful and cruel giant, and also that she had one night admitted a poor, hungry, friendless boy,

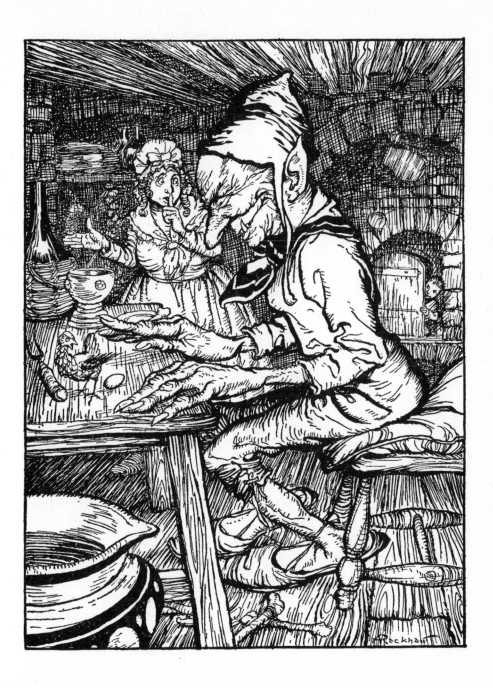

that the ungrateful fellow had stolen one of the giant's treasures, and ever since that her husband had been worse than before. Jack did his best to persuade her to admit him, but found it a very hard task. At last she consented, and took him into the kitchen, and after he had done eating and drinking she hid him in an old lumber-closet. The giant returned at the usual time, and walked in so heavily that the house was shaken to its foundation. He seated himself by the fire, and shouted, "Fee-fi-fo-fum, I smell the blood of an Englishman! Wife, what does this mean?"

The wife replied that it was the crows, which had brought a piece of raw meat, and left it at the top of the house. While supper was preparing the giant was very ill-tempered and impatient, frequently lifting up his hand to strike his wife for not being quick enough.

At last, having ended his supper, he cried, "Give me my money-bags."

She brought them, staggering under the weight: two bags —one filled with new guineas, and the other with new shillings; she emptied them out on the table; and the giant began counting them in great glee. "Now you may go to bed," he said, and his wife crept away.

Jack from his hiding-place watched the counting of the money, and wished it was his own; it would give him much less trouble than going about selling the golden eggs. The giant, little thinking he was so narrowly observed, reckoned it all up, and then replaced it in the two bags, which he tied up very carefully and put beside his chair, with his little dog to guard them. At last he fell asleep as before, and snored so loud that Jack stole out in order to carry off the two bags of money; but just as he laid his hand upon one of them the little dog, which he had not noticed before, started from under the giant's chair and barked most furiously. Too frightened to try to escape, Jack stood still, expecting his enemy to awake every instant. However, to his surprise the giant continued in a sound sleep, and Jack, seeing a piece of meat, threw it to the dog, who at once ceased barking and began to devour it. So Jack carried off the bags, one on each shoulder. Then he climbed down as quickly as he could, and found his mother waiting for him by the beanstalk, overjoyed when he appeared safe and sound.

For three years Jack went no more up the beanstalk, for fear of making his mother unhappy. He did his utmost to conquer the great desire he had for another adventure. Finding, however, that his inclination grew too powerful for him, he began to make secret preparations for his journey. He got ready a new disguise, better and more complete than the former; and when summer came on the longest day he woke as soon as it was light and, without telling his mother, ascended the beanstalk. He arrived at the giant's mansion in the evening, and found the wife standing as usual at the door. Jack had disguised himself so completely that she did not appear to have the least recollection of him; however, when he pleaded hunger and poverty in order to gain admittance he found it very difficult indeed to persuade her. At last he prevailed, and was concealed in the copper. When the giant returned he said furiously, "Fee-fi-fo-fum!" and started up suddenly, and, notwithstanding all his wife could say, he searched all round the room. While this was going on Jack was exceedingly terrified, wishing himself at home a thousand times; but when the giant approached the copper and put his hand upon the lid Jack thought his death was certain. However, nothing happened; for the giant did not take the trouble to lift up the lid, but sat down shortly by the fireside and began to eat his enormous supper. When he had finished he commanded his wife to fetch down his harp. Jack peeped under the copper-lid, and saw a most beautiful harp. The giant placed it on the table, said "Play!" and it played of its own accord, without anybody touching it, the most exquisite music imaginable. The harp lulled him to sleep earlier than usual. As for the wife, she had gone to bed as soon as ever she could.

As soon as he thought all was safe Jack got out of the copper, and, seizing the harp, was eagerly running off with it. But the harp was enchanted, and as soon as it found itself in strange hands it called out loudly, just as if it had been alive, "Master! Master!"

The giant awoke, started up, and saw Jack scampering away as fast as his legs could carry him.

"Oh, you villain! It is you who have robbed me of my hen and my money-bags, and now you are stealing my harp also! Wait till I catch you, and I'll eat you up alive!"

"Very well, try!" shouted Jack, who was not a bit afraid, for he saw the giant was old and could not run very fast, whereas he himself had young legs, and also he had a considerable start of the giant. He was first to reach the top of the beanstalk, and scrambled down, the harp playing all the while the most melancholy music, and crying out, "Master! Master!"

Down climbed Jack as fast as he could, and down climbed the giant after him, but he couldn't catch him. Jack reached the bottom first, and shouted out to his mother, who was at the cottage door, "Mother! Mother! Bring me an axe! Make haste, Mother!" For he knew there was not a moment to spare. However, he was just in time. Jack seized the hatchet and chopped through the beanstalk close to the root; the giant fell headlong into the garden, and was killed on the spot.

So all ended well. Jack and his mother had now plenty of money and nothing to fear. Jack became a gallant gentleman, and married a princess, of course, and, better still, he was a good son to his mother, and made her happy till the end of her days.

As for the wonderful beanstalk, after it had been cut through it withered to the roots, and as no seeds of it had been kept there never was such another grown again.

BEAUTY AND THE BEAST

THERE was once a very rich merchant, who had six children, three boys and three girls, for whose education he very wisely spared no expense. The three daughters were all handsome, but particularly the youngest, who was so very beautiful that in her childhood every one called her Beauty. Being equally lovely when she was grown up, nobody called her by any other name, which made her sisters very jealous of her. This youngest daughter was not only more handsome than her sisters, but also was better tempered. The others were vain of their wealth and position. They gave themselves a thousand airs, and refused to visit other merchants' daughters; nor would they condescend to be seen except with persons of quality. They went every day to balls, plays, and public places, and always made game of their youngest sister, who often spent her leisure in reading or other useful work. As it was well known that these young ladies would have large fortunes many great merchants wished to get them for wives; but the two eldest always answered that, for their parts, they had no thought of marrying anyone below a duke or an earl at least. Beauty had quite as many offers as her sisters, but she always answered, with the greatest civility, that though she was much obliged to her lovers she would rather live some years longer with her father, as she thought herself too young to marry.

It happened that by some unlucky accident the merchant suddenly lost all his fortune, and had nothing left but a small cottage in the country. Upon this he said to his daughters, while the tears ran down his cheeks, "My children, we must now go and dwell in the cottage, and try to get a living by labour, for we have no other means of support."

The two eldest replied that they did not know how to work, and would not leave town, for they had lovers enough who would be glad to marry them, though they had no longer any fortune. But in this they were mistaken, for when the lovers heard what had happened they said that as the girls were so proud and ill-tempered they were not sorry at all to see their pride brought down. They could now show off to their cows and sheep. But everybody pitied poor Beauty, because she was so sweet-tempered and kind to all, and several gentlemen offered to marry her, though she had not a penny; but Beauty still refused, and said she could not think of leaving her poor father in this trouble. At first Beauty could not help sometimes crying in secret for the hardships she was now obliged to suffer; but in a very short time she said to herself, "All the crying in the world will do me no good, so I will try to be happy without a fortune."

When they had removed to their cottage the merchant and his three sons employed themselves in ploughing and sowing the fields and working in the garden. Beauty also did her part, for she rose by four o'clock every morning, lighted the fires, cleaned the house, and got ready the breakfast for the whole family. At first she found all this very hard; but she soon grew quite used to it, and thought it no hardship. Indeed, the work greatly benefited her health, and made her more beautiful still, and when she had done all that was necessary she used to amuse herself with reading, playing her music, or singing while she spun. But her two sisters were at a loss what to do to pass the time away. They had their breakfast in bed, and did not rise till ten o'clock. Then they commonly walked out, but always found themselves very soon tired, when they would often sit down under a shady tree and grieve for the loss of their carriage and fine clothes, and say to each other, "What a mean-spirited, poor, stupid creature our young sister is to be so content with this low way of life!" But their father thought differently, and loved and admired his youngest child more than ever.

After they had lived in this manner about a year the merchant received a letter which informed him that one of his richest ships, which he thought was lost, had just come into port. This news made the two eldest sisters almost mad with joy, for they thought they would now leave the cottage and have all their finery again. When they found that their father must take a journey to the ship the two eldest begged he would not fail to bring them back some new gowns, caps, rings, and all sorts of trinkets. But Beauty asked for nothing; for she thought in herself that all the ship was worth would hardly buy everything her sisters wished for. "Beauty," said the merchant, "how comes it that you ask for nothing? What can I bring you, my child?"

"Since you are so kind as to think of me, dear Father," she answered, "I should be glad if you would bring me a rose, for we have none in our garden."

Now Beauty did not indeed wish for a rose, nor anything else, but she only said this that she might not affront her sisters; otherwise they would have said she wanted her father to praise her for desiring nothing.

The merchant took his leave of them, and set out on his journey; but when he got to the ship some persons went to law with him about the cargo, and after a deal of trouble and several months' delay he started back to his cottage as poor as he had left it. When he was within thirty miles of his home, in spite of the joy he felt at again meeting his children, he could not help thinking of the presents he had promised to bring them, particularly of the rose for Beauty, which, as it was now mid-winter, he could by no means have found for her. It rained hard, and then it began to snow, and before long he had lost his way.

Night came on, and he feared he would die of cold and hunger, or be torn to pieces by the wolves that he heard howling round him. All at once he cast his eyes towards a long avenue, and saw at the end a light, but it seemed a great way off. He made the best of his way towards it, and found that it came from a splendid palace, the windows of which were all blazing with light. It had great bronze gates, standing wide open, and fine courtyards, through which the merchant passed; but not a living soul was to be seen. There were stables too, which his poor, starved horse entered at once, making a good meal of oats and hay. His master then tied him up and walked towards the entrance-hall, but still without seeing a single creature. He went on to a large dining-parlour, where he found a good fire and a table covered with some very appetizing dishes, but only one plate with a knife and fork. As the snow and rain had wetted him to the skin he went up to the fire to dry himself. "I hope," said he, "the master of the house or his servants will excuse me, for it surely will not be long now before I see them." He waited some time, but still nobody came; at last the clock struck eleven, and the merchant, being quite faint for the want of food, helped himself to a chicken and to a few glasses of wine, yet all the time trembling with fear. He sat till the clock struck twelve, and then, taking courage, began to think he might as well look about him, so he opened a door at the end of the hall, and went through it into a very grand room, in which there was a fine bed; and as he was feeling very weary he shut the door, took off his clothes, and got into it.

It was ten o'clock in the morning before he awoke, when he was amazed to see a handsome new suit of clothes laid ready for him, instead of his own, which were all torn and spoiled. "To be sure," said he to himself, "this place belongs to some good fairy who has taken pity on my ill-luck." He looked out of the window, and though far away there were the snow-covered hills and the wintry wood where he had lost himself the night before within the palace grounds, he

He heard a loud noise, and saw coming towards him a beast,
so frightful to look at that he was ready to faint with fear

saw the most charming arbours covered with all kinds of summer flowers blooming in the sunshine. Returning to the hall where he supped, he found a breakfast-table, ready prepared. "Indeed, my good fairy," said the merchant aloud, "I am vastly obliged to you for your kind care of me." He then made a hearty breakfast, took his hat, and was going to the stable to pay his horse a visit; but as he passed under one of the arbours, which was loaded with roses, he thought of what Beauty had asked him to bring back to her, and so he took a bunch of roses to carry home. At that same moment he heard a loud noise, and saw coming towards him a beast, so frightful to look at that he was ready to faint with fear.

"Ungrateful man!" said the Beast in a terrible voice. "I have saved your life by admitting you into my palace, and in return you steal my roses, which I value more than anything I possess. But you shall atone for your fault: you shall die in a quarter of an hour."

The merchant fell on his knees, and, clasping his hands, said, "Sir, I humbly beg your pardon. I did not think it would offend you to gather a rose for one of my daughters, who had entreated me to bring her one home. Do not kill me, my lord!"

"I am not a lord, but a beast," replied the monster. "I hate false compliments, so do not fancy that you can coax me by any such ways. You tell me that you have daughters; now I will suffer you to escape if one of them will come and die in your stead. If not, promise that you will yourself return in three months, to be dealt with as I may choose."

The tender-hearted merchant had no thoughts of letting any one of his daughters die for his sake; but he knew that if he seemed to accept the Beast's terms he should at least have the pleasure of seeing them once again. So he gave his promise, and was told he might then set off as soon as he liked. "But," said the Beast, "I do not wish you to go back empty-handed. Go to the room you slept in, and you will find a chest there; fill it with whatsoever you like best, and I will have it taken to your own house for you."

When the Beast had said this he went away. The good merchant, left to himself, began to consider that as he must die—for he had no thought of breaking a promise, made even to a Beast—he might as well have the comfort of leaving his children provided for. He returned to the room he had slept in, and found there heaps of gold pieces lying about. He filled the chest with them to the very brim, locked it, and, mounting his horse, left the palace and the garden full of flowers as sorrowful as he had been glad when he first beheld it.

The horse took a path across the snowy forest of his own accord, and in a few hours they reached the merchant's house. His children came running to meet him, but, instead of kissing them with joy, he could not help weeping as he looked at them. He held in his hand the bunch of roses, which he gave to Beauty, saying, "Take these roses, Beauty; but little do you think how dear they have cost your poor father." Then he gave them an account of all that he had seen or heard in the palace of the Beast.

The two eldest sisters now began to shed tears, and to lay the blame upon Beauty, who, they said, would be the cause of her father's death. "See," said they, "what happens from the pride of the little wretch. Why did not she ask for such things as we did? But, of course, she could not be like other people, and though she will be the cause of her father's death, yet she does not shed a tear."

"It would be useless," replied Beauty, "for my father shall not die. As the Beast will accept of one of his daughters, I will give myself up, and be only too happy to prove my love for the best of fathers."

"No, sister," said the three brothers with one voice, "that cannot be; we will go in search of this monster, and either he or ourselves shall perish."

"Do not hope to kill him," said the merchant: "his power is far too great. But Beauty's young life shall not be sacrificed. I am old, and cannot expect to live much longer, so I shall but give up a few years of my life, and shall only grieve for the sake of my children."

"Never, Father!" cried Beauty. "If you go back to the palace you cannot hinder my going after you. Though young, I am not overfond of life; and I would much rather be eaten up by the monster than die of grief for your loss."

The merchant in vain tried to reason with Beauty, who still obstinately kept to her purpose, which, in truth, made her two sisters glad, for they were jealous of her because everybody loved her.

The merchant was so grieved at the thought of losing his child that he never once thought of the chest filled with gold; but at night, to his great surprise, he found it standing by his bedside. He said nothing about his riches to his eldest daughters, for he knew very well it would at once make them want to return to town; but he told Beauty his secret, and she then said that while he was away two gentlemen had been on a visit at their cottage, who had fallen in love with her two sisters. She entreated her father to marry them without delay, for she was so sweet-natured she only wished them to be happy.

Three months went by, only too fast, and then the merchant and Beauty got ready to set out for the palace of the Beast. Upon this the two sisters rubbed their eyes with an onion, to make believe they were crying, but both the merchant and his sons cried in earnest. Only Beauty shed no tears. They reached the palace in a very few hours, and the horse, without bidding, went into the same stable as before. The merchant and Beauty walked towards the large hall, where they found a table covered with every dainty, and two plates laid ready. The merchant had very little appetite; but Beauty, that she might the better hide her grief, placed herself at the table, and helped her father. She then began to eat herself, and thought all the time that to be sure the Beast had a mind to fatten her before he ate her up, since he had provided such good cheer for her. When they had done their supper they heard a great noise, and the good old man began to bid his poor child farewell, for he knew it was the Beast coming to them. When Beauty first saw that frightful form she was very much terrified, but tried to hide her fear. The creature walked up to her, and eyed her all over, then asked her in a dreadful voice if she had come quite of her own accord.

"Yes," said Beauty.

"Then you are a good girl, and I am very much obliged to you."

This was such an astonishingly civil answer that Beauty's courage rose; but it sank again when the Beast, addressing the merchant, desired him to leave the palace next morning and never return to it again. "And so good night, merchant. And good night, Beauty."

"Good night, Beast," she answered, as the monster shuffled out of the room.

"Ah, my dear child," said the merchant, kissing his daughter, "I am half dead already at the thought of leaving you with this dreadful Beast; you shall go back and let me stay in your place."

"No," said Beauty boldly, "I will never agree to that; you must go home to-morrow morning."

They then wished each other good night, and went to bed, both of them thinking they should not be able to close their eyes; but they immediately fell into a deep sleep, and did not wake till morning. Beauty dreamt that a lady came up to her, who said, "I am very pleased, Beauty, that you have been willing to give your life to save that of your father. Do not be afraid; you shall not go without a reward."

As soon as Beauty awoke she told her father this dream;

but though it gave him some comfort he was a long time before he could be persuaded to leave the palace. At last Beauty succeeded in getting him safely away.

When her father was out of sight poor Beauty began to weep sorely; still, having naturally a courageous spirit, she soon resolved not to make her sad case still worse by useless sorrow, but to wait and be patient. She walked through the rooms of the palace, and the elegance of every part of it much charmed her.

But what was her surprise when she came to a door on which was written "BEAUTY'S ROOM"! When she opened it her eyes were dazzled by the splendour and taste of the apartment. What made her wonder more than all the rest was a large library filled with books, a harpsichord, and many pieces of music. "The Beast surely does not mean to eat me up immediately," said she, "since he takes care I shall not be at a loss how to amuse myself." She opened the library, and saw these verses written in letters of gold on the back of one of the books:

> Beauteous lady, dry your tears;
> Here's no cause for sighs or fears.
> Command as freely as you may,
> For you command, and I obey.

"Alas," said she, sighing, "I wish I could only command a sight of my poor father, and know what he is doing at this moment." Just then, by chance, she cast her eyes on a looking-glass that stood near her, and in it she saw a picture of her old home, and her father riding mournfully up to the door. Her sisters came out to meet him, and although they tried to look sorry it was easy to see that in their hearts they were very glad. In a short time all this picture disappeared, but it caused Beauty to think that the Beast, besides being very powerful, was also very kind. About the middle of the day she found a table laid ready for her, and sweet music was played all the time she was dining, although she could not see anybody. But at supper, when she was going to seat herself at table, she heard the noise of the Beast, and could not help trembling with fear.

"Beauty," said he, "will you give me leave to see you sup?"

"That is as you please," answered she, very much afraid.

"Not in the least," said the Beast. "You alone command in this place. If you should not like my company you need only say so, and I will leave you this moment. But tell me, Beauty, do you not think me very ugly?"

"Why, yes," said she, "for I cannot tell a falsehood; but then I think you are very good."

"Am I?" sadly replied the Beast. "Yet, besides being ugly, I am also very stupid; I know well enough that I am but a beast."

"Very stupid people," said Beauty, "are never aware of it themselves."

At this kindly speech the Beast looked pleased, and replied, not without an awkward sort of politeness, "Pray do not let me detain you from supper, and be sure that you are well served. All you see is your own, and I should be deeply grieved if you wanted for anything."

"You are very kind—so kind that I almost forgot you are so ugly," said Beauty earnestly.

"Ah, yes!" answered the Beast with a great sigh. "I hope I am good-tempered, but still I am only a monster."

"There is many a monster who wears the form of a man. It is better of the two to have the heart of a man and the form of a monster."

"I would thank you, Beauty, for this speech, but I am too stupid to say anything that would please you," returned the Beast in a melancholy voice; and altogether he seemed so gentle and so unhappy that Beauty, who had the tenderest heart in the world, felt her fear of him gradually vanish.

She ate her supper with a good appetite, and talked in her

own sensible and charming way, till at last, when the Beast rose to depart, he terrified her more than ever by saying abruptly, in his gruff voice, "Beauty, will you marry me?"

Now Beauty, frightened as she was, would speak only the exact truth: her father had told her that the Beast liked only to have the truth spoken to him. So she answered in a very firm tone, "No, Beast."

He did not go into a passion, or do anything but sigh deeply and depart.

When Beauty found herself alone she began to feel pity for the poor Beast. "Oh," said she, "what a sad thing it is that he should be so very frightful, since he is so good-tempered!"

Beauty lived three months in this palace very well pleased. The Beast came to see her every night, and talked with her while she supped; and though what he said was not very clever, yet she saw in him every day some new goodness. So, instead of dreading the time of his coming, she soon began continually looking at her watch, to see if it were nine o'clock, for that was the hour when he never failed to visit her. One thing only vexed her, which was that every night before he went away he always made it a rule to ask her if she would be his wife, and seemed very much grieved when she firmly answered, "No." At last, one night, she said to him, "You wound me greatly, Beast, by forcing me to refuse you so often; I wish I could take such a liking to you as to agree to marry you; but I must tell you plainly that I do not think it will ever happen. I shall always be your friend; so try to let that content you."

"I must," sighed the Beast, "for I know well enough how frightful I am; but I love you better than myself. Yet I think I am very lucky in your being pleased to stay with me. Now promise me, Beauty, that you will never leave me."

Beauty would almost have agreed to this, so sorry was she for him but she had that day seen in her magic glass, which

she looked at constantly, that her father was dying of grief
for her sake.

"Alas," she said, "I long so much to see my father that if
you do not give me leave to visit him I shall break my heart."

"I would rather break mine, Beauty," answered the Beast.
"I will send you to your father's cottage: you shall stay
there, and your poor Beast shall die of sorrow."

"No," said Beauty, crying, "I love you too well to be the
cause of your death; I promise to return in a week. You
have shown me that my sisters are married and my brothers
are gone for soldiers, so that my father is left all alone. Let
me stay a week with him."

"You shall find yourself with him to-morrow morning,"
replied the Beast; "but, mind, do not forget your promise.
When you wish to return you have nothing to do but to
put your ring on a table when you go to bed. Good-bye,
Beauty!" The Beast sighed as he said these words, and
Beauty went to bed very sorry to see him so much grieved.
When she awoke in the morning she found herself in her
father's cottage. She rang a bell that was at her bedside, and
a servant entered; but as soon as she saw Beauty the woman
gave a loud shriek, upon which the merchant ran upstairs,
and when he beheld his daughter he ran to her and kissed her
a hundred times. At last Beauty began to remember that
she had brought no clothes with her to put on; but the
servant told her she had just found in the next room a large
chest full of dresses, trimmed all over with gold, and adorned
with precious stones.

Beauty, in her own mind, thanked the Beast for his kindness, and put on the plainest gown she could find among
them all. She then desired the servant to lay the rest aside, for
she intended to give them to her sisters; but as soon as she
had spoken these words the chest was gone out of sight in a
moment. Her father then suggested that perhaps the Beast
chose for her to keep them all for herself; and as soon as he

had said this they saw the chest standing again in the same place. While Beauty was dressing herself a servant brought word to her that her sisters were come with their husbands to pay her a visit. They both lived unhappily with the gentlemen they had married. The husband of the eldest was very handsome, but was so proud of this that he thought of nothing else from morning till night, and did not care a pin for the beauty of his wife. The second had married a man of great learning; but he made no use of it, except to torment and affront all his friends, and his wife more than any of them. The two sisters were ready to burst with spite when they saw Beauty dressed like a princess, and looking so very charming. All the kindness that she showed them was of no use, for they were vexed more than ever when she told them how happy she lived at the palace of the Beast. The spiteful creatures went by themselves into the garden, where they cried to think of her good fortune.

"Why should the little wretch be better off than we?" said they. "We are much handsomer than she is."

"Sister," said the eldest, "a thought has just come into my head: let us try to keep her here longer than the week for which the Beast gave her leave; and then he will be so angry that perhaps when she goes back to him he will eat her up in a moment."

"That is a good idea," answered the other; "but to do this we must pretend to be very kind."

They then went to join her in the cottage, where they showed her so much false love that Beauty could not help crying for joy.

When the week was ended the two sisters began to pretend such grief at the thought of her leaving them that she agreed to stay a week more; but all that time Beauty could not help fretting for the sorrow that she knew her absence would give her poor Beast, for she tenderly loved him, and much wished for his company again. Among all the grand and clever people she saw she found nobody who was half so sensible, so affectionate, so thoughtful, or so kind. The tenth night of her being at the cottage she dreamed she was in the garden of the palace, that the Beast lay dying on a grass-plot, and with his last breath put her in mind of her promise, and laid his death to her forsaking him. Beauty awoke in a great fright, and burst into tears. "Am not I wicked," said she, " to behave so ill to a Beast who has shown me so much kindness? Why do I not marry him? I am sure I should be more happy with him than my sisters are with their husbands. He shall not be wretched any longer on my account, for I should do nothing but blame myself all the rest of my life."

She then rose, put her ring on the table, got into bed again, and soon fell asleep. In the morning she with joy found herself in the palace of the Beast. She dressed herself very carefully, that she might please him the better, and thought she had never known a day pass away so slowly. At last the clock struck nine, but the Beast did not come. Beauty, dreading lest she might truly have caused his death, ran from room to room, calling out, "Beast, dear Beast"; but there was no answer. At last she remembered her dream, rushed to the grass-plot, and there saw him lying apparently dead beside the fountain. Forgetting all his ugliness, she threw herself upon him, and, finding his heart still beating, she fetched some water and sprinkled it over him, weeping and sobbing the while.

The Beast opened his eyes. "You forgot your promise, Beauty, and so I determined to die, for I could not live without you. I have starved myself to death, but I shall die content, since I have seen your face once more."

"No, dear Beast," cried Beauty passionately, "you shall not die; you shall live to be my husband. I thought it was only friendship I felt for you, but now I know it was love."

The moment Beauty had spoken these words the palace was suddenly lighted up, and all kinds of rejoicings were heard around them, none of which she noticed, but continued to hang over her dear Beast with the utmost tenderness. At last, unable to restrain herself, she dropped her head over her hands, covered her eyes, and cried for joy; and when she looked up again the Beast was gone. In his stead she saw at her feet a handsome, graceful young prince, who thanked her with the tenderest expressions for having freed him from enchantment.

"But where is my poor Beast? I only want him, and nobody else," sobbed Beauty.

"I am he," replied the prince. "A wicked fairy condemned me to this form, and forbade me to show that I had any wit or sense till a beautiful lady should consent to marry me. You alone, dearest Beauty, judged me neither by my looks nor by my talents, but by my heart alone. Take it, then, and all that I have besides, for all is yours."

Beauty, full of surprise, but very happy, suffered the prince to lead her to his palace, where she found her father and sisters, who had been brought there by the fairy-lady whom she had seen in a dream the first night she came.

"Beauty," said the fairy, "you have chosen well, and you have your reward, for a true heart is better than either good looks or clever brains. As for you, ladies"—and she turned to the two elder sisters—"I know all your ill-deeds, but I have no worse punishment for you than to see your sister happy. You shall stand as statues at the door of her palace, and when you repent of and have amended your faults you shall become women again. But, to tell you the truth, I very much fear you will remain statues for ever."

HENNY-PENNY

ONE day Henny-Penny was picking up corn in the rick-yard, when—*whack!*—something fell and hit her on the head. "Goodness gracious me!" said Henny-Penny. "The sky's a-going to fall! I must go and tell the King."

So off she goes, and after a bit she met Cocky-Locky. "Good day, Cocky-Locky," says she.

"Good day, Henny-Penny," says Cocky-Locky. "Where are you off to so early?" says he.

"Oh, I'm going to tell the King the sky's a-falling," says Henny-Penny.

"May I come with you?" says Cocky-Locky.

"Certainly," says Henny-Penny.

So Henny-Penny and Cocky-Locky went off together to tell the King the sky was a-falling. They went along and they went along, and after a bit they met Ducky-Daddles.

"Where are you going to, Henny-Penny and Cocky-Locky?" says Ducky-Daddles.

"Oh, we're going to tell the King the sky's a-falling," said Henny-Penny and Cocky-Locky.

"May I come with you?" says Ducky-Daddles.

"Certainly," said Henny-Penny and Cocky-Locky.

So Henny-Penny, Cocky-Locky, and Ducky-Daddles went off together to tell the King the sky was a-falling. And they went along and they went along, and after a bit they met Goosey-Poosey.

"Where are you going to, Henny-Penny, Cocky-Locky, and Ducky-Daddles?" says Goosey-Poosey.

"Oh, we're going to tell the King the sky's a-falling," said Henny-Penny and Cocky-Locky and Ducky-Daddles.

"May I come with you?" said Goosey-Poosey.

"Certainly," said Henny-Penny, Cocky-Locky, and Ducky-Daddles.

So Henny -Penny, Cocky-Locky, Ducky-Daddles, and Goosey-Poosey went off together to tell the King the sky was a-falling. So they went along and they went along, and after a bit they met Turkey-Lurkey.

"Where are you going to, Henny-Penny, Cocky-Locky, Ducky-Daddles, and Goosey-Poosey?" says Turkey-Lurkey.

"Oh, we're going to tell the King the sky's a-falling," said Henny-Penny, Cocky-Locky, Ducky-Daddles, and Goosey-Poosey.

"May I come with you?" said Turkey-Lurkey.

"Certainly," said Henny-Penny, Cocky-Locky, Ducky-Daddles, and Goosey-Poosey.

So Henny-Penny, Cocky-Locky, Ducky-Daddles, Goosey-Poosey, and Turkey-Lurkey all went together to tell the King the sky was a-falling. And so they went along and they went along, until after a bit they met Foxy-Woxy.

"Where are you off to so early, Henny-Penny, Cocky-Locky, Ducky-Daddles, Goosey-Poosey, and Turkey-Lurkey?" says Foxy-Woxy.

And so Henny-Penny, Cocky-Locky, Ducky-Daddles, Goosey-Poosey, and Turkey-Lurkey told Foxy-Woxy that they were going to tell the King the sky was a-falling.

"Oh, but this isn't the way to the King, Henny-Penny, Cocky-Locky, Ducky-Daddles, Goosey-Poosey, and Turkey-Lurkey," says Foxy-Woxy. "I know the right way. Shall I show it you?"

"Oh, that would be very kind of you, Foxy-Woxy," said Henny-Penny, Cocky-Locky, Ducky-Daddles, Goosey-Poosey, and Turkey-Lurkey.

So Henny-Penny, Cocky-Locky, Ducky-Daddles, Goosey-Poosey, Turkey-Lurkey, and Foxy-Woxy all went along together to tell the King the sky was a-falling. And they went along and went along, until they came to a dark, narrow hole.

Now this was the door of Foxy-Woxy's earth. But what he said to Henny-Penny, Cocky-Locky, Ducky-Daddles, Goosey-Poosey, and Turkey-Lurkey was, "This is a short cut to the King's Palace: you'll soon get there if you'll follow me. I'll go first, and you come after, Henny-Penny, Cocky-Locky, Ducky-Daddles, Goosey-Poosey, and Turkey-Lurkey."

"Oh, certainly we will, Foxy-Woxy," said Henny-Penny,

Cocky-Locky, Ducky-Daddles, Goosey-Poosey, and Turkey-Lurkey.

So Foxy-Woxy went on ahead into his earth, and he didn't go very far, but turned round and waited for Henny-Penny, Cocky-Locky, Ducky-Daddles, Goosey-Poosey, and Turkey-Lurkey to come after him. And it was Turkey-Lurkey who was the first, and he hadn't got very far in when "*Hrumph!*" Foxy-Woxy snapped off Turkey-Lurkey's head. Then Goosey-Poosey came next, and—"*Hrumph!*"—Foxy-Woxy snapped off her head too, and threw her body alongside Turkey-Lurkey's. Then in came Ducky-Daddles, and—

"*Hrumph!*"—off came her head, and her body was thrown beside Turkey-Lurkey's and Goosey-Poosey's. And then in came Cocky-Locky, and "*Hrumph!*" went Foxy-Woxy, but he had to take two snaps to bite off Cocky-Locky's head, and after the first bite Cocky-Locky managed to call out to Henny-Penny, and round she turned, and off she ran home as fast as her legs could take her; and so she never told the King the sky was a-falling at all.

THE STORY OF SINDBAD THE SAILOR

IN the reign of the Caliph Haroun Al Raschid there lived in Bagdad a poor porter, whose name was Hindbad. It happened one day that he was carrying a heavy burden. The day was so hot that he was wearied by the load. In this state he passed by a fine house, before which the ground was swept and sprinkled and the air was cool. There came forth from the door a pleasant breeze laden with an exquisite odour. The porter was delighted, and sat down upon the bench by the door and listened to the melodious sounds of stringed instruments, and to joyous voices laughing and singing. He also heard the voices of nightingales warbling and praising Allah, whose name be exalted.

The porter was moved with curiosity, and he looked and saw within the house a lovely garden, wherein he beheld slaves and servants hurrying to and fro, and from the charming melody and the smell of savoury dishes he concluded there was a feast within. He asked the name of the owner of the house, and, learning that it was Sindbad, the famous voyager, he lifted up his eyes to heaven, and said, "O Allah! Thou enrichest whom thou wilt, and whom Thou wilt Thou abasest! Thou hast bestowed wealth upon the owner of this palace, while I am wretched and weary, and spend the day carrying other people's burdens!" Scarcely had Hindbad finished lamenting when there came forth from the door a servant, who took the porter by the hand and said to him, "Enter! My master calleth for thee."

The porter entered the house with the servant, and found himself in a grand chamber, in which he beheld noblemen and great lords. A feast was spread with all kinds of delicious viands and beverages. On both sides were beautiful slave-girls performing upon instruments of music, and at the upper end of the chamber was a great and venerable man, who requested him to seat himself, and placed before him delicious food. So Hindbad advanced, and, having said, "In the name of Allah, the Compassionate, the Merciful," ate until he was satisfied, and then said, "Praise be to Allah!" and washed his hands, and thanked his host.

"Thou art welcome," said the master of the house. "What is thy name, and what trade dost thou follow?" "O my master," answered the porter, "my name is Hindbad, and I am a porter." At this the master of the house smiled, and said, "I heard thy lamentation at my door, and I will now inform thee of all that happened to me and befell me before I attained this prosperity. My story is wonderful, for I have suffered severe fatigue and great troubles and many terrors. I have performed seven voyages, and connected with each voyage is a wonderful tale."

Thereupon Sindbad related as follows:

THE FIRST VOYAGE: THE ISLAND-FISH

Know, O masters, that my father was a merchant of first rank, who possessed abundant wealth and ample fortune, which I inherited from him, but which I squandered in my youth in dissipation.

Repenting of my prodigality, I arose and sold my apparel and all else that I still possessed. And with the money that I obtained I bought commodities and merchandise, and such other things as were required for travel. I embarked in a ship with a company of merchants, and we steered our course towards the Indies through the Persian Gulf. We touched at several islands, where we bought and sold and exchanged our merchandise.

One day we arrived at an island lovely as one of the gardens of Paradise, where the master of the ship brought us to anchor.

All who were on the ship landed, and took with them fire-pots and lighted fire in them. Some cooked, others washed, and others amused themselves.

Suddenly the master of the ship called out in his loudest voice, "O ye passengers, come quickly into the ship! Flee for your lives! This island upon which ye are is not really an island, but it is a great fish floating in the midst of the sea. When ye lighted the fires it felt the heat and began to move, and now it will sink with you to the bottom of the sea!" We hastened to the vessel, which was reached by some, but others reached it not, for the island moved, and sank into the sea with all that were upon it, while the ship set sails and departed.

I was among those who were left, but Allah, whose name be exalted, delivered me and saved me from drowning. There floated towards me a great wooden bowl, in which the passengers had been washing, and I got into it, and, tossed by the waves, drifted for a day and a night, until the bowl stopped under a high island, whereon were trees overhanging the sea. I laid hold upon the branch of a tree, and, climbing up by its means, I threw myself upon the island like one dead. I became unconscious, and remained in this condition until the next day, when I awoke, and found that I was reduced to a state of excessive weakness. There were in the island fruits in abundance and springs of sweet water. I ate some of the fruits and drank, and continued to live in this manner for several days. My spirit then revived, and my strength returned, and, having made myself a staff to lean upon, I walked farther into the island, until at last I reached a meadow where in the distance I could see some horses feeding. I went towards them, when I perceived a man, who came forth from a cave and called to me and pursued me, saying, "Who art thou? Whence hast thou come?" I told him of my adventure, and he then took my hand and led me into a cave, where he seated me and brought food.

Then said the man, "Know that we are the grooms of the King Mihrage, having under our care all his horses, which we bring here to graze." And as he spoke his companions came, each leading a mare, and, seeing me with him, they inquired who I might be, and when they heard they drew near and invited me to eat with them. After which they rose and mounted the horses, taking me with them.

We journeyed until we arrived at the city of King Mihrage, and the grooms went in to him and related my story. He welcomed me in an honourable manner, saying, "O my son, verily thou hast experienced an extraordinary preservation! Praise be to Allah for thy safety!" He then treated me with beneficence, and made me keeper of the seaport, and I became a person of high importance.

In this state I continued for some time, during which I amused myself with the sight of the islands belonging to King Mihrage. I saw there an island called Kasil, in which at night is heard mysterious beatings of tambourines and drums, and the people told me that it is inhabited by that strange being called Dagial, the false and one-eyed. I saw also in the sea in which is that island a fish two hundred cubits long, and a fish whose face is like an owl's, and many other wonderful and strange things.

I stood one day on the shore of the sea with a staff in my hand, as was my custom, and, lo, a great vessel approached the harbour of the city. The master furled its sails, brought it to anchor, and the sailors brought out everything that was in the vessel to the shore. Then said I to the master, "Doth aught remain in thy vessel?" "Yes, my master," he answered, "I have goods in the hold, but their owner was drowned, and we desire to sell them, in order to convey their price to his family in the city of Bagdad, the Abode of Peace." "And what," said I, "was the name of this man, the owner of the goods?" "His name was Sindbad the Sailor," answered the master, "and he was drowned on his voyage with us."

When I heard this I looked attentively at the master, and recognized him, and I cried out with a great cry, "I am the owner of the goods! I am Sindbad himself!" And I told him all that had happened to me. But the master said, "Thou verily art a deceiver. Because thou heardest me say that I had goods whose owner was drowned therefore thou desirest to take them without price. We saw Sindbad when he sank, and with him were many of the passengers, not one of whom escaped." But I related to the master all that I had done from the time that I went forth with him from the city of Bagdad, and I related to him some circumstances that had occurred between him and me, and the master and merchants were convinced of my truthfulness and recognized me.

They then gave me my goods, and I found nothing missing. So I opened the bales and took forth precious and costly things and carried them as a present to the King. When he heard what had occurred he treated me with exceeding honour, giving me a large gift in return. Then I sold my bales, and purchased other goods and commodities of that city —sandal-wood, and aloes, camphire, nutmegs, cloves, and ginger—after which I begged the King to grant me permission to depart to my country and my family. So he bade me farewell, and gave me an abundance of rich and costly things.

I embarked in the vessel, and Fortune aided us so that we arrived in safety at the city of Balsora, whence I proceeded to the city of Bagdad. I had an abundance of bales and goods and merchandise of the value of one hundred thousand sequins, with which I procured servants and slave-girls and black slaves, and houses and furniture, more than I had at first. I enjoyed the society of my friends and companions, and forgot the fatigue and difficulty and terror of travel. I occupied myself with delights and pleasures, and delicious meats and exquisite drinks, and continued to live in this manner for some time. Such were the events of my first voyage, and to-morrow, if it be the will of Allah, whose name be exalted, I will relate to you the tale of the second of my seven voyages.

Sindbad the Sailor then made Hindbad the porter sup with him, after which he presented him with a hundred pieces of gold, and the porter thanked him and went his way. He slept that night in his own home, rejoicing with his wife and children, and when the morning came he performed his morning prayers and repaired to the house of Sindbad the Sailor, who welcomed him with honour. After the rest of his companions had come, and food and drink were set before them, and they were merry, then Sindbad began his story thus:

THE SECOND VOYAGE: THE VALLEY OF DIAMONDS

Know, O my brothers, I lived most comfortably, as I told ye yesterday, until one day I felt a longing to travel again to lands of other peoples, and for the pleasure of seeing the countries and islands of the world. I decided to set forth at once, and, taking a large sum of money, I purchased with it goods and merchandise suitable for trade, and packed them up. Then I went to the banks of the river, and found there a handsome new vessel, manned by a numerous crew. So I embarked my bales in it, as did also a party of merchants, and we set sail that day.

The voyage was pleasant, and we passed from sea to sea, and from island to island, and at every place where we cast anchor we sold, bought, and exchanged goods. Thus we continued to voyage until we arrived at a beautiful island, abounding with trees of ripe fruit, but where there was not an inhabitant on the whole island. I landed with the rest, and sat by a spring of pure water among the trees. And soon I fell asleep, enjoying the sweet shade and the fragrant air. When I awoke I found that the master had forgotten me, and the vessel had sailed with all the passengers, leaving me alone on the island.

I had with me neither food nor drink nor worldly goods, and I was desolate and despairing of life. I began to weep and wail, and to blame myself for having undertaken the voyage and fatigue when I was reposing at ease in my home and country, in want of nothing, either of money or goods or merchandise. I repented of having gone forth from the city of Bagdad, and of having set out on a voyage over sea.

After a while I arose and walked about the island. I climbed a lofty tree, and saw naught save sky and water, and trees and birds, and islands and sand. Looking attentively, I saw an enormous white object, indistinctly seen in the distance. I descended from the tree, and proceeded in that direction without stopping. And, lo, it was a huge white dome, of great height and immense circumference. I drew near to it, and walked around it, but found no door, and I could not climb it because of its excessive smoothness. I made a mark at the place where I stood, and went around the dome measuring it, and, lo, it was fifty full paces!

Suddenly the sky became dark, and the sun was hidden. I imagined a cloud had passed over it, and I raised my head, and saw a bird of enormous size, bulky body, and wide wings, flying in the air, and this it was that concealed the sun and darkened the island. My wonder increased, and I remembered a story which travellers and voyagers had told me long before. How in certain islands there is a bird of enormous size called the Roc, and it feedeth its young ones with elephants. I was convinced, therefore, that the dome was the egg of a Roc, and I wondered at the works of Allah, whose name be exalted!

The bird alighted upon the dome, and, brooding over it with its wings, stretched out its legs behind upon the ground and slept over it. Thereupon I arose and unwound my turban from my head, and twisted it into a rope. I fastened it tightly about my waist, and tied myself to one of the feet of the bird, saying to myself, "Perhaps this bird will convey me to a land of cities and inhabitants, and that will be better than my remaining on this island."

I passed the night sleepless, and when the dawn came the bird rose from its egg, uttered a great cry, and flew up into the sky, drawing me with it. It soared higher and higher, and then it descended gradually, until it alighted with me upon the earth. When I reached the ground I hastily unbound myself from its foot, loosed my turban, shaking with fear as I did so, and walked away. The Roc took something from the earth in its talons, and soared aloft, and I looked and saw that it was a serpent of enormous size which the bird had taken and was carrying off towards the sea.

I walked about the place, and found myself in a large, deep, wide valley, shut in by a great mountain, whose summit I could not see because of its excessive height, and I could not ascend it because of its steepness. Seeing this, I blamed myself for what I had done. "Would that I had remained on the island," I said, "since it is better than this deserted place! For on that island are fruits that I might have eaten, and I might have drunk from its rivers, but in this place are neither trees nor fruits nor rivers! Verily every time I escape from one calamity I fall into another that is greater and more severe!" Then I arose, and, encouraging myself, walked down the valley, and, lo, its ground was covered with magnificent diamonds, a stone so hard that neither iron nor rock can have any effect upon it.

All that valley was likewise occupied by venomous serpents of enormous size, big enough to swallow an elephant. These serpents came out of their holes in the night, and during the day they hid themselves, fearing lest the Rocs should carry them off and tear them to pieces. The day departed, and I began to search for a place in which to pass the night, fearing

the serpents who were beginning to come forth. I found a cave near by with a narrow entrance. I therefore entered, and, seeing a large stone, I pushed it and stopped up the mouth of the cave. I said to myself I am safe in this cave, and when daylight cometh I will go forth and look for some means of escape from this valley.

I prepared to repose, when, looking towards the upper end of the cave, I saw a huge serpent sleeping over its eggs. At this my flesh quaked, and I raised my head, and passed the night sleepless until dawn, when I removed the stone and went forth, giddy from sleeplessness and hunger and fear.

I walked along the valley, when, of a sudden, the carcass of a great animal fell before me. I looked, but could see no one, so I wondered extremely, and I remembered a story which I had heard long ago from merchants and travellers: how in the mountains of diamonds are experienced great horrors, and that no one can gain access to the diamonds. To obtain these stones the merchants employ a stratagem. They take a sheep and slaughter it, and skin it, and cut up its flesh, which they throw down from the mountain to the bottom of the valley, and, the meat being fresh and moist, some of the diamonds stick to it. The merchants leave it until midday, when large birds descend to the valley, and, taking the meat up in their talons, carry it to the top of the mountain, whereupon the merchants cry out and frighten away the birds. They then remove the diamonds sticking to the meat, and carry them to their own country, leaving the flesh for the birds and wild beasts. No one can procure the diamonds but by this stratagem.

Therefore when I beheld that slaughtered animal and remembered this story I arose and selected a great number of large and beautiful diamonds, which I put into my pocket, and wrapped in my turban, and within my clothes. While I was doing this, behold, another great slaughtered animal fell before me. I bound myself to it with my turban, and, lying down on my back, placed the meat upon my bosom, and grasped it firmly. Immediately an enormous bird descended upon it, seized it with its talons, and flew up with it into the air, with me attached to it. It soared to the summit of the mountain, where it alighted. Then a great and loud cry arose near by, and a piece of wood fell clattering upon the mountain, and the bird, frightened, flew away.

I disengaged myself from the carcass, and stood up by its side, when, lo, the merchant who had cried out at the bird advanced and saw me standing there. He was very much terrified, and when he saw that there were no diamonds on the meat he uttered a cry of disappointment. "Who art thou," exclaimed he, "who hath brought this misfortune upon me?" "Fear not, nor be alarmed," answered I, "for I am a human being, a merchant like thyself, and my tale is prodigious, and my story wonderful! I have with me an abundance of diamonds, and I will share them with thee to repay thee for those thou hast lost." The man thanked me for this and conversed with me, and, behold, the other merchants heard me talking with their companion, and they came and saluted me. I acquainted them with my whole story, relating to them all I had suffered upon the voyage. Then I gave the owner of the slaughtered animal to which I had attached myself a number of the diamonds that I had brought with me from the valley. And I passed the night with the merchants, full of utmost joy at my escape from the valley of serpents.

When the next day came we arose and journeyed together until we arrived at a city, where I exchanged a part of my diamonds for merchandise and gold and silver. After which I journeyed from country to country, and from city to city, selling and buying, until I arrived at the city of Bagdad, the Abode of Peace. I entered my house, bringing with me a great quantity of diamonds and money and goods. I made presents to my family and relations, and bestowed alms and gifts, and feasted with my friends and companions, and thus

I forgot all that I had suffered. This is the end of the account of what befell and happened to me during the second voyage. To-morrow, if it be the will of Allah, whose name be exalted, I will relate to you the events of the third of my seven voyages.

When Sindbad had finished his story all the company marvelled. They supped with him, and he presented to Hindbad a hundred pieces of gold. Next day, when the party had gathered together again, Sindbad the Sailor began thus:

THE THIRD VOYAGE: THE WONDER VOYAGE

Know, O my brothers, that my third voyage was more wonderful than the preceding ones. When I returned from my second voyage I resided in the city of Bagdad for a length of time, in the most perfect prosperity, delight, joy, and happiness. Then my soul became desirous of travel and diversion. So I considered the matter, and decided to set forth immediately. I bought an abundance of goods suited to a sea-voyage, and departed in a great vessel, in which were many merchants and other passengers. We proceeded from sea to sea, and from island to island, and from city to city, and at every place we amused ourselves and bought and sold.

One day we pursued our course in the midst of a raging sea, when, lo, the master, standing at the side of the vessel, suddenly slapped his face, furled the sails, cast the anchors, plucked his beard, rent his clothes, and uttered a great cry. "Know, O passengers," exclaimed he, "that the wind hath driven us out of our course in the midst of the sea, and destiny hath cast us, through our evil fortune, towards the Mountain of Apes. No one hath ever arrived at this place and escaped!"

Scarcely had the master spoken before a band of apes, numerous as locusts, surrounded the ship on every side. Their numbers were so excessive that we feared to kill one or strike him or drive him away, lest the others should fall upon us and destroy us. They were the most hideous of beasts, and covered with hair like black felt. They had yellow eyes and black faces, and were of small size. They climbed up the cables and severed them with their teeth, and they severed all the ropes, so that the vessel drifted with the wind, and stopped at the island. The apes then put all the merchants and passengers ashore, and, taking the ship, sailed away in it, leaving us upon the island, and we knew not whither they went.

We wandered about until we discovered a pavilion, with high walls, having an entrance with folding-doors which were open, and the doors were made of ebony. We entered, and found a wide, large court, around which were many lofty doors. Over the fire-pots hung cooking utensils, and on the floor were many bones. As we were fatigued we sat down on a great bench and fell asleep. Suddenly the earth trembled, and we heard a dreadful noise, and there entered the pavilion a creature of enormous size in human form. He was black and of lofty stature, like a great palm-tree. He had two eyes like two flames, and tusks like the tusks of swine, and a mouth of prodigious size, and lips like the lips of a camel, hanging down upon his bosom. His ears hung down upon his shoulders, and the nails of his hands were like the claws of lions.

When we beheld him we were so filled with dread and terror that we became as dead men. The creature came to us and seized me in his hand, lifted me from the ground, and felt me over and turned me over, and I was in his hand like a little mouthful, but he found me lean and having no flesh. He therefore put me down, and took another from among my companions, and turned him over, then let him go. In this manner he felt us, and turned us over one by one, until he came to the master of our ship, who was a fat, broad-shouldered man. He seized him as does the butcher the animal that he is about to slaughter, and, having thrown him upon the ground, put his foot upon his neck and broke it.

Then he brought a long spit and thrust it through him. After which he built a fierce fire, and placed over it the spit, turning it about over the burning coals, until the master was thoroughly roasted, when he took him off the fire and separated his joints as a man separates the joints of a chicken. He ate his flesh and after gnawing his bones tossed them by the side of the fire-pot. He then threw himself down and slept upon the bench, making a fearful noise with his throat.

We wept and said, "Would that we had been drowned in the sea, or that the apes had eaten us! For it would be better than being roasted upon burning coals!" We then arose, and went forth to find a place to hide in. But we could find no hiding-place, and when night came we returned to the pavilion by reason of our fear. We had sat there a little while, when, lo, the earth trembled beneath us, and the black creature approached us, and took us one by one, and turned us over, until one pleased him, whereupon he seized him, and killed and roasted him, as he had done with the master of the ship. He then slept, making a dreadful noise with his throat as before. When morning came he arose and went his way.

Then said one of our company, "Verily we must contrive some stratagem to kill him, and rid the earth of such a monster!" "Hear, O my brothers," I answered, "if we must kill him, let us first make some rafts of this firewood, each raft to bear three men, after which we will kill him, and embark on our rafts, and proceed over the sea to whatsoever place Allah shall desire. And if we be not able to kill him we will embark anyway, and if we be drowned we shall be preserved from being roasted over the fire!" We all agreed upon this matter, and commenced the work. We took the pieces of firewood out and constructed rafts, moored them to the shore and stowed upon them some provisions, after which we returned to the pavilion.

When it was evening again the black came in like a biting dog! He turned us over, and felt us, one after another, and, having taken one of us, did with him as he had done with the others. He ate him, and slept upon the bench, and the noise in his throat was like thunder.

We then arose, and took two iron spits, and put them in the fierce fire until they were red-hot and became like burning coals. We grasped them firmly, and went to the black, while he lay asleep snoring, and thrust them into his eyes, all of us pressing upon them with our united strength and force. Thus we pushed them into his eyes as he slept, and his eyes were destroyed, and he uttered a terrible cry. He arose, and began to search for us, while we fled in every direction, and he saw us not, for his sight was blinded. Then he sought the door, feeling for it, and went forth crying out so that the earth trembled.

We hastened to the rafts, and scarcely had we reached them before the black returned, accompanied by a female, greater than he, and more hideous in form. As soon as we beheld the horrible female with him we loosed the rafts, and pushed them out to sea. But each of the two blacks took masses of rock, and they cast them at us, until they had destroyed all the rafts but one, and the persons upon them were drowned. There remained of us only three, I and two others, and the raft we were on conveyed us to another island.

We landed, and walked about this island until the close of day, when night overtook us, so we slept a little. We awoke from our sleep, and, lo, a serpent of enormous size, of large body and wide belly, had surrounded us. It approached one of us, and swallowed him to his shoulders, then it swallowed the rest of him, and we heard his ribs crack. After which the serpent went away. We mourned for our companion, and were in the utmost fear for ourselves, saying, "Verily every death we witness is more horrible than the preceding one!"

When night came my companion and myself found a lofty

tree, so we climbed up it, and slept. When it was day the serpent came, looking to the right and left, and, advancing to the tree upon which we were, climbed to my companion, swallowed him to his shoulders, and then it wound itself around the tree, and I heard his bones break. The serpent swallowed him entire, descended from the tree, and went its way.

I remained upon that tree the rest of the night, and when day came I descended, more dead than alive from excessive fear and terror. I desired to cast myself into the sea, but it was no light matter, for to live was sweet, so I tied a wide piece of wood upon the soles of my feet crosswise, and I tied one like it upon my left side, and a similar one on my right side, and another on the front of my body, and I tied a long and wide one on the top of my head, crosswise, like that which was on the soles of my feet. I bound them tightly, and threw myself upon the ground. Thus I lay in the midst of the pieces of wood, and they enclosed me like a box.

When evening arrived the serpent approached, but could not swallow me, as I had the pieces of wood on every side. It went round me, then retired from me, and returned again to me. Every time it tried to swallow me the pieces of wood prevented it. It continued to attack me thus, from sunset until daybreak arrived and the light appeared, then the serpent went its way in the utmost vexation and rage.

I loosed myself from the pieces of wood in a state like that of the dead. I arose, and walked along the island, and, looking towards the sea, beheld a ship in the distance in the midst of the deep. I took a great branch of a tree, and made signs with it, calling out, and the sailors saw me. They approached the shore, and took me with them in the ship. They asked me my story, and I informed them of all that had happened to me from beginning to end. They then clad me in some of their garments, and put food before me, and I ate until I was satisfied, and my soul was comforted.

We proceeded on our voyage until we came in sight of an island, called the Isle of Selahit, where sandal-wood is abundant. The master anchored the ship, and the merchants and other passengers took forth their goods to sell and buy. Then said the master to me, "Thou art a stranger and poor, and hast suffered many horrors, and I desire to aid thee to reach thy country. Know that there was with us a merchant who was lost at sea, and I will commit to thee his bales of goods, that thou mayest sell them in this island, after which we will take the price to his family. If thou wilt take charge of the sale we will give thee something for thy trouble and service." For this kind and beneficent offer I was full of gratitude, and readily agreed to look after the goods.

The master ordered the porters and sailors to land the goods upon the island, and to deliver them to me. "Write upon them," said he, "the name of Sindbad the Sailor, who was left behind at the island of the Roc, and of whom no tidings have come to us." Upon this I uttered a great cry, saying, "O master, I am Sindbad the Sailor! I was not drowned." And I told him all that had happened unto me. While we were talking one of the merchants, on hearing me mention the Valley of Diamonds, advanced and said, "Hear, O company, my words. I have already related to you the wonderful thing I saw on my travels. I told you that when I cast my slaughtered animal into the Valley of Diamonds that there came up with my beast a man attached to it, and ye believed me not, but accused me of lying. This is the man, and he gave me diamonds of high price, and he informed me that his name was Sindbad the Sailor, and he told me how the ship had left him on the island of the Roc."

When the master heard the words of the merchant he looked at me awhile with a searching glance, then said, "What is the mark of thy goods?" "Know," I answered, "that the mark of my goods is of such and such a kind." He therefore was convinced that I was Sindbad the Sailor, and embraced and saluted me, and congratulated me upon my safety.

I disposed of my merchandise with great gain, selling and buying at the islands, until we arrived at Balsora, where I remained a few days. In due time I came back to the city of Bagdad, and entered my house, and saluted my family, companions, and friends. I rejoiced at my safety, and forgot all the horrors I had suffered. To-morrow, if it be the will of Allah, whose name be exalted, I will relate to thee the story of my fourth voyage, for it is more wonderful than the stories of the preceding voyages.

Then Sindbad gave the porter a hundred pieces of gold, and the company supped, wondering at that story, and at the events described. When the morning came the company assembled again, and Sindbad the Sailor related to them the fourth story, saying:

THE FOURTH VOYAGE: THE BURIAL CAVE

Know, O my brothers, that after I returned to the city of Bagdad, and met my friends and companions, and was enjoying the utmost pleasure, after a time I felt a longing to see different races, and for selling and gains. So I purchased precious goods, and, having packed up my merchandise, I went to the city of Balsora, where I embarked my bales, and joined myself to a party of the chief men of that city, and we set forth.

The voyage was pleasant, and we went from island to island, and from sea to sea, until a contrary wind arose. The master cast anchor, and stayed the ship in the midst of the sea, fearing that she would sink in the deep. Suddenly a great tempest arose, which rent the sails, the ship sank, and the merchants were cast into the sea. I was submerged among the rest, and swam in the sea for half a day. But Allah, whose name be exalted, enabled me to lay hold of one of the planks

from the ship, and I and a party of merchants got upon it.
The next day a wind arose against us, the sea became boister-
ous, and the waves and wind violent, and the water cast us
upon an island.

We passed the night on the shore, and when morning came
we walked until there appeared a building in the distance.
When we reached its door, lo, there came forth from it a
party of naked black men. Without speaking they seized us
and carried us to their King. He commanded us to sit down,
and the blacks brought us disgusting food, which my stomach
revolted against, therefore I ate scarcely any, but my companions ate most ravenously.

I was filled with fear for myself and my companions, for I
saw that the men were cannibals, and I discovered that every
one who arrived at their country, or whom they met, they
caught and brought to their King. And they fed the captive
until he became fat, when they slaughtered and roasted him,
and served him as meat to their King. As for myself, I became,
through hunger and fear, wasted and thin, and my flesh dried
on my bones. When the blacks saw me in this state they left
me, and forgot all about me.

One day I walked along the island, and, seeing a road on
my right hand, I proceeded along it day and night, eating of
the herbs and vegetables and drinking of the springs whenever
I was hungry, until the eighth day, when I saw in the distance
a party of men gathering peppers. When they saw me they
surrounded me on every side, saying, "Who art thou?
Whence hast thou come?" I informed them of my whole
case, and of the horrors and distresses that I had suffered.

Their work being completed, they embarked with me in
a ship, and went to their island and took me to their King.
He treated me with honour, and inquired of me my story, at
which he wondered greatly, and commanded a repast to be
spread. After I had eaten I arose, and, leaving his presence,
diverted myself with a sight of his city. It was a flourishing

place, abounding with inhabitants and wealth, and with food and markets and goods and sellers and buyers.

After a few days I saw that its men, great and little, rode excellent, fine horses without saddles, whereat I wondered. On inquiry I discovered that no one in that land had ever seen a saddle, or knew of its make or use. I sought out a clever carpenter, and took wool, and leather, and felt, and caused a saddle to be made; I then sought a blacksmith, and described to him the form of stirrups, and he forged an excellent pair, to which I attached a fringe of silk.

Having done this, I placed the saddle on one of the King's horses, attached to it the stirrups, bridled the horse, and led him forward to the King, who thanked me, and seated himself upon it, and was greatly delighted with that saddle, and gave me a large present as a reward. When his Vizier saw that I had made a saddle he desired one like it, so I made one for him. The grandees and great lords likewise desired saddles, and I made them, with the help of the carpenter and blacksmith, and for these I received large sums. Thus I collected abundant wealth, and became in high estimation with all the people.

I sat one day with the King in the utmost happiness and honour, and he said to me, "Know, O thou, that thou art honoured among us, and we cannot part with thee, nor can we suffer thee to depart from our city. Therefore I desire to marry thee to a beautiful wife, possessed of wealth and loveliness. I will lodge thee by me in a palace, so do not oppose me in this matter." I could not refuse to do as the King commanded me, so he sent immediately for the Cadi and witnesses to come, and married me forthwith to a woman of high rank and surprising beauty, possessing abundant wealth and fortune. He presented me with a great and handsome house, and gave me servants and other dependants. I loved my wife, and she loved me with great affection, and we lived together in a most delightful manner.

One day the wife of my neighbour and companion died,

and I went in to console him. He was anxious, weary in soul and body, and I comforted him, saying, "Mourn not for thy wife, for Allah will perhaps give thee one better than she!" But he wept bitterly, and said, "O my companion, how can I marry another when I have but one more day to live! This day they will bury my wife, and they will bury me with her in the sepulchre, for it is a custom in our country when the wife dieth to bury with her the husband alive, and when the husband dieth they bury with him the wife alive, that neither of them may enjoy life after the other."

While he was thus speaking behold the people of the city came. They prepared the body for burial, according to their custom, brought a bier, and carried the woman on it, with all her apparel, ornaments, and wealth. Taking the husband with them, they went forth from the city, and came to a mountain by the sea. They advanced to a certain spot, and lifted up a great stone from the mouth of a hole like a well, and threw the woman into a pit beneath the mountain. They brought the man, tied beneath his arms a rope of fibres of the palm-tree, and lowered him into the pit. They let down to him a great jug of sweet water and seven cakes of bread. When they had let him down he loosed himself from the rope, and they drew it up, and covered the mouth of the pit with that great stone, as it was before.

On my return to the city I went to the King, and said to him, "O King of the age, if the wife of a foreigner like myself die do ye do with him after the manner of the country?" "Yea, verily," answered the King, "we bury him with her, and do with him as thou hast seen." When I heard those words my mind was stupefied, and I became fearful lest my wife should die before me, and they should bury me alive with her.

But a short time elapsed before my wife fell sick of a fever, and she remained ill for a few days, and died. Great numbers of people assembled to console me, and the King also came to comfort me. They washed my wife and decked her with the richest of her apparel, and ornaments of gold, and necklaces and jewels. They then placed her on the bier, and carried her to the mountain, and lifted the stone from the mouth of the pit, and cast her in. The family of my wife then advanced to bid me farewell, but I cried out that I was a foreigner, and would not submit to their custom. They laid hold upon me, and bound me by force, tying to me seven cakes of bread and a jug of sweet water, and let me down into the pit. They commanded me to loose myself from the ropes, but I would not do so; thereupon they threw down the ropes upon me, and covered the mouth of the pit with the great stone, and went their way.

I found that I was in an immense cavern beneath the mountain, and all about me lay the dead. I walked about, feeling the sides of the cavern, and found that it was spacious and had many cavities in its sides, and in one of these I made a place for myself and sat down. "Alas!" said I. "Would that I had not married in this country! Would that I had been drowned at sea, or had died upon the mountains! It would have been better than this evil death!"

I remained thus for several days, eating and drinking a little at a time, fearing to exhaust the food and water. One day I awoke and heard something make a noise in the cavern. I arose and walked towards it, and when it heard me coming it fled from me, and, lo, it was a wild beast! I followed it to the upper end of the cavern, where a light appeared like a star. I advanced, and the light grew larger, so that I was convinced that it was a hole in the cavern, communicating with open country. I continued to advance, and, lo, it was an aperture in the back of the mountain, which wild beasts had made, and through which they entered the cavern. I managed to force my way through the hole, and found myself on the shore of the sea, with a great mountain between me and the city from whence I came.

I praised Allah, whose name be exalted, and rejoiced exceedingly, and my heart was strengthened. I returned through the hole to the cavern, where I collected an abundance of jewels, necklaces of pearls, ornaments of gold and silver, which had been buried with the dead, and these I carried forth to the shore of the sea. One day I was sitting upon the shore of the sea, and I beheld a vessel passing along through the midst of the roaring waves. So I took a white cloth and tied it to a staff, and ran along the seashore, signalling the sailors until they saw me. They sent a boat to me, and carried me to the master, who kindly embarked me and my goods in his ship. I offered him a considerable portion of my property, but he would not accept it of me, saying, "We take nothing from anyone whom we find stranded on a lonely shore or on an island; instead we act towards him with kindness and favour for the sake of Allah, whose name be exalted."

We proceeded on our voyage from island to island, and from sea to sea, until at length we reached the city of Balsora, where I landed, and in due time returned to my home in Bagdad. O porter, if thou wilt sup with me to-morrow I will inform thee what befell me during my fifth voyage, for it was more wonderful and extraordinary than the preceding voyage.

Sindbad the Sailor then presented the porter with a hundred pieces of gold, and the party supped, after which they went their ways, wondering extremely. Next day Sindbad the Sailor began his narrative, saying thus:

THE FIFTH VOYAGE: THE OLD MAN OF THE SEA

Know, O my brothers, that in course of time my mind again suggested to me to travel and to divert myself with the sight of other countries and peoples. So again I joined a company of merchants, and we set sail in the utmost joy and happiness, and pursued our voyage from island to island, and from sea to sea, buying and selling goods.

We arrived one day at a large island, deserted and desolate, but on it was an enormous white dome, of great bulk, and, lo, it was the egg of a Roc. When the merchants had landed to amuse themselves, not knowing that it was the egg of a Roc, they struck it with stones, so that it broke, and there poured from it a great quantity of liquid, and the young Roc appeared within the shell. The merchants pulled it out, killed it, and cut from it an abundance of meat. I was then in the ship, and knew not of it, and, looking forth, I saw the merchants striking the egg. I called out to them, "Do not this deed! It is a Roc's egg, and the bird will come and demolish our ship and destroy us!" But they would not hear my words.

Suddenly the sun was veiled, and the day grew dark, and we raised our eyes, and, lo, the wings of the Roc darkened the sky! When the bird came and beheld its egg broken it cried out fiercely, whereupon its mate, the female bird, came to it, and they flew in circles over the ship, uttering cries like thunder. So I called out to the master and sailors, "Push off the vessel and seek safety before we perish!" The master hastened, and, the merchants having embarked, he loosed the ship, and we departed from the island. When the Rocs saw that we had put out to sea they flew away, and soon returned, each of them having in its claws a huge mass of stone from a mountain. The male bird threw upon us the stone he had brought, but the master steered away the ship, and the stone missed it and fell into the sea. Then the mate of the male Roc threw upon us the stone she had brought, and it fell upon the stern of the ship and crushed it, and the vessel sank with all that was in it.

I strove to save myself, and Allah, whose name be exalted, placed within my reach a plank from the ship, on which I clung, and was at last cast exhausted on the shore of an island. At last I arose and walked along the island, and saw that it resembled a garden of Paradise. There was an abundance of trees and fruits and flowers. So I ate of the fruits until I was satisfied, and I drank of the flowing rivers. Then I lay down and slept.

In the morning I beheld an old man sitting beside a stream, and he was clad from the waist down in a covering made of the leaves of trees. I approached and saluted him, but he returned the salutation by a sign, without speaking. "O sheikh," said I, "what is the reason of thy sitting in this place?" He shook his head and sighed, and made a sign as though to say, "Carry me upon thy back, and transport me across this stream."

I said to myself, "I will act kindly to this old man, and perhaps I shall obtain a reward in heaven!" So I stooped, and took him upon my shoulders, and carried him over the stream to the place he had indicated. When I said, "Descend in peace," he did not descend from my shoulders. He had wound his legs round my neck, and I looked at them, and saw that they were black and rough, like the hide of a buffalo. I was frightened, and tried to throw him from my shoulders, but he pressed his feet on my neck, and squeezed my throat, so that the world became black before my face, and I fell upon the ground in a fit. He then raised his legs, and beat me upon my back and shoulders, and caused me such violent pain that I was forced to rise.

He still kept his seat upon my shoulders, and when I became fatigued with bearing him he made a sign that I should go among the trees to the best of the fruit. If I disobeyed him he inflicted upon me with his feet blows more violent than those of whips, and he directed me with his hand to every place where he desired to go, and to that place I went with him. If I loitered or went leisurely he beat me, and I was a captive to him. He descended not from my shoulders by night nor by day, and when he desired to sleep he would wind his legs about my neck and sleep a little, and then he would beat me until I arose.

Thus I remained for some time, until one day I carried the old man to a place on the island where I found an abundance of dried pumpkins. I took a large one, and cleansed it. I then went to a grape-vine, and filled the pumpkin with the juice of the grapes. I stopped up the aperture, and put the juice in the sun, and left it for some days until it became pure wine. Every day I used to drink of it to help me endure the fatigue. So, seeing me one day drinking, the old man made a sign with his hand for me to hand him the pumpkin, and, fearing greatly, I handed it to him immediately. Whereupon he drank all the wine that remained, and threw the pumpkin upon the ground. He then became intoxicated, and began to sway from side to side upon my shoulders. When I knew that he was drunk I put my hand to his feet and loosed them from my neck, and I stooped with him and sat down, and threw him upon the ground. Fearing lest he should rise from his intoxication and torment me, I took a great mass of stone and struck him upon the head until he was dead.

After that I walked about the island with a happy mind, and came to the place where I was at first, on the shore of the sea, and, lo, a vessel approached from the midst of the roaring waves, and it ceased not its course until it anchored at the island. The passengers landed, and when they saw me they approached and inquired the cause of my coming to that place. I therefore acquainted them with all that had befallen me. Whereat they wondered extremely, and said, "This old man who rode upon thy shoulders is called the Old Man of the Sea, and no one was ever beneath his limbs and escaped from him excepting thee."

They then brought me food, and I ate until I was satisfied, and they gave me clothes, which I put on, covering myself decently. After this they took me with them to their ship, and proceeded night and day, until destiny drove us to a city of lofty buildings overlooking the sea.

The next day one of the party with whom I was said to me, "Hast thou any trade or art whereby thou mayest earn thy bread?" "No, my brother," I answered, "I am acquainted with no art, nor do I know how to make anything." Whereupon he gave me a large bag, and at that moment, a party of men going forth from the gates, my companion said to them, "This is a stranger, so take him with you and teach him your mode of earning your livelihood; perhaps he may in this way gain means of providing himself with food and drink; and ye will obtain a reward and recompense from Allah, whose name be exalted."

I accompanied them until we arrived at a wide valley, wherein were lofty trees, which no one could climb. In that valley were many apes, and when they saw us they fled and ascended the trees. Then the men began to pelt the apes with stones, and the apes plucked off the fruit of the trees and threw them at the men. I looked at the fruit which they threw down, and, lo, they were coconuts.

I chose a tree in which were many apes, and proceeded to pelt them with stones, and they broke off the nuts from the tree and threw them at me. So I collected a great quantity, and when the men returned home I carried off as many nuts as I could. Entering the city, I went to the man, my companion, and gave him all the coconuts I had collected, and thanked him for his kindness. "Take these," he said, "and sell them, and make use of the price." I did as he told me, and continued every day to go forth with the men and do as they did. I collected a great quantity of good coconuts, which I sold, and for which I received a large sum of money.

One day I was standing by the seaside when a vessel arrived and cast anchor. In it were merchants, who proceeded to exchange their goods for coconuts and other things. So I bade farewell to my companion and embarked in that vessel with my coconuts and the other merchandise I had collected; after which we set sail the same day.

We passed by an island in which are cinnamon and pepper, and there I exchanged coconuts for a great quantity of each. We passed also the island of Asirat, wherein is aloes-wood, and after that others, where I traded my coconuts for aloes-wood, and later for pearls.

In time as before I regained the city of Bagdad, and entered my house and saluted my family and friends. Allah had compensated me with four times as much as I had lost, and I forgot all the fatigue and terror I had suffered, and resumed my feasting and merrymaking.

When he had finished Sindbad the Sailor presented Hindbad with one hundred pieces of gold as before. He took them and departed, wondering at this affair. Next morning Sindbad the Sailor related the story of the sixth voyage, saying:

THE SIXTH VOYAGE: THE TREASURE-WRECKS

Know, O my brothers and my friends and my companions, that as time passed I forgot what I had suffered, and my soul longed again to see other countries. So I went to the city of Balsora, where I beheld a large vessel, in which were merchants with their precious goods. I therefore embarked with them, and we departed in safety.

We were proceeding one day, and, lo, the master of the ship called out in grief and rage, threw down his turban, slapped his face, plucked his beard, and fell in the hold of the ship. The merchants and other passengers gathered about him, saying, "O master, what is the matter?" "Know, O company," he answered, "that we have wandered from our course, and have entered an unknown sea! If Allah help us not to escape we shall perish!"

Then the master arose, and ascended the mast, and tried to

loose the sails, but the wind became violent, and drove back the ship, and her rudder broke near a lofty mountain. The waves threw the vessel upon rocks, and it broke to pieces, its planks were scattered, and the merchants fell into the sea. Some of them were drowned, and some were thrown upon the mountain.

I was of the number of those who landed upon this mountain. We crossed it, and on the other side found a wide shore, whereon were treasures thrown up by the sea from ships that had been wrecked. My reason was confounded by the abundance of commodities and wealth cast up on the shore. And I beheld there a river of sweet water, flowing forth from beneath the nearest part of the mountain, and entering at the farthest part of it; and in the bed of this stream were various kinds of jewels, jacinths and large pearls suitable for kings. They were like gravel in the channel of the river, which flowed through the fields, and all the bottom of the stream glittered by reason of ornaments of gold and silver.

We continued to wander about the island, and collected from the wreckage of the ship a small quantity of food, which we used sparingly, eating of it every day or two days, only one meal. At last our stock became exhausted, and my companions died one by one, until I alone was left upon the shore. Then I wept, and said, "Would that I had died before my companions!" And I blamed myself for leaving my country and my people, after all that I had suffered during my former voyages.

Then thought I, "This river must have a beginning and an end, and it must have a place of egress into an inhabited country. I will construct for myself a raft, and I will depart on it, and hope to find safety." Accordingly I arose and collected planks and pieces of aloes-wood, and bound them together with ropes from the ships that had been wrecked. I piled the raft high with jewels and ornaments of gold and silver, and with the pearls that were like gravel, and with ambergris. I then launched the raft upon the river, and made for it two pieces of wood like oars.

And so I departed on the raft, following the current towards the mountain, and entered a tunnel through which the river ran. There was intense darkness within, and the raft continued to carry me along to a narrow place beneath the mountain, where my head rubbed the roof of the tunnel. I threw myself down upon my face on the raft, and continued to proceed, not knowing night from day, until the intensity of the darkness wearied me so that I was overcome with slumber, and the current ceased not to bear me along while I slept.

At length I awoke, and found myself in the light, and, opening my eyes, beheld wide fields on either side of the river, and the raft tied to the shore, and around me a number of negroes. When they saw that I had awakened they spoke to me in their language, but I knew not what they said, and imagined that it was a dream, and that this occurred in sleep. Then a man from among them advanced, and said to me in the Arabic language, "Peace be on thee, O our brother! Who art thou? Whence hast thou come? We are people of the sown lands and the fields, and we came to irrigate our lands, and we found thee asleep upon thy raft. We tied it here, waiting for thee to arise at thy leisure. Now tell us what is the cause of thy coming unto this place."

"O my master," I replied, "I entreat thee to bring to me some food, for I am hungry, and after that ask of me what thou wilt!" Thereupon he brought food, and I ate until I was at ease, and my fear subsided, and I then acquainted the people with all that had happened to me from beginning to end, and with what I had experienced upon the river.

They took me with them, and conveyed with me the raft, together with all that was upon it of riches and goods, and jewels and minerals, and ornaments of gold and silver, and they led me to their King, who was the King of India, and acquainted him with my story. He wondered at this exceedingly, and welcomed me with great honours, and congratulated me on my safety. Then I arose and took a quantity of jewels and aloes-wood and ambergris, and presented them to the King. He accepted it all, treated me with the greatest honour, and lodged me in a place in his abode.

I remained in this country for some time, then begged of the King that I might return to my own land. He gave me permission after great pressing, and bestowed upon me abundant gifts from his treasury. He also gave me a present and a sealed letter, saying, "Convey these to the Caliph Haroun Al Raschid, and give him many salutations from us." The letter was on yellow parchment, and the writing was ultramarine. The words that he wrote to the Caliph were these:

> Peace be on thee from the King of India, before whom are a thousand elephants, and on the battlements of whose palace are a thousand jewels.
> To proceed: we have sent to thee a trifling present; accept it then from us. Thou art to us a brother and sincere friend, and the affection for you that is in our hearts is great; therefore favour us by a reply. The present is not suited to thy dignity; but we beg thee, O brother, to accept it graciously. And peace be on thee!

And the present was a ruby cup a span high, the inside of which was set with precious pearls, and a bed covered with the spotted skin of the serpent that swalloweth an elephant, and a hundred thousand mithkals of Indian aloes-wood, and a slave-girl like the shining full moon.

So I embarked, and departed thence, and we continued our voyage from island to island, and from country to country, until we arrived at Bagdad, whereupon I entered my house and met my family and my brethren, after which I took the present of the King of India to the Caliph the Commander of the Faithful, Haroun Al Raschid. On entering his presence I kissed his hand, and placed before him the ruby cup, the serpent's skin, and the other things, all of which pleased the

Sindbad carries the Old Man of the Sea on his shoulders

Caliph greatly, and he read the letter, and showed me utmost honour, and said, "O Sindbad, is that true which this King hath stated in his letter?" And I kissed the ground and answered, "O my lord, I witnessed in his kingdom much more than he hath mentioned. On the day of his public appearance a throne is set for the King upon a huge elephant, eleven cubits high, and he sitteth upon it, with his chief officers and pages and guests standing in two ranks, on his right and on his left. At his head standeth a man holding a golden javelin in his hand, and behind him a man in whose hand is a mace of gold, at the top of which is an emerald of the thickness of a thumb. And when the King mounteth he is accompanied by a thousand horsemen clad in gold and silk. Moreover, by reason of the King's justice and good government there is no need of a Cadi in his city, and all the people of his country know the truth from falsity."

And the Caliph wondered at my words, and conferred favours upon me, and commanded me to depart to my abode. I did so, and continued to live in the same pleasant manner as at present. I forgot the arduous troubles that I had experienced, and betook myself to eating and drinking and pleasures and joy.

And when Sindbad the Sailor had finished his story every one present wondered at the events that had happened to him. He then ordered his treasurer to give to Hindbad a hundred pieces of gold, and commanded him to depart, and to return the next day with the boon-companions to hear the seventh story. Sindbad the Sailor next day began as follows:

THE SEVENTH VOYAGE: THE ELEPHANT HUNT

After my sixth voyage I determined to go to sea no more, and my time was spent in joy and pleasures. But one day some one knocked on the door of my house, and the door-keeper opened, and a page entered and summoned me to the

Caliph. I immediately went with him, and kissed the ground before the Commander of the Faithful, who said, "O Sindbad, I have an affair for thee to perform. I desire that thou go to the King of India, and convey to him our letter and our present."

I trembled thereat, and replied, "O my lord, I have a horror of voyaging, and when it is mentioned to me my limbs tremble. And this is because of the terrors and troubles I have experienced. Moreover, I have bound myself by an oath not to go forth from Bagdad." Then I informed the Caliph of all that had befallen me from first to last, and he wondered exceedingly thereat, and said, "Verily, O Sindbad, it hath not been heard from times of old that such events have befallen anyone as have befallen thee. But for our sake thou wilt go forth this time, and convey our letter and our present to the King of India." So I replied, "I hear and obey," being unable to oppose this command.

I went from Bagdad to the sea, and embarked in a ship, and we proceeded nights and days, by the aid of Allah, whose name be exalted, until we arrived at the capital of India. As soon as I entered the city I took the present and the letter, and went in with them to the King, and kissed the ground before him. "A friendly welcome to thee, O Sindbad," said he. "We have longed to see thee, and praise be to Allah, who hath shown us thy face a second time!" Then he took me by the hand, and seated me by his side, and treated me with familiar kindness. "O my lord," I said, "I have brought thee a present and a letter from the Caliph Haroun Al Raschid." I then offered to him the letter and the present, which consisted of a horse worth ten thousand pieces of gold, with a saddle adorned with gold set with jewels; and a book; and a sumptuous dress; and a hundred different kinds of white cloths and silks of Egypt; and Greek carpets; and a wonderful, extraordinary cup of crystal; and also the table of Solomon, the son of David, on whom be peace!

And the contents of the letter were as follows:

Peace from the King Al Raschid, strengthened by Allah (who hath given to him and to his ancestors the rank of nobles and widespread glory), on the fortunate Sultan!

To proceed: thy letter hath reached us, and we rejoiced thereat. And we send thee the book entitled *The Delight of the Intelligent and the Rare Present for Friends,* together with varieties of royal rarities. Therefore do us the honour to accept them, and peace be on thee!

Then the King bestowed upon me abundant gifts, and treated me with the utmost honour. After some days I begged his permission to depart, but he permitted me not, save after great pressing. Thereupon I took leave of him, and went forth from his city, and set out on my journey, without any desire for travel or commerce. But after three or four days at sea we were attacked by corsairs, who seized our ship by force, slaying some and taking others captive. Those, with me among them, they conveyed to an island, where they sold us as slaves.

A rich man purchased me, and took me to his house, fed me and gave me to drink, and clad and treated me in a friendly manner. So my soul was tranquillized, and I rested a little. One day my master said to me, "Dost thou know any art or trade?" I answered him, "O my lord, I am a merchant. I know nothing but traffic." "But dost thou know," he asked, "the art of shooting with the bow and arrow?" "Yes," I answered, "I know that." Thereupon he brought me a bow and arrows, and mounted me behind him upon an elephant. He departed from the city at the close of night, and conveyed me to a grove of large trees, where, selecting a lofty, firm tree, he made me climb it, and gave me the bow and arrows, saying, "Sit here, and when the elephants come in the daytime shoot at them with the arrows. If thou kill one come and inform me." He then left me and departed.

I was terrified and frightened. I remained concealed in the tree until the sun rose, when the elephants came forth wandering through the grove. I discharged my arrows until I shot one, and then I went to my master and informed him of this. He was delighted with me, and treated me with honour, and removed the slain elephant. In this way I continued every day, shooting one and my master coming and removing it, until one day I was sitting in the tree, concealed, when suddenly elephants innumerable came towards me, roaring and growling, so that the earth trembled beneath them. They surrounded the tree in which I was sitting, and a huge elephant, enormously great, wound his trunk around it, pulled it up by the roots, and cast it upon the ground.

I fell down senseless among the elephants, and the great one approached me, wound his trunk around me, raised me on his back, and went away with me, the other elephants following. He carried me a long distance, then threw me from his back and departed, the other elephants accompanying him. When my terror had subsided I looked about, and found myself among the bones of elephants, and the ground was covered with ivory tusks. I knew then that this was the burial-place of the elephants, and that the great one had brought me here on account of the tusks.

I arose, and journeyed a night and a day, until I arrived at the house of my master, who saw that I was pale from fright and hunger. "Verily thou hast pained my heart," said he, "for I went and found the tree torn up, and I imagined that the elephants had destroyed thee. Tell me what happened to thee." So I informed him of all that had occurred, and he took me upon his elephant, and together we journeyed to the burial-place. When my master beheld those numerous ivory tusks he rejoiced greatly, and carried away as many as he desired, and we returned to his house.

He treated me with increased favour, and said, "O my son, thou hast directed me to a means of very great gain!"

May Allah recompense thee well! Thou art freed for the sake of Allah, whose name be exalted! Those elephants used to destroy many of us, but Allah hath preserved thee from them." "O my master," I replied, "may Allah bless thee! And I request, O my master, that thou give me permission to depart to mine own country." At my request he allowed me to leave the country, loaded with presents, with which in due time I regained my home in Bagdad, where I have since lived.

Sindbad here finished the relation of his seventh and last voyage, and Hindbad departed for his home, bearing with him as before one hundred pieces of gold, which Sindbad gave him.

THE PRINCESS AND THE PEA

ONCE upon a time there was a prince, and he wanted a princess; but she would have to be a *real* princess. He travelled all round the world to find one, but always there was something wrong. There were princesses enough, but he found it difficult to make out whether they were *real* ones. There was always something about them that was not quite right. So he came home again, and was very sad, for he would have liked very much to have a real princess.

One evening a terrible storm came on; it thundered and lightened, and the rain poured down in torrents. It was really dreadful! Suddenly a knocking was heard at the city gate, and the old King himself went to open it.

It was a princess standing out there before the gate. But, good gracious, what a sight she was after all the rain and the dreadful weather! The water ran down from her hair and her clothes; it ran down into the toes of her shoes and out again at the heels. And yet she said that she was a real princess.

"Yes, we'll soon find that out," thought the old Queen. But she said nothing, went into the bedroom, took all the bedding off the bedstead, and laid a pea at the bottom; then she took twenty mattresses and laid them on the pea, and then twenty eiderdown beds on top of the mattresses.

On this the Princess was to lie all night. In the morning she was asked how she had slept.

"Oh, terribly badly!" said the Princess. "I have scarcely shut my eyes the whole night. Heaven only knows what was in the bed, but I was lying on something hard, so that I am black and blue all over my body. It is really terrible!"

Now they knew that she was a real princess, because she

had felt the pea right through the twenty mattresses and the twenty eiderdown beds.

Nobody but a real princess could be as sensitive as that.

So the prince took her for his wife, for now he knew that he had a real princess; and the pea was put in the Art Museum, where it may still be seen, if no one has stolen it.

There, that is a real story!

BLUE BEARD

Near the city of Bagdad there once lived a man who had fine houses, both in town and country, silver and gold plate, chests of jewels, embroidered furniture, coaches gilded all over with gold, and all that riches can give. But this man had the misfortune to have a blue beard, which made him so frightfully ugly that all the women and girls ran away from him.

One of his neighbours, a lady of quality, had two sons and daughters who were perfect beauties. He desired of her one of them in marriage, leaving to her the choice which of the two, Anne or Fatima, she would bestow upon him. They would neither of them have him, and each made the other welcome of him, being not able to bear the thought of marrying a man who had a blue beard. And what besides gave them disgust and aversion was his having already been married to several wives, and nobody ever knew what became of them.

Blue Beard, to engage their affection, took them, with the lady their mother, and three or four ladies of their acquaintance, with other young people of the neighbourhood, to one of his country seats, where they stayed a whole week. There was nothing then to be but parties of pleasure, hunting, fishing, dancing, mirth, and feasting. Nobody went to bed, but all passed the night in playing tricks upon each other. In short, everything succeeded so well that the younger daughter began to think the beard of the master of the house was not so very blue after all, and that he was a mighty pleasant gentleman. And in the end, soon after they returned home, the marriage was concluded.

About a month afterwards Blue Beard told his wife that

he was obliged to take a country journey for six weeks at least, about affairs of very great consequence, desiring her to divert herself in his absence, to send for her friends and acquaintances, to carry them into the country, if she pleased, and to make good cheer wherever she was.

"Here," said he, "are the keys of the two great wardrobes, wherein I have my best furniture; these keys open the strong-rooms, where are kept my silver and gold plate, which is not every day in use; these open my strong-boxes, which hold my money, both gold and silver; these my caskets of jewels; and this is the master-key to all my apartments. But for this little one here, it is the key of the closet at the end of the gallery on the ground floor. Open them all, go into all and every one of them except that little closet, which I forbid you, and forbid it in such a manner that if you happen to open it there will be no bounds to my just anger and resentment."

She promised to observe very exactly whatever he had ordered; when he, after having embraced her, got into his coach and proceeded on his journey.

Her neighbours and good friends hardly stayed to be sent for by the newly married young lady, so great was their impatience to see all the rich furniture of her house, not having dared to come while her husband was there, because of his blue beard, which frightened them. They ran through all the rooms, closets, and wardrobes, which were all so rich and fine that each seemed to surpass the other.

After that they went up into the two great rooms, where were the best and richest furniture; they could not suffi-ciently admire the quantity and beauty of the tapestry, bed, couches, cabinets, stands, tables, and looking-glasses, in which you might see yourself from head to foot; some of them were framed with glass, others with silver, plain and gilded, the finest and most magnificent which were ever seen. They ceased not to extol and envy the happiness of their friend, who in the meantime no way diverted herself in looking upon all these rich things, because of the impatience she had to go and open the closet on the ground floor. She was so much pressed by her curiosity that, without considering that it was very uncivil to leave her company, she went down a little back staircase, and with such excess haste that once or twice she had all but broken her neck.

Being come to the closet door, she made a stop for some time, thinking upon her husband's orders, and considering what unhappiness might attend her if she was disobedient; but the temptation was so strong that she could not overcome it. She took then the little key, and opened it, trembling; but could not at first see anything plainly, because the window-shutters were closed. After some moments she began to perceive that the floor was all covered over with clotted blood, and in a row in front of her were hanging the bodies of several dead women against the wall: these, then, were all the wives whom Blue Beard had married, and murdered one after another! She was like to have died for fear, and the key, which she pulled out of the lock, fell out of her hand.

After having somewhat recovered her senses she picked up the key, locked the door, and went upstairs into her chamber to recover herself; but she could not, so much was she frightened. Having observed that the key of the closet was stained with blood, she tried two or three times to wipe it off, but the blood would not come off; in vain did she wash it, and even rub it with soap and sand, the blood still remained, for the key was a magic key, and she could never make it quite clean; when the blood was gone off from one side it came again on the other.

Blue Beard returned from his journey the same evening, and said he had received letters upon the road informing him that the affair he went about was ended to his advantage. Fatima did all she could to convince him that she was extremely glad of his speedy return. Next morning he asked her for the keys, which she gave him, but with such a trembling hand that he easily guessed what had happened.

"What," said he, "is not the key of my closet among the rest?"

"I must certainly," answered she, "have left it above upon the table."

"Fail not," said Blue Beard, "to bring it me presently."

After putting him off several times she was forced to bring him the key. Blue Beard, having very attentively considered it, said to his wife:

"How comes this blood upon the key?"

"I do not know," cried poor Fatima, paler than death.

"You do not know!" replied Blue Beard. "But *I* know well enough. You were resolved to go into the closet, were you not? Very well, madam; you *shall* go in, and you shall take your place among the ladies you saw there."

Upon this she threw herself at her husband's feet, weeping and begging his pardon with all the signs of a true repentance for her disobedience. She would have melted a rock, so beautiful and sorrowful was she; but Blue Beard had a heart harder than any rock.

"You must die, madam," said he, "and that at once!"

"Since I must die," answered she, looking upon him with her eyes all bathed in tears, "give me some little time to say my prayers."

"I give you," replied Blue Beard, "half a quarter of an hour, but not one moment more!"

She left him, and went to find her sister, and she said to her, "Sister Anne, Sister Anne, I beg you, go up to the top of the tower and look if my brothers are coming; they promised me that they would come to-day, and if you see them give them a sign to make haste."

She said this with such agitation that her sister dared not wait to ask the reason, but ran up to the roof of the tower and watched and watched, while poor Fatima below cried out to her, "Sister Anne, Sister Anne, do you see anybody coming?"

And Sister Anne said, "I see nothing but dust blowing and the green grass growing."

Meanwhile Blue Beard had taken a great scimitar in his hand, and now cried out to her as loud as he could bawl, "Wife, come down instantly, or I shall come up to you!"

"One moment, just one moment, longer, if you please," said his wife, and then she called very softly, "Anne, Sister Anne, do you see anybody coming?"

And Sister Anne answered, "I see nothing but the dust blowing and the green grass growing."

"Come down quickly," cried Blue Beard, "or I shall come up to you!"

"I am coming," answered his wife. And then she cried again, "Sister Anne, Sister Anne, do you see anybody coming?"

"I see," replied Sister Anne, "a great cloud of dust that comes this way."

"Are they my brothers?"

"Alas, no, my dear sister; I see a flock of sheep."

"Will you not come down?" shouted Blue Beard.

"One moment longer," said his wife, and then she cried out, "Anne, Sister Anne, do you see nobody coming?"

"I see," said she, "two horsemen coming, but they are yet a great way off.

"God be praised!" she cried presently. "They are my brothers; I am waving to them, as well as I can, for them to make haste."

Then Blue Beard bawled out so loud that he made the whole house tremble. The distressed wife came down, and threw herself at his feet, all in tears, with her hair about her shoulders.

"Naught will avail," said Blue Beard. "You must die." Then, taking hold of her hair with one hand and waving his scimitar with the other, he was on the very point of cutting off her head.

The poor lady turning about to him, and looking at him with dying eyes, desired him to afford her one little moment to recollect herself.

"No, no!" said he. "Recommend thyself to God," and again he raised his scimitar ready to strike.

At this very instant there was such a loud knocking at the gate that Blue Beard made a sudden stop. The gate burst open, and in flew two horsemen, drawing their swords, and rushed furiously upon Blue Beard. He knew them at once to be his wife's brothers and fled to save himself; but the

She took then the little key, and opened the door, trembling

two brothers pursued so close that they overtook him before he could get to the steps of the porch, when they ran their swords through his body, and left him dead. Poor Fatima, almost as dead as her husband, sank on to the ground, and had not strength enough to rise and welcome her brothers.

Blue Beard had no heirs, and so his wife became mistress of all his estates. She made use of part of his wealth to marry her sister Anne to a young gentleman who had loved her a long while; another to buy captains' commissions for her brothers; and the rest to marry herself to a very worthy gentleman, who made her forget the terrible time she had passed with Blue Beard.

JACK THE GIANT-KILLER

IN the reign of King Arthur there lived in the county of Cornwall a worthy farmer, who had an only son named Jack.

Jack was a boy of a bold temper; he took pleasure in hearing or reading stories of wizards, conjurers, giants, and fairies. He was a leader in all the sports of youth, and hardly anyone could equal him at wrestling; or if he met with a match for himself in strength his skill and cunning always made him the victor.

In those days there lived on St Michael's Mount, off the coast of Cornwall, a huge giant. He was eighteen feet high and three yards round; and his fierce and savage looks were the terror of all his neighbours. He dwelt in a gloomy cavern on the very top of the mountain, and used to wade over to the mainland in search of his prey. When he came near the people left their houses; and, after he had glutted his appetite upon their cattle, he would throw half a dozen oxen upon his back, and tie as many sheep and hogs round his waist like a bunch of candles, and march back home. The giant had done this for many years, and all Cornwall was greatly hurt by his thefts, when Jack boldly resolved to destroy him.

Early in a long winter's evening Jack took a horn, a shovel, a pickaxe, and a dark lantern, and went over to the Mount. There he fell to work at once, and before morning he had dug a pit twenty-two feet deep, and almost as many broad. He covered it over with sticks and straw, and strewed some of the earth over them, to make it look just like solid ground. He then put his horn to his mouth, and blew such a loud and long tantivy that the giant awoke, and came towards Jack, roaring like thunder, "You saucy villain, you shall pay dearly for breaking my rest; I will broil you whole for breakfast." He had scarcely spoken these words when he tumbled headlong into the pit, and his fall shook the very mountain.

"Oho, Giant!" said Jack, "where are you now? Have you found your way so soon into Lob's Pound? Will nothing serve you now for breakfast this cold morning but broiling poor Jack?"

The giant now tried to rise, but Jack struck him a blow on the crown of the head with his pickaxe, which killed him at once.

Jack now made haste back, to rejoice his friends with the news of the giant's death. When the justices of Cornwall heard of this valiant action they sent for Jack, and declared that he should always be called Jack the Giant-killer; and they also gave him a sword and belt, upon which was written, in letters of gold:

> This is the valiant Cornishman
> Who slew the giant Cormoran.

The news of Jack's victory soon spread over all the west of England; and another giant, called Blunderbore, vowed to have revenge on Jack, if it should ever be his fortune to get him into his power. The giant kept an enchanted castle in

the midst of a lonely wood. About four months after the death of Cormoran, as Jack was taking a journey into Wales, he passed through this wood; and, as he was very weary, he sat down to rest by the side of a pleasant fountain, and there he fell into a deep sleep. The giant came to the fountain for water just at this time, and found Jack there; and as the lines on Jack's belt showed who he was, the giant lifted him gently on to his shoulder, to carry him to his castle; but, as he passed through the thicket, the rustling of the leaves awakened Jack; and he was sadly afraid when he found himself in the clutches of Blunderbore. Yet this was nothing to his fright soon after; for when they reached the castle he beheld the floor covered all over with the bones of men and women. The giant quickly locked Jack up, while he went to fetch another giant, who lived in the same wood, to come to dinner with him. While he was away Jack heard dreadful shrieks, groans, and cries from many parts of the castle; and soon after he heard a mournful voice repeat these lines:

> Haste, valiant stranger, haste away,
> Lest you become the giant's prey.
> On his return he'll bring another,
> Still more savage than his brother.

Then Jack, looking out of the window, saw the two giants coming along arm in arm. This window was right over the gates of the castle. "Now," thought Jack, "either my death or freedom is at hand."

There were two strong ropes in the room. Jack made a large noose, with a slip-knot, at the ends of both these, and as the giants were coming through the gates he threw the ropes over their heads. He then made the other ends fast to a beam in the ceiling, and pulled with all his might till he had almost strangled them. When he saw that they were both quite black in the face and had not the least strength left, he drew his sword and slid down the ropes; he then killed the giants, and thus saved himself from a cruel death. Jack next took a great bunch of keys from the pocket of Blunderbore, and went into the castle again. He made a

search through all the rooms, and in them found three ladies tied up by the hair of their heads, and almost starved to death.

"Sweet ladies," said Jack, "I have killed the monster and his wicked brother, and now I set you free." He then gave them the keys of the castle, and went farther on his journey to Wales.

Jack then went on his way, travelling as fast as he could. At length he lost his way, and when night came on he was in a lonely valley between two lofty mountains, where at last he found a large house. He went up to it boldly and knocked loudly at the gate, when, to his surprise, there came forth a monstrous giant with two heads. He spoke to Jack very civilly, for he was a Welsh giant, and all the mischief he did was by private and secret malice, under the show of friendship and kindness. Jack told him that he was a traveller who had lost his way, on which the huge monster made him welcome, and led him into a room where there was a good bed in which to pass the night. But soon after he had gone to bed he heard the giant in the next room saying to himself:

> Though here you lodge with me this night,
> You shall not see the morning light;
> My club shall dash your brains outright.

"Say'st thou so?" quoth Jack. "Are these your Welsh tricks? But I hope to prove as cunning as you." Then, getting out of bed, he found a billet of wood; he laid it in his own place in the bed and hid himself in a corner of the room. In the middle of the night the giant came in with his club and struck many heavy blows on the bed, in the very place where Jack had laid the billet, thinking he had broken all the bones in Jack's skin. Early in the morning Jack put on a bold face and walked into the giant's room to thank him for his lodging.

"How have you rested?" quoth the giant; "did you not feel anything in the night?"

"No," said Jack, "nothing but a rat, I believe, that gave me three or four slaps with his tail."

The giant wondered at this; yet he did not answer a word, and went to bring two great bowls of hasty-pudding for their breakfast.

Jack wished to make the giant believe that he could eat as much as himself; so he contrived to button a leathern bag inside his coat and slipped the hasty-pudding into this bag, while he seemed to put it into his mouth. Then telling the giant he would show him a trick he took hold of the knife, ripped up the bag, and all the hasty-pudding tumbled out upon the floor.

"Ods splutter hur nails," cried the Welsh giant, "hur can do that trick hurself." So he snatched up the knife, plunged it into his stomach, and fell down dead.

As soon as Jack had thus tricked the Welsh monster he went farther on his journey; and, a few days after, he met with King Arthur's only son, who had got his father's leave to travel into Wales, to deliver a beautiful lady from the power of a wicked magician, by whom she was held in enchantment.

When Jack found that the young prince had no servants with him he begged leave to attend him; and the prince at once agreed to this, and gave Jack many thanks for his kindness.

King Arthur's son was a handsome, polite, and brave knight, and so good-natured that he gave money to everybody he met. At length he gave his last penny to an old woman, and then as the sun began to grow low he said, "Jack, since we have no money left where can we lodge this night?"

"Master," said Jack, "be of good heart; two miles farther on there lives an uncle of mine: he is a huge and monstrous giant with three heads. He will fight five hundred men in armour, and make them fly before him."

"Alas!" cried the King's son, "we had better never have been born than meet with such a monster."

"My lord, leave me to manage that; but tarry here till I return."

Then Jack rode on at full speed; and when he came to the gates of the castle he gave a loud knock. The giant, with a voice like thunder, roared out, "Who is there?"

Jack made answer, and said, "None but your poor Cousin Jack."

Quoth he, "What news with my poor Cousin Jack?"

"Dear Uncle," he replied, "heavy news, God wot!"

"Prithee!" said the giant, "what heavy news can come to me? I am a giant with three heads, and can fight five hundred men in armour, and make them fly like chaff before the wind."

"Alas!" said Jack, "here is the King's son coming with a thousand men to kill you, and to destroy all that you have."

"Oh, Cousin Jack," said the giant, "this is heavy news indeed! But I have a large cellar underground, where I will hide myself, and you shall lock, bolt, and bar me in, and keep the keys till the King's son is gone."

Now when Jack had barred the giant fast in the vault he went back and fetched the prince, and they both made themselves happy while the poor giant lay trembling with fear in the cellar underground.

Early in the morning Jack gave the King's son gold and silver out of the giant's treasure, and accompanied him three miles forward on his journey, by which time he was pretty well out of the smell of the giant. He then went back to let out his uncle, who asked him what he should give him for saving his castle.

"Why, good Uncle," said Jack, "I desire nothing but the

old coat and cap, with the old rusty sword and slippers, which are hanging at your bed's head."

"Then," said the giant, "you shall have them: and pray keep them for my sake, for they are things of great use. The coat will keep you invisible, the cap will give you knowledge, the sword will cut through anything, and the shoes are of vast swiftness. They may be useful to you, so take them with all my heart."

Jack gave many thanks to the giant, and when he had come up with the King's son they soon arrived at the dwelling of the lady who was under the power of a wicked magician. She received the prince very politely, and made a noble feast for him. When it was ended she rose and, wiping her mouth with a fine handkerchief, said, "My lord, you must submit to the custom of my palace; to-morrow morning I command you to tell me on whom I bestow this handkerchief, or lose your head." She then left the room.

The young prince went to bed very mournful, but Jack put on his cap of knowledge, which told him that the lady was forced, by the power of enchantment, to meet the wicked magician every night in the middle of the forest. Jack put on his coat of darkness, and his shoes of swiftness, and was there before her. When the lady came she gave the handkerchief to the magician. Jack, with his sword of sharpness, at one blow cut off his head; the enchantment was then ended in a moment, and the lady restored to her former beauty and goodness. She was married to the prince on the next day, and they soon after went back to the Court of King Arthur, where they were received with joyful welcomes; and Jack, for his many great deeds, was made one of the Knights of the Round Table.

As Jack had been so lucky he resolved not to be idle, but still to do what he could for his king and country. He therefore begged his Majesty for a horse and money, that he might travel in search of new and strange exploits. "For," said he, "there are many giants yet living in the farthest parts of Wales, to the great distress of your Majesty's subjects; therefore, if it please you, sire, to favour me in my design, I will soon rid your kingdom of these giants and monsters in human shape."

When the King heard this offer he gave Jack everything proper for such a journey, and taking with him his cap of knowledge, his sword of sharpness, his shoes of swiftness, and his invisible coat, the better to perform the great exploits that might fall in his way, Jack set off on his journey. He went along over hills and mountains; and on the third day he came to a wide forest. He had hardly entered it when on a sudden he heard dreadful shrieks and cries, and, forcing his way through the trees, saw a monstrous giant dragging along by the hair of their heads a handsome knight and a beautiful lady. Their tears and cries melted the heart of honest Jack; he alighted from his horse, and, tying him to an oak-tree, put on his invisible coat, under which he carried his sword of sharpness.

When he came up to the giant he made several strokes at him, and at length, putting both hands to his sword, and aiming with all his might, he cut off both the giant's legs just below the garter, and the earth itself trembled with the force of his fall. At this the noble knight and the virtuous lady not only returned Jack hearty thanks for their deliverance, but also invited him to their house, to refresh himself after his dreadful encounter, as likewise to receive a reward for his good services.

"No," said Jack, "I cannot be at ease till I find out the giant's den."

The knight, on hearing this, grew very sorrowful, and replied: "Noble stranger, it is too much to run a second hazard; this monster lived in a den under yonder mountain, with a brother more fierce and cruel than himself; therefore, if you should go thither, and perish in the attempt, it would be a heart-breaking thing to me and my lady; so let me persuade you to go back with us, and desist from any further pursuit."

"Nay," answered Jack, "if there be another, even if there were twenty, not one of them should escape my fury. But when I have finished this task I will come and pay my respects to you."

Jack had not ridden a mile and a half before he came in sight of the mouth of the cavern; and, nigh the entrance of it, he saw the other giant sitting on a huge block of timber, with a knotted iron club lying by his side, waiting for his brother. His eyes looked like flames of fire, his face was grim and ugly, and his cheeks were like two flitches of bacon; the bristles of his beard seemed to be thick rods of iron wire; and his long locks of hair hung down upon his broad shoulders like curling snakes. Jack got down from his horse and turned him into a thicket; then he put on his coat of darkness and drew a little nearer, and said softly, "Oh! are you there? It will not be long before I shall take you fast by the beard!"

The giant all this while could not see him, by reason of his invisible coat ; so Jack came quite close to him, and struck a blow at his head with his sword of sharpness; but he missed his aim, and only cut off his nose, which made him roar like loud claps of thunder. He took up his iron club, and began to lay about him like one that was mad with pain and fury.

But Jack slipped nimbly behind him, and drove his sword up to the hilt in the giant's back. This done, Jack cut off his head, and sent it, with the head of his brother, to King Arthur, by a wagon he hired for that purpose. When Jack had thus killed these two monsters he went into their cave in search of their treasure. He passed through many turnings and windings, which led him to a room paved with free-stone; at the end of it was a boiling cauldron, and on the right hand stood a large table, where the giants used to dine. He then came to a window that was secured with iron bars, through which he saw a number of wretched captives, who cried out when they saw Jack, "Alas! alas!

young man, you are come to be one among us in this horrid den."

"Ay," said Jack, "but pray tell me what is the meaning of your being here at all?"

"Alas!" said one poor old man, "I will tell you, sir. We are persons that have been taken by the giants who hold this cave, and are kept till they choose to have a feast; then one of us is to be killed, and cooked to please their taste. It is not long since they took three for the same purpose."

"Say you so," quoth Jack, and straightway he unlocked the gate, and set the captives all free. Then they searched the giant's coffers, and Jack divided among them all the treasures. The next morning they set off to their homes, and Jack to the knight's house, whom he had left with his lady not long before.

He was received with the greatest joy by the thankful knight and his lady, who, in honour of Jack's exploits, gave a grand feast, to which all the nobles and gentry were invited, and gave him also a fine ring, on which was engraved the picture of the giant dragging the knight and the lady by the hair, with this motto round it:

> Behold in dire distress were we,
> Under a giant's fierce command;
> But gain'd our lives and liberty
> From valiant Jack's victorious hand.

In the midst of their mirth a messenger brought the dismal tidings that Thunderdell, a savage giant with two heads, had heard of the death of his two kinsmen, and was come to take his revenge on Jack; and that he was now within a mile of the knight's seat, the people flying before him like chaff. But Jack only drew his sword, and said, "Let him come. I have here a tool to pick his teeth. Pray, ladies and gentlemen, do me the favour to walk into the garden, and you shall soon behold the giant's defeat and death."

The knight's house stood in the middle of a moat, thirty feet deep and twenty wide, over which lay a drawbridge. Jack set men to work to cut through the bridge on both sides, almost to the middle, and then dressed himself in his coat of darkness and went against the giant with his sword of sharpness. As he came close to him, though the giant could not see him for his invisible coat, yet he found some danger was near, which made him cry out:

> " Fee, fi, fo, fum,
> I smell the blood of an Englishman!
> Let him be alive, or let him be dead,
> I'll grind his bones to make me bread!"

"Say'st thou so?" said Jack; "then thou art a monstrous miller, indeed!"

"Art thou the villain that killed my kinsmen? Then I will tear thee with my teeth and grind thy bones to powder."

"You must catch me first," quoth Jack; and throwing off his coat of darkness, and putting on his shoes of swiftness, he began to run, the giant following him like a walking castle, making the earth shake at every step.

Jack led him round and round the walls of the house, that the company might see the monster; then, to finish the work, he ran over the drawbridge, the giant going after him with his club; but when he came to the middle, where the bridge had been cut on both sides, the great weight of his body made it break, and he tumbled into the water, where he rolled about like a large whale. Jack stood by the side of the moat and laughed at him the while. The giant foamed to hear him scoff, and plunged from side to side of the moat; but he could not get out to be revenged. At last Jack ordered a cart-rope to be brought to him; he then cast it over his two heads, and by the help of a team of horses dragged him to the edge of the moat, where he cut off his heads, and sent them both to the Court of King Arthur.

After staying with the knight for some time, Jack set out again in search of new adventures. He went over hills and dales without meeting any, till he came to the foot of a very high mountain. Here he knocked at the door of a small and lonely house, and an old man, with a head as white as snow, let him in.

"Good father," said Jack, "can you lodge a traveller who has lost his way?"

"Yes," said the old man, "I can, if you will accept such fare as my poor house affords."

Jack entered, and the old man set before him some bread and fruit for his supper. When Jack had eaten as much as he chose the old man said: "My son, I know you are the famous conqueror of giants; now, at the top of this mountain is an enchanted castle, kept by a giant named Galligantus, who, by the help of a vile magician, gets many knights into his castle, where he changes them into the shape of beasts. Above all, I lament the hard fate of a duke's daughter whom they seized as she was walking in her father's garden, and brought hither through the air in a chariot drawn by two fiery dragons, and turned her into the shape of a deer. Many knights have tried to destroy the enchantment and deliver her, yet none have been able to do it, by reason of two fiery griffins, who guard the gate of the castle and destroy all who come nigh; but as you, my son, have an invisible coat you may pass by them without being seen; and on the gates of the castle you will find engraved by what means the enchantment may be broken."

Jack promised that in the morning, at the risk of his life, he would break the enchantment; and after a sound sleep he arose early, put on his invisible coat, and got ready for the attempt. When he had climbed to the top of the mountain he saw the two fiery griffins; but he passed between them without the least fear of danger, for they could not see him because of his invisible coat. On the castle-gate he found a golden trumpet, under which were written these lines:

> Whoever can this trumpet blow
> Shall cause the giant's overthrow.

As soon as Jack had read this he seized the trumpet and blew a shrill blast, which made the gates fly open and the very castle itself tremble. The giant and the conjurer now knew that their wicked course was at an end, and they stood biting their thumbs and shaking with fear. Jack, with his sword of sharpness, soon killed the giant, and the magician was then carried away by a whirlwind. All the knights and beautiful ladies, who had been changed into birds and beasts, returned to their proper shapes. The castle vanished away like smoke, and the head of the giant Galligantus was sent to King Arthur. By then Jack's fame had spread through the whole country; and at the King's desire the duke gave him his daughter in marriage, to the joy of all the kingdom. After this the King gave him a large estate, on which he and his lady lived the rest of their days in joy and content.

THE UGLY DUCKLING

It was delightful out in the country: it was summer, and the cornfields were golden, the oats were green, the hay had been put up in stacks in the green meadows, and the stork went about on his long red legs and chattered Egyptian, for this was the language he had learned from his mother. Round the fields and meadows were great forests, and in the midst of the forests lay deep lakes. Yes, it was really delightful out in the country! In the midst of the sunshine there lay an old manor-house, with deep canals round it, and from the wall down to the water grew large burdocks, so high that little children could stand upright under the tallest of them. It was just as wild there as in the deepest wood. Here sat a duck upon her nest, for she had to hatch her ducklings, but she was almost tired out, for it took such a long time; and she so seldom had visitors. The other ducks liked better to swim about in the canals than to climb up to sit under a burdock and cackle with her.

At last one egg after another cracked open. "Piep! piep!" they cried; all the yolks had come to life, and little heads were peeping out.

"Quack! quack!" said the duck, and they all came out, quacking as fast as they could, looking all round them under the green leaves, and the mother let them look as much as they wished, for green is good for the eyes.

"How wide the world is!" said the young ones, for they truly had much more room now than when they were in the eggs.

"Do you think this is the whole world?" said the mother. "That stretches far across the other side of the garden, quite into the parson's field; but I have never been there yet! I hope you are all here," she said, and she stood up. "No, I haven't got you all. The biggest egg is still there. How long is this going to last? I am getting tired of it." And she sat down again.

"Well, how goes it?" said an old duck who had come to pay her a visit.

"It's taking so long with that one egg," said the duck sitting there. "It will not break. But look at the others! They are the prettiest ducklings I have ever seen! They are all just like their father, the rascal! He never comes to see me."

"Let me see the egg which will not break," said the old one. "Depend upon it, it is a turkey's egg! I was once cheated in that way, and had a lot of bother and trouble with the young ones, for they are afraid of the water. I could not get them into it. I quacked and pecked, but it was no use! Let me see the egg. Yes, that's a turkey's egg! Let it alone, and teach the other children to swim."

"I think I'll just sit on it a little longer," said the duck. "I've sat so long now that I may as well sit a few days more."

"As you please," said the old duck, and she went away.

At last the big egg broke. "Piep! piep!" said the little one, and crept out. It was very big and ugly. The duck looked at it.

"That's a terribly big duckling!" said she; "none of the others look like that: can it really be a turkey-chick? Well, we shall soon find that out! Into the water he shall go, even if I have to push him in myself!"

Next day the weather was splendidly bright, and the sun shone on all the green burdocks. The mother-duck went down to the canal, with all her little ones. Splash!—she sprang into the water. "Quack! quack!" she said, and one duckling after another plumped in. The water closed over their heads, but they came straight up again and swam capitally; their legs went of themselves, and there they were, all in the water, and the ugly grey duckling swimming with them.

"No, he's not a turkey," said she; "see how well he uses his legs, and how upright he holds himself! He's my own child! On the whole he's quite pretty, if only you look at him properly. Quack! quack! come along with me, and I'll lead you out into the world, and present you in the poultry-yard; but keep close to me, so that no one may tread on you, and take care of the cats!"

And so they came into the poultry-yard. There was a terrible riot going on there, for two families were quarrelling about an eel's head, and the cat got it after all.

"See, that's the way of the world!" said the mother-duck; and she whetted her beak, for she too wanted the eel's head. "Only use your legs," said she. "See that you bustle about, and bow your heads before the old duck yonder. She's the grandest of all of them here; she's of Spanish blood—that's why she's so fat—and, do you see, she has a red rag round her leg; that's something unusually fine, and the greatest dis-tinction any duck can enjoy: it means that they don't want to lose her, and that she's to be recognized by man and beast. Stir yourselves—don't turn in your toes! A well-brought-up duck turns its toes right out, just like his father and mother —so! Now bend your necks and say 'Quack!'"

And so they did; but the other ducks round about looked at them, and said out loud:

"Look there! Now we're to have that lot too, as if there were not enough of us already! And—fie!—look how ugly that duckling is! We won't stand that!" And one duck flew straight at him, and bit him in the neck.

"Let him alone," said the mother; "he is doing no harm to anyone."

"Yes, but he's too big and so different," said the duck who had bitten him, "and therefore he must be pecked."

"Those are pretty children that mother has there!" said the old duck with the rag on her leg. "They're all pretty but that one. That's not a lucky one! I wish she could hatch him over again!"

"That cannot be, your Highness," said the duckling's mother. "He is not pretty, but he has a really good disposition, and swims as well as any other—yes, I may even say better! I think he will grow pretty, and may become smaller in time! He has lain too long in the egg, and therefore has not got the proper shape." And she stroked his neck and smoothed his feathers. "Moreover, he is a drake," said she, "and so it does not matter so much. I think he will be very strong, and make his way in the world."

"The other ducklings are graceful enough," said the old duck. "Make yourself at home; and if you find an eel's head you may bring it me."

So now they felt at home. But the poor duckling which had crept last out of the egg, and looked so ugly, was bitten and pushed and made a fool of, as much by the ducks as by the chickens.

"He is too big!" they all said. And the turkey-cock, who had been born with spurs, and therefore thought himself an emperor, puffed himself up like a ship in full sail, and bore down upon him, and gobbled, and grew quite red in the face. The poor duckling did not know where to stand or where to go; he was quite miserable because he looked ugly, and was the butt of the whole yard.

So it went on the first day, and afterwards it became worse and worse. The poor duckling was hunted about by them all; even his brothers and sisters were quite cross with him, and said, "If only the cat would catch you, you ugly sight!" And his mother said, "If you were only far away!" And the ducks bit him, and the chickens pecked at him, and the girl who fed the poultry kicked at him with her foot.

Then he ran and flew over the hedge, and the little birds in the bushes flew up in fear.

"That is because I am so ugly!" thought the duckling; and he shut his eyes, but ran on farther; so he came out into the great moor, where the wild ducks lived. Here he lay the whole night long: he was so tired and sorrowful.

Towards morning the wild ducks flew up and looked at their new comrade.

"What sort of a one are you?" they asked; and the duckling turned in every direction, and bowed to them as best he could. "You are remarkably ugly!" said the wild ducks. "But that's all the same to us, so long as you do not marry into our family."

Poor thing! He certainly was not thinking of marrying, and only hoped to get leave to lie among the reeds and drink some of the marsh water.

Thus he lay two whole days, and then there came two wild

geese, or, rather, ganders, for both were males. It was not long since each came out of the egg, and that's why they were so saucy.

"Listen, comrade," said one of them. "You're so ugly that I like you. Will you go with us, and become a bird of passage? Near here, in another moor, there are a few sweet, lovely wild geese, all unmarried, and all able to say 'Quack!' You've a chance of making your fortune, ugly as you are!

"Bang! bang!" sounded in the air above, and the two ganders fell dead in the swamp, and the water became blood-red. "Bang! bang!" it sounded again, and whole flocks of wild geese rose up from the reeds. And then there was another shot. A great hunt was going on. The hunters were lying in wait all round the moor—yes, some were even sitting up in the branches of the trees, which stretched far over the reeds. The blue smoke rose up like clouds among the dark trees and drifted far over the water; into the mud came the hunting dogs—splash, splash!—and the rushes and the reeds bent on every side. That was a fright for the poor duckling! He turned his head to put it under his wing, but at that moment a frightful great dog stopped close to the duckling. His tongue hung far out of his mouth and his eyes gleamed horribly; he thrust out his nose close to the duckling, showed his sharp teeth, and—splash, splash!—on he went, without touching him.

"Oh, thank heaven!" sighed the duckling. "I am so ugly that even the dog does not want to bite me!"

And so he lay quite still, while the shots rattled through the reeds, and gun after gun went off. At last, late in the day, all was quiet again; but the poor duckling did not dare to move; he waited several hours before he looked round him, and then made off out of the marsh as fast as he could. He ran on over field and meadow, and such a storm was blowing that it was difficult to get along at all.

Towards evening the duckling came to a miserable little peasant's hut. It was so tumbledown that it did not know which side to fall, and that's why it remained standing. The storm whistled so fiercely about the duckling that he was obliged to sit down to withstand it; and the tempest grew worse and worse. Then the duckling noticed that one of the hinges of the door had given way, and the door hung so askew that he could slip through the crack into the room; and so he did.

Here there lived a woman, with her tom-cat and her hen. And the tom-cat, whom she called 'Sonnie,' could arch his back and purr, and he could even give out sparks, but for that one had to stroke his fur the wrong way. The hen had very little short legs, and therefore she was called 'Chickabiddy-shortlegs'; she laid good eggs, and the woman loved her as her own child.

In the morning the strange duckling was noticed at once, and the tom-cat began to purr, and the hen to cluck.

"What's all this?" said the woman, and looked about her; but she could not see well, and so she thought the duckling was a fat duck that had strayed in. "This is a rare catch!" she said. "Now I shall have duck's eggs. I hope it is not a drake. That we must find out!"

And so the duckling was taken on trial for three weeks; but no eggs came. And the tom-cat was master of the house, and the hen was mistress, and always said, "We and the world!" for she thought they were half the world, and by far the better half too. The duckling thought it might be possible to hold another opinion, but the hen would not allow it.

"Can you lay eggs?" she asked.

"No."

"Then you'd better hold your tongue."

And the tom-cat said, "Can you arch your back, and purr, and give out sparks?"

"No."

"Then you mustn't have any opinion of your own when sensible folk are talking."

And the duckling sat in a corner and was in a sad humour; then the fresh air and the sunshine streamed in; and he was seized with such a strange longing to swim on the water that he could not help telling it to the hen.

"What are you thinking of?" cried the hen. "You have nothing to do, that's why you have these fancies. Lay eggs or purr, and they will pass away."

"But it is so delightful to swim on the water!" said the duckling, "so delightful to let it close over your head, and dive down to the bottom!"

"Yes, that must be a great pleasure truly," said the hen. "You must be going crazy. Ask the cat about it—he's the wisest creature I know—ask him if he likes to swim on the water or to dive under it: I won't speak of myself. Ask our mistress, the old woman; no one in the world is wiser than she. Do you think she has any longing to swim, and to let the water close over her head?"

"You don't understand me," said the duckling.

"We don't understand you? Then pray who will understand you? You surely don't pretend to be wiser than the tom-cat and the old woman—to say nothing of myself. Don't be conceited, child; and be grateful for all the kindness that has been shown you. Have you not come into a warm room, and into company where you may learn something? But you are an idle chatterer, and it's no pleasure to be with you. You may believe me, I speak for your own good. I say unpleasant things to you, and that's the way you may always know your true friends! Just you learn to lay eggs, or to purr and give out sparks!"

"I think I'll go out into the wide world," said the duckling.

"Yes, do, by all means," said the hen.

And away went the duckling. He swam on the water and dived, but he was slighted by all the other creatures because of his ugliness.

Then autumn came. The leaves in the forest turned yellow and brown, the wind caught them so that they danced about, and the air turned very cold. The clouds hung low, heavy with hail and snow, and on the fence stood the raven and croaked, "Caw! caw!" from sheer cold; yes, it makes one shiver only to think of it. The poor duckling certainly had not a good time. One evening—the sun was just setting in all its beauty—there came a whole flock of great handsome birds out of the bushes. The duckling had never seen anything so beautiful. They were dazzlingly white, with long, slender necks. They were swans; they uttered a very peculiar cry, spread their lovely long wings, and flew away from that cold region to warmer lands, to open lakes. They rose so high, so high, that the ugly little duckling felt quite queer as he watched them. He turned round and round in the water like a wheel, stretched out his neck towards them, and uttered such a strange loud cry that he frightened even himself. Oh! he could not forget those beautiful, those happy birds; and as soon as he could see them no longer he dived right down to the bottom, and when he came up again he was quite beside himself. He knew not what birds they were, nor whither they were flying; but he loved them more than he had ever loved anyone before. He was not at all envious of them. How could he think of wishing for such loveliness as they had? He would have been quite happy if only the ducks would have allowed him to be with them—the poor ugly little thing!

And the winter grew so cold, so cold! The duckling was forced to swim about in the water to prevent it from freezing all over; but every night the hole in which he swam became smaller and smaller. It froze so hard that the icy covering creaked; and the duckling had to use his legs all the time to keep the hole from freezing up. At last he became exhausted, and lay quite still, and soon froze fast into the ice.

Early in the morning a peasant came by and saw him. And he went on to the ice, and took his wooden shoe and broke the ice to pieces, and carried the duckling home to his wife. There he came to again. The children wanted to play with him, but the duckling thought they would hurt him, and in his fright he fluttered up into the milk-pan, so that the milk splashed all over the room. The woman cried out and clapped her hands, at which the duckling flew into the butter-tub, and then into the meal-barrel and out again. What a sight he was then! The woman screamed, and struck at him with the fire-tongs; the children tumbled over one another in trying to catch the duckling; and they laughed and they screamed! Luckily the door stood open, and the poor creature was able to slip out among the shrubs into the newly fallen snow.

But it would be too sad to tell you all the misery and trouble the duckling had to bear through the hard winter. He was lying out on the moor among the reeds, when the sun began to shine warmly again. The larks were singing, and it was lovely springtime.

Then all at once the duckling flapped his wings: they beat the air more strongly than before, and bore him quickly away; and before he knew it he found himself in a large garden, where the apple-trees were in bloom, and lilacs scented the air and hung their long green branches down to the winding canals. Oh, here it was so beautiful, in the freshness of spring! and right in front of him from the thicket came three lovely white swans; they ruffled their feathers, and swam lightly over the water. The duckling knew the splendid creatures, and was seized with a strange sadness.

"I will fly to them, the royal birds! and they will kill me, because I, that am so ugly, dare to go near them. But that will not matter! Better be killed by them than snapped at by ducks, pecked by fowls, and kicked by the girl who takes care of the poultry-yard, and suffer hunger in winter!" And he flew into the water, and swam towards the beautiful swans; they saw him, and came sailing up with ruffled feathers. "Only kill me!" said the poor creature, and bent his head down to the water and awaited his death. But what did he see in the clear water? He saw below him his own image; but he was no longer a clumsy, dark grey bird, ugly and ungainly—he was himself a swan.

It matters little to be born in a duck-yard when one comes from a swan's egg!

He felt quite glad at all the trouble and misfortune he had suffered now he realized his good fortune in all the beauty that surrounded him. And the big swans swam round him, and stroked him with their beaks.

Into the garden came some little children, and threw bread and corn into the water; and the youngest cried, "There is a new one!" and the other children shouted with joy, "Yes, a new one has come!" And they clapped their hands and danced about, and ran to their father and mother; and bread and cake were thrown into the water; and they all said, "The new one is the most beautiful of all! so young and handsome!" and the old swans bowed their heads to him.

Then he felt quite shy, and hid his head under his wings, for he did not know what to do; he was so happy, and yet not at all proud, for a good heart is never proud. He thought of how he had been persecuted and despised; and now he heard them all saying that he was the most beautiful of all beautiful birds. Even the lilac bent its branches straight down into the water before him, and the sun shone warm and mild. He ruffled his feathers and lifted his slender neck, and from his heart he cried joyfully:

"Of so much happiness I never dreamed when I was the ugly duckling!"

THE STORY OF ALADDIN, OR
THE WONDERFUL LAMP

THERE lived in ancient times in the capital of China a tailor named Mustapha, who was so poor that he could scarcely support his wife and son. Now his son, whose name was Aladdin, was idle and careless and disobedient to his father and mother, and he played from morning till night in the streets with other bad and idle lads. Mustapha chastised him, but Aladdin remained incorrigible, and his father was so much troubled that he became ill and died in a few months. His mother, finding that Aladdin would not work, did all she could by spinning cotton to maintain herself and him.

Now Aladdin, who was no longer restrained by fear of a father, gave himself over entirely to his idle habits. As he was one day playing according to custom with his vagabond associates, a stranger, passing by, stood and regarded him earnestly. This stranger was a sorcerer, an African magician. By means of his magic he saw in Aladdin's face something necessary for the accomplishment of a deed in which he was engaged. And the wily magician, taking Aladdin aside from his companions, said, "Boy, is not thy father called Mustapha the tailor?" "Yes," answered the boy, "but he has been dead a long time."

At these words the African magician threw his arms about Aladdin's neck, and kissed him several times, with tears in his eyes. "Alas, O my son," he cried, "I am thine uncle. I have been abroad for many years, and now I am come home with the hope of seeing thy father, but thou tellest me that he is dead! I knew thee at first sight, because thou art so like him, and I see that I was not deceived!" Then, putting his hand into his pocket, he asked Aladdin where his mother lived, and gave him a small handful of money, saying, "Go, O my son, to thy mother, and give her my love, and tell her that I will visit her to-morrow."

As soon as the African magician had departed Aladdin ran to his mother overjoyed. "Mother," he said, "I have met my uncle!" "No, my son," answered his mother, "thou hast no uncle by thy father's side or mine." Then Aladdin related to her all that the African magician had told him.

The next day Aladdin's mother made ready a repast, and when night came some one knocked upon the door. Aladdin opened it, and the African magician entered, laden with wine and various fruits. He saluted Aladdin's mother, and shed tears, and lamented that he had not arrived in time to see his brother Mustapha. "I have been forty years absent from my country," said the wily magician, "travelling in the Indies, Persia, Arabia, Syria, and Egypt. At last I was desirous of seeing and embracing my dear brother, so I immediately prepared for the journey and set out. Reaching this city, I wandered through the streets, where I observed my brother's features in the face of my nephew, thy son."

The African magician, perceiving that the widow began to weep at these words, turned to Aladdin, and asked him what trade or occupation he had chosen. At this question Aladdin hung down his head, blushing and abashed, while his mother replied that he was an idle fellow, living on the streets. "This is not well," said the magician. "If thou hast no desire to learn a handicraft I will take a shop for thee, and furnish it with fine linens and rich stuffs." This plan greatly flattered Aladdin, for he knew that the owners of such shops were much respected, so he thanked the African magician, saying that he preferred such a shop to any trade or handicraft. Aladdin's mother, who had not till then believed that the magician was the brother of her husband, now could no longer doubt. She thanked him for his kindness to Aladdin, and exhorted the lad to repay his uncle with good behaviour.

The next day, early in the morning, the African magician came again, and took Aladdin to a merchant, who provided the lad with a rich and handsome suit, after which the magician took him to visit the principal shops, where they sold the richest stuffs and linens. He showed him also the largest and finest mosques, and entertained him at the most frequented inns. Then the magician escorted Aladdin to his mother, who, when she saw her son so magnificently attired, bestowed a thousand blessings upon his benefactor.

Aladdin rose early the next morning, and dressed himself in his elegant new garments. Soon after this the African magician approached the house, and entered it, and, caressing him, said, "Come, my dear son, and I will show thee fine things to-day!" He then led the lad out of the city, through magnificent parks and gardens, past fine palaces and buildings, enticing him beyond the gardens, across the country, until they arrived at some mountains. He amused Aladdin all the way by relating to him pleasant stories, and feasting him with cakes and fruit.

When at last they arrived at a valley between two mountains of great height the magician said to Aladdin, "We will go no farther. I will now show thee some extraordinary things. While I strike a light do thou gather up loose sticks for a fire." Aladdin collected a pile of sticks, and the African magician set fire to them, and when they began to burn he muttered several magical words, and cast a perfume upon the fire. Immediately a great smoke arose, and the earth, trembling, opened and uncovered a stone with a brass ring fixed in the middle.

Aladdin became so frightened at what he saw that he would have run away, but the magician caught hold of him, and gave him such a box on the ear that he knocked him down. Aladdin rose up trembling, and with tears in his eyes inquired what he had done to merit such a punishment. "I have my reasons," answered the magician harshly. "Thou seest what I have just done! But, my son," continued he, softening, "know that under this stone is hidden a treasure destined to be thine. It will make thee richer than the greatest monarch in the world. Fate decrees that no one but thou mayest lift the stone or enter the cave, but to do this successfully thou must promise to obey my instructions."

Aladdin was amazed at all he saw, and, hearing that the treasure was to be his, his anger was appeased, and he said quickly, "Command me, Uncle, for I promise to obey." The magician then directed him to take hold of the ring and lift the stone, and to pronounce at the same time the names of his father and grandfather. Aladdin did as he was bidden, and raised the heavy stone with ease, and laid it on one side. When the stone was pulled up there appeared a cave several feet deep, with a little door, and with steps to go farther down.

"Observe, my son," said the African magician, "what I direct. Descend, and at the bottom of these steps thou wilt find a door open. Beyond the door are three great halls, in each of which thou wilt see four large brass chests, full of gold and silver. Take care that thou dost not touch any of the wealth. Before thou enterest the first hall tuck up thy vest, and pass through the first and the second and the third hall without stopping. Above all things do not touch the walls, not even with thy clothing, for if thou do so thou wilt die instantly.

"At the end of the third hall thou wilt find a door which opens into a garden planted with fine trees, loaded with fruits. Walk directly across the garden by a path that will lead thee to five steps, which will bring thee to a terrace, where thou wilt see a niche, and in that niche a lighted lamp. Take down the lamp, extinguish the flame, throw away the wick, pour out the oil, and put the lamp into thy bosom, and bring it to me. If thou shouldst wish for any of the fruits of the garden thou mayest gather as much as thou pleasest."

The magician then took a ring from his finger, and placed it upon Aladdin's hand, telling him that it would preserve him from all evil. Aladdin sprang into the cave, descended the steps, and found the three halls just as the African magician had described. He passed through, taking care not to touch the walls, crossed the garden without stopping, took down the lamp from the niche, threw away the wick, poured out the oil, and placed the lamp in his bosom.

But as he came down from the terrace he stopped to observe the fruits. All the trees were loaded with extraordinary fruits of different colours. Some trees bore fruit entirely white, and some clear and transparent as crystal; some red, some green, blue, purple, and others yellow—in short, there were fruits of all colours. The white were pearls, the clear and transparent diamonds, the red rubies, the green emeralds, the blue turquoises, the purple amethysts, and those that were yellow sapphires. Aladdin was altogether ignorant of their worth, and would have preferred figs and grapes, or any other fruits. But though he took them for coloured glass of little value, yet he was so pleased with the variety of bright colours and with the beauty and extraordinary size of the seeming fruits that he gathered some of every sort, and filled the two new purses his uncle had given him, and crammed his bosom as full as it could hold.

Aladdin, having thus loaded himself with riches he knew not the value of, returned through the three halls to the mouth of the cave, where the magician was expecting him with the utmost impatience. Now the African magician intended, as soon as he should receive the lamp from Aladdin, to push the lad back into the cave, so that there should remain no witness of the affair. But as soon as Aladdin saw him he cried out, "Pray, Uncle, lend me thy hand to help me out." "Give me the lamp first," said the magician; "it will be troublesome to thee." "Indeed, Uncle," answered Aladdin, "I am unable to give it to thee now, but I will do so as soon as I am up." But the magician was obstinate, and insisted on having the lamp, and Aladdin, whose bosom was so stuffed with the fruits that he could not well get at it, refused to give up the lamp until he was out of the cave. The magician, provoked at this refusal, flew into a rage, threw some incense into the fire, pronounced two magical words, and instantly the stone which had covered the mouth of the cave moved back into its place. Then the African magician, having lost all hope of obtaining the wonderful lamp, returned that same day to Africa.

When Aladdin found himself thus buried alive he cried, and called out to his uncle that he was ready to give him the lamp, but in vain, since his cries could not be heard. He descended to the bottom of the steps, desiring to enter the garden, but the door, which had been open before by enchantment, was now closed by the same means. He then redoubled his cries and tears, and sat down upon the steps, without any hopes of ever seeing the light again.

Aladdin remained in this state for two days, without eating or drinking. On the third day, clasping his hands in despair, he accidentally rubbed the ring which the magician had placed upon his finger. Immediately a Genie of enormous size and frightful aspect rose out of the earth, his head reaching the roof of the cave, and said to him, "What wouldest thou have? I will obey thee as thy slave, and the slave of all who may possess the ring on thy finger, I and the other slaves of that ring!"

At any other time Aladdin would have been frightened at the sight of so extraordinary a figure, but the danger that he was in made him answer without hesitation, "Whoever thou art, deliver me from this place!" He had no sooner spoken these words than he found himself on the very spot where the magician had caused the earth to open.

Thankful to find himself safe, he quickly made his way home. When he reached his mother's door the joy at seeing her and the weakness due to lack of food made him faint, and he remained for a long time as dead. His mother did all she could to bring him to himself, and the first words he spoke were, "Pray, Mother, give me something to eat." His mother brought what she had, and set it before him.

Aladdin then related to his mother all that had happened to him, and showed her the transparent fruits of different colours which he had gathered in the garden. But though these fruits were precious stones, brilliant as the sun, the mother was ignorant of their worth, and she laid them carelessly aside.

Aladdin slept very soundly till the next morning, but on waking he found that there was nothing to eat in the house, nor any money with which to buy food.

"Alas, my son," said his mother, "I have not a bit of bread to give thee, but I have a little cotton which I have spun, and I will go and sell it." "Mother," replied Aladdin, "keep thy cotton for another time, and give me the lamp I brought home with me yesterday. I will go and sell it, and the money I shall get for it will serve both for breakfast and dinner, and perhaps for supper also."

Aladdin's mother brought the lamp, and as it was very dirty she took some fine sand and water to clean it, but she no sooner began to rub than in an instant a hideous Genie, of gigantic size, appeared before her, and said in a voice like thunder, "What wouldest thou have? I am ready to obey thee as thy slave, and the slave of all those who hold the lamp in their hands, I and the other slaves of the lamp!"

Aladdin's mother, terrified at the sight of the Genie, fainted, but Aladdin snatched the lamp out of her hand, and said to him, "I am hungry. Bring me something to eat." The Genie disappeared immediately, and in an instant returned with a large silver tray, holding twelve covered dishes of the same metal, which contained the most delicious viands, six large white bread cakes, two flagons of wine, and two silver cups. All these he placed upon a carpet, and disappeared. This was done before Aladdin's mother recovered from her swoon.

Aladdin fetched some water and sprinkled it in her face, and she recovered. Great was her surprise to see the silver tray, twelve dishes, six loaves, the two flagons and cups, and to smell the savoury odour which exhaled from the dishes. When, however, Aladdin informed her that they were brought by the Genie whom she had seen she was greatly alarmed, and urged him to sell the enchanted lamp and have nothing to do with the Genie. "With thy leave, Mother," answered Aladdin, "I will keep the lamp, as it has been of service to us. Thou mayest be sure that my false and wicked uncle would not have taken so much pains and undertaken such a long journey if he had not known that this wonderful lamp was worth more than all the gold and silver which were in those three halls. He knew too well the worth of this lamp not to prefer it to so great a treasure. Let us make profitable use of it, without exciting the envy and jealousy of our neighbours. However, since the Genie frightens thee I will take the lamp out of thy sight, and put it where I may find it when I want it." His mother, convinced by his arguments, said he might do as he wished, but for herself she would have nothing to do with Genii.

The mother and son then sat down to breakfast, and when they were satisfied they found that they had enough food left for dinner and supper, and also for two meals for the next day. By the following night they had eaten all the provisions the Genie had brought, and the next day Aladdin, putting one of the silver dishes under his vest, went to the silver market and sold it. Before returning home he called at the baker's and bought bread, and on his return gave the rest of the money to his mother, who went and purchased provisions enough to last for some time.

After this manner they lived, till Aladdin had sold all the dishes and the silver tray. When the money was spent he had recourse again to the lamp. He took it in his hand, rubbed it, and immediately the Genie appeared, and said, "What wouldst thou have? I am ready to obey thee as thy slave, and the slave of all those who hold that lamp in their hands, I and the other slaves of the lamp!" "I am hungry," said Aladdin. "Bring me something to eat." The Genie immediately disappeared, and instantly returned with a tray containing the same number of dishes as before, and he set them down and vanished. And when the provisions were gone Aladdin sold the tray and dishes as before. Thus he and his mother continued to live for some time, and though they had an inexhaustible treasure in their lamp they dwelt quietly with frugality.

Meanwhile Aladdin frequented the shops of the principal merchants, where they sold cloth of gold, and silver, linens, silk stuffs, and jewellery, and, oftentimes joining in their conversation, he acquired a knowledge of the world and a polished manner. By his acquaintance among the jewellers he came to know that the fruits which he had gathered in the subterranean garden, instead of being coloured glass, were jewels of inestimable value.

One day as Aladdin was walking about the town he heard an order proclaimed, commanding the people to close their shops and houses and to keep within doors while the Princess Badroulboudour, the Sultan's daughter, went to the baths and returned. When Aladdin heard this he became filled with curiosity to see the face of the Princess. So he placed himself behind the outer door of the bath, which was so situated that he could not fail to see her.

He had not long to wait before the Princess came, and he could see her plainly through a chink in the door without being discovered. She was attended by a great crowd of ladies, and slaves, and eunuchs, who walked on each side and behind her. When she came near to the door of the bath she took off her veil, and Aladdin saw her face.

The Princess was the most beautiful brunette in the world. Her eyes were large, lively, and sparkling, her looks sweet and modest, her nose without a fault, her mouth small, and her lips vermilion red. It was not surprising that Aladdin, who had never before seen such a blaze of charms, was dazzled, and that his heart became filled with admiration and love.

After the Princess had passed by Aladdin returned home in a state of great dejection, which he could not conceal from his mother, who was surprised to see him thoughtful and melancholy. She inquired the cause of this, and Aladdin told her all that had occurred, saying, "This, my mother, is the cause of my melancholy! I love the Princess more than I can express, I cannot live without the beautiful Badroulboudour, and I am resolved to ask her in marriage of the Sultan, her father."

Aladdin's mother listened in surprise to what her son told her, but when he spoke of asking the Princess in marriage she burst into a loud laugh. "Alas, my son," she said, "what art thou thinking of? Thou must be mad to talk thus!" "I assure thee, my mother," replied Aladdin, "that I am not mad, but I am resolved to demand the Princess in marriage, and thy remonstrances shall not prevent me; instead I will expect thee to use thy persuasion with the Sultan." "I go to the Sultan?" answered his mother, amazed and surprised. "I assure thee I cannot undertake such an errand. And who art thou, my son," continued she, "to think of the Sultan's daughter? Hast thou forgotten that thy father was one of the poorest tailors in the city? How can I open my mouth to make such a proposal to the Sultan? His majestic presence and the lustre of his Court would confound me! There is another reason, my son, which thou dost not think of, which is that no one ever asks a favour of the Sultan without taking him a fitting present."

Aladdin heard very calmly all that his mother had to say; then he replied, "I love the Princess, or rather I adore her, and shall always persevere in my design to marry her. Thou sayest that it is not customary to go to the Sultan without a present. Would not those fruits that I brought home from the subterranean garden make an acceptable present? For what thou and I took for coloured glass are really jewels of inestimable value, and I am persuaded that they will be favourably received by the Sultan. Thou hast a large porcelain dish fit to hold them; fetch it, and let us see how the stones will look when we have arranged them according to their different colours."

Aladdin's mother brought the porcelain dish, and he arranged the jewels on it according to his fancy. But the brightness and lustre they emitted in daylight and the variety of colours so dazzled the eyes of both mother and son that they were astonished beyond measure. After they had admired the beauty of the jewels Aladdin said to his mother, "Now thou canst not excuse thyself from going to the Sultan under the pretext of not having a present for him!" But his mother did not believe in the beauty and value of the stones, and she used many arguments to make her son change his mind. Aladdin, however, could not be changed from his purpose, and continued to persuade her, until out of tenderness she complied with his request.

The next morning Aladdin's mother took the porcelain dish, in which were the jewels, and, wrapping it in two fine napkins, set out for the Sultan's palace. She entered the audience chamber, and placed herself just before the Sultan, the Grand Vizier, and the great lords of the Court, who sat in council, but she did not venture to declare her business, and when the audience chamber closed for the day she returned home. The next morning she again repaired to the audience chamber, and left it when it closed without having dared to address the Sultan, and she continued to do thus daily, until at last one morning the chief officer of the Court approached her, and at a sign from him she followed him to the Sultan's throne, where he left her.

Aladdin's mother saluted the Sultan, and kissing the ground before him, bowed her head down to the carpet which covered the steps of the throne, and remained in that posture until he bade her rise, which she had no sooner done than he said to her, "My good woman, I have observed thee to stand for a long time from the opening to the closing of the audience chamber. What business brings thee thither?"

When Aladdin's mother heard these words she prostrated herself a second time, and when she arose said, "O King of Kings, I will indeed tell thee the incredible and extraordinary business that brings me, but I presume to beg of thee to hear what I have to say in private." The Sultan then ordered all but the Grand Vizier to leave the audience chamber, and directed her to proceed with her tale.

Thus encouraged, Aladdin's mother humbly entreated the Sultan's pardon for what she was about to say. She then told him faithfully how Aladdin had seen the Princess Badroulboudour, and of the love that the fatal sight had inspired him with, and she ended by formally demanding the Princess in marriage for her son. After which she took the porcelain dish, which she had set down at the foot of the throne, unwrapped it, and presented it to the Sultan.

The Sultan's amazement and surprise were inexpressible when he saw so many large, beautiful, and valuable jewels. He remained for some time motionless with admiration. At length, when he had recovered himself, he received the present from the hand of Aladdin's mother, crying out in a transport of joy, "How rich, how beautiful!" After he had admired and handled all the jewels one by one he turned to his Grand Vizier, and, showing him the dish, said, "Behold, admire, wonder! Confess that thine eyes never beheld precious stones so rich and beautiful before! What sayest thou to such a present? Is it not worthy of the Princess my daughter?"

These words agitated the Grand Vizier, for the Sultan had for some time intended to bestow the Princess his daughter upon the Vizier's son. Therefore, going to the Sultan, the Vizier whispered in his ear and said, "I cannot but own that the present is worthy of the Princess, but I beg thee to grant me three months' delay, and before the end of that time I hope that my son may be able to make a nobler present than Aladdin, who is an entire stranger to thy Majesty."

The Sultan granted his request, and, turning to Aladdin's mother, said to her, "My good woman, go home and tell thy son that I agree to the proposal thou hast made me, but that I cannot marry the Princess my daughter until the end of three months. At the expiration of that time come again." Aladdin's mother, overjoyed at these words, hastened home and informed Aladdin of all the Sultan had said. Aladdin thought himself the most happy of all men at hearing this news. He waited with great impatience for the expiration of the three months, counting not only the hours, days, and weeks, but every moment.

When two of the three months were passed his mother one evening, finding no oil in the house, went out to purchase some. She found in the city a general rejoicing. The shops were decorated with foliage, silks, and gay carpets; the streets were crowded with officers, magnificently dressed, mounted on horses richly caparisoned, each attended by numerous footmen. Aladdin's mother asked the oil-merchant what was the meaning of all this festivity. "Whence comest thou, my good woman?" he answered. "Know that to-night the Grand Vizier's son is to marry the Princess Badroulboudour, the Sultan's daughter!"

Aladdin's mother hastened home, and related all the news to Aladdin. He was thunderstruck on hearing her words, and, hastening to his chamber, closed the door, took the lamp in his hand, rubbed it in the same place as before, and immediately the Genie appeared, and said to him, "What wouldest thou have? I am ready to obey thee as thy slave, and the slave of all those who hold that lamp in their hands, I and the other slaves of the lamp!"

"Genie," said Aladdin, "I have demanded the Princess Badroulboudour in marriage of the Sultan her father. He promised her to me, only requiring three months' delay. But instead of keeping his word he has this night married her to the Grand Vizier's son. What I require of thee is this: as soon as the bride and bridegroom are alone bring them both hither."

"Master," said the Genie, "I hear and obey!" The Genie then disappeared, flew to the palace, took up the bed with the bride and bridegroom in it, returned, and set it down in Aladdin's room. The Genie then took up the bridegroom, who was trembling with fear, and shut him up in a dark closet. Aladdin then approached the Princess and said most respectfully, "Adorable Princess, thou art here in safety! The Sultan thy father promised thee in marriage to me, and as he has now broken his word I am thus forced to carry thee away, in order to prevent thy marriage with the Grand Vizier's son. Sleep in peace until morning, when I will restore thee to the Sultan thy father." Having thus reassured the Princess, Aladdin laid himself down and slept until morning.

Aladdin had no occasion the next morning to summon the Genie, who appeared at the hour appointed. He brought the bridegroom from the closet, and, placing him beside the Princess, transported the bed to the royal palace. The bridegroom, pale and trembling with fear, sought the Sultan, related to him all that had happened, and implored him to break off his marriage with the Princess. The Sultan did so, and commanded all rejoicings to cease.

Aladdin waited until the three months were completed, and the next day sent his mother to the palace to remind the Sultan of his promise. The Sultan no sooner saw her than he remembered her business, and as he did not wish to give his daughter to a stranger thought to put her off by a request impossible of fulfilment. "My good woman," he said, "it is true that sultans should keep their promises, and I am willing to do so as soon as thy son shall send me forty trays of massy gold, full of the same sort of jewels thou hast already made me a present of. The trays must be carried by a like number of black slaves, who shall be led by as many young and handsome white slaves magnificently dressed."

Aladdin's mother prostrated herself a second time before the Sultan's throne, and retired. She hastened home, laughing within herself at her son's foolish ambition. She then gave him an exact account of what the Sultan had said to her, and the conditions on which he consented to the marriage. Aladdin immediately retired to his room, took the lamp, and rubbed it. The Genie appeared, and with the usual salutation offered his services. "Genie," said Aladdin, "the Sultan gives me the Princess his daughter in marriage, but demands first forty large trays of massy gold, full of the fruits of the subterranean garden; these he expects to be carried by as many black slaves, each preceded by a young and handsome white slave, richly clothed. Go and fetch me this present as soon as possible." The Genie told him that his command should be instantly obeyed, and disappeared.

In a short time the Genie returned with forty black slaves, each bearing upon his head a heavy tray of pure gold, full of pearls, diamonds, rubies, emeralds, and every sort of precious stone, all larger and more beautiful than those already presented to the Sultan. Each tray was covered with silver tissue, richly embroidered with flowers of gold. These, together with the white slaves, quite filled the house, which was but a small one, as well as the little court before it and a small garden behind. The Genie, having thus fulfilled his orders, disappeared.

Aladdin found his mother in great amazement at seeing so many people and such vast riches. "Mother," he said, "I would have you return to the palace with this present as a dowry, that the Sultan may judge by the rapidity with which I fulfil his demands of the ardent and sincere love I have for the Princess his daughter." And, without waiting for his mother's reply, Aladdin opened the door into the street, and made the slaves walk out, each white slave followed by a black with a tray upon his head. When they were all out his mother followed the last black slave, and Aladdin shut the door and retired to his chamber, full of hopes.

The procession of slaves proceeded through the streets, and the people ran together to see so extraordinary and magnificent a spectacle. The dress of each slave was rich in stuff and decorated with jewels, and the noble air and fine shape of each was unparalleled. Their grave walk, at an equal distance from each other, the lustre of the jewels curiously set in their girdles of gold, the aigrettes of precious stones in their turbans, all filled the spectators with wonder and amazement. At length they arrived at the Sultan's palace, and the first slave, followed by the rest, advanced into the audience chamber, where the Sultan was seated on his throne, surrounded by his viziers and the chief officers of the Court. After all the slaves were entered they formed a semicircle before the Sultan's throne, the black slaves laid the golden trays upon the carpet, and all the slaves prostrated themselves, touching the ground with their foreheads. They then arose, the black slaves uncovering the trays, and stood with their arms crossed over their breasts.

In the meantime Aladdin's mother advanced to the foot of the throne and prostrated herself before the Sultan. When he cast his eyes on the forty trays filled with the most precious and brilliant jewels and gazed upon the fourscore slaves so richly attired he no longer hesitated, as the sight of such immense riches and Aladdin's quickness in satisfying his demand easily persuaded him that the young man would make a most desirable son-in-law. Therefore he said to Aladdin's mother, "Go and tell thy son that I wait with open arms to embrace him, and the more haste he makes to come and receive the Princess my daughter the greater pleasure he will do me."

Aladdin's mother hastened home and informed her son of this joyful news. He, enraptured at the prospect of his marriage with the Princess, retired to his chamber, again rubbed the lamp, and the obedient Genie appeared as before. "Genie," said Aladdin, "provide me with the richest and most magnificent raiment ever worn by a king, and with a charger that surpasses in beauty the best in the Sultan's stable, with a saddle, bridle, and other caparisons worth a million of gold pieces. I want also twenty slaves, richly clothed, to walk by my side and follow me, and twenty more to go before me in two ranks. Besides these, bring my mother six female slaves to attend her, as richly dressed as any of the Princess Badroulboudour's, each carrying a dress fit for a sultan's wife. I want also ten thousand pieces of gold in ten purses. Go, and make haste."

As soon as Aladdin had given these orders the Genie disappeared, but returned instantly with the horse, the forty slaves, ten of whom carried each a purse containing ten thousand pieces of gold, and six female slaves, each carrying on her head a dress for Aladdin's mother, wrapped in silver tissue. The Genie presented all these to Aladdin and disappeared.

Of the ten purses Aladdin took four, which he gave to his mother; the other six he left in the hands of the slaves who brought them, with an order to throw the gold by handfuls among the people as they went to the Sultan's palace. The six slaves who carried the purses he ordered likewise to march before him, three on the right hand and three on the left.

Aladdin then clad himself in his new garments, and, mount-

New lamps for old

ing his charger, began the march to the Sultan's palace. The streets through which he passed were instantly filled with a vast concourse of people, who rent the air with their acclamations. When he arrived at the palace everything was prepared for his reception. He was met at the gate by the Grand Vizier and the chief officers of the empire. The officers formed themselves into two ranks at the entrance of the audience chamber, and their chief led Aladdin to the Sultan's throne.

When the Sultan perceived Aladdin he was surprised at the elegance of his attire, and at his fine shape and air of dignity, very different from the meanness of his mother's late appearance. Rising quickly from the throne, the Sultan descended two or three steps, and prevented Aladdin from throwing himself at his feet. He embraced him with demonstrations of joy, held him fast by the hand, and obliged him to sit close to the throne.

The marriage feast was begun, and the Sultan ordered that the contract of marriage between the Princess Badroulboudour and Aladdin should be immediately drawn up; then he asked Aladdin if he wished the ceremony solemnized that day. To which Aladdin answered, "Though great is my impatience, I beg leave to defer it until I have built a palace fit to receive the Princess; therefore, I pray thee, give me a spot of ground near thy palace where I may build." "My son," said the Sultan, "take what ground thou thinkest proper." And he embraced Aladdin, who took his leave with as much politeness as though he had always lived at Court.

As soon as Aladdin reached home he dismounted, retired to his own chamber, took the lamp, and called the Genie as before, who in the usual manner offered him his services. "Genie," said Aladdin, "I would have thee build me as soon as possible a palace near the Sultan's fit to receive my wife, the Princess Badroulboudour. Build it of porphyry, jasper, lapis lazuli, or the finest marbles of various colours. On the

terraced roof build me a large hall, crowned with a dome.
Let the walls be of massy gold and silver. On each of the
four sides of this hall let there be six windows. Leave one
window lattice unfinished, but enrich all the others with
diamonds, rubies, and emeralds. I would have also a spacious
garden and a treasury full of gold and silver. There must be
kitchens, offices, storehouses, and stables full of the finest
horses. I want also male and female slaves and equerries and
grooms. Come and tell me when all is finished."

The next morning before break of day the Genie presented
himself to Aladdin, and said, "Master, thy palace is finished.
Come and see if it pleaseth thee." Aladdin had no sooner
signified his consent than the Genie transported him thither
in an instant, and led him through richly furnished apartments,
and Aladdin found nothing but what was magnificent.
Officers, slaves, and grooms were busy at their tasks, and the
treasury was piled to the ceiling with purses of gold, and the
stables were filled with the finest horses in the world. When
Aladdin had examined the palace from top to bottom, and
particularly the hall with four-and-twenty windows, he found
all beyond anything he had imagined. "Genie," he said,
"there is only one thing wanting, which I forgot to mention,
that is a carpet of fine velvet for the Princess to walk upon,
between my palace and the Sultan's." The Genie disappeared,
and instantly a carpet of fine velvet stretched across the park
to the door of the Sultan's palace.

When the porters of the Sultan's palace came to open the
gates they were amazed to see a carpet of velvet stretching
from the grand entrance across the park to a new and magnificent palace. The Grand Vizier, who arrived soon after
the gates were opened, being no less amazed than the others,
hastened to acquaint the Sultan with the wonderful news.
The hour of going to the audience chamber put an end
to their conjectures, but scarcely were they seated before
Aladdin's mother arrived, dressed in her most sumptuous

garments, and attended by the six female slaves, who were clad richly and magnificently. She was received at the palace with honour, and introduced into the Princess Badroulboudour's apartment by the chief of the eunuchs. As soon as the Princess saw her she arose and saluted her, and desired her to sit beside her upon a sofa. A collation was served, and then the slaves finished dressing the Princess and adorning her with the jewels which Aladdin had presented to her.

The Sultan immediately ordered bands of trumpets, cymbals, drums, fifes, and hautboys, placed in different parts of the palace, to play, so that the air resounded with concerts, which inspired the city with joy. The merchants began to adorn their shops and houses with fine carpets and silks, and to prepare illuminations for the coming festival.

When night arrived the Princess took tender leave of her father, and, accompanied by Aladdin's mother, set out across the velvet carpet, amid the sound of trumpets and lighted by a thousand torches. Aladdin received her with joy, and led her into the large, illuminated hall, where was spread a magnificent repast. The dishes were of massy gold, and contained the most delicious viands, and after the supper there was a concert of the most ravishing music, accompanied by graceful dancing, performed by a number of female slaves.

The next morning Aladdin mounted and went in the midst of a large troop of slaves to the Sultan's palace. The Sultan received him with honours, embraced him, placed him upon the throne near him, and ordered a collation. Aladdin then said, "I entreat thee to dispense with my eating with thee this day, as I came to invite thee to partake of a repast in the Princess's palace, attended by thy Grand Vizier and all the lords of thy Court." The Sultan consented with pleasure, rose up immediately, and, followed by all the officers of his Court, accompanied Aladdin.

The nearer the Sultan approached Aladdin's palace the more

he was struck with its beauty, but he was much more amazed when he entered it, and could not forbear breaking out into exclamations of wonder. But when he came into the hall of the four-and-twenty windows enriched with diamonds, rubies, emeralds, all large and perfect stones, he was so much surprised that he remained for some time motionless. "This palace," exclaimed he at length, "is surely one of the wonders of the world, for where in all the world besides shall we find walls built of massy gold and silver, and diamonds, pearls, and rubies adorning the windows!"

The Sultan examined and admired all the windows, but on counting them he found that there were but three-and-twenty so richly adorned, and that the four-and-twentieth was left imperfect, and in great astonishment he inquired the reason of this. "It was by my orders that the workmen left it thus," said Aladdin, "since I wished that thou shouldst have the glory of finishing this hall." The Sultan was much pleased with this compliment, and immediately ordered his jewellers and goldsmiths to complete the four-and-twentieth window. When the Sultan returned to his palace he ordered his jewels to be brought out, and the jewellers took a great quantity, which they soon used without making any great advance in their work. They worked steadily for a whole month, but could not finish half the window, although they used all the jewels the Sultan had and borrowed off the Vizier.

Aladdin, who knew that all the Sultan's endeavours to complete the window were in vain, sent for the jewellers and goldsmiths, and commanded them not only to desist, but to undo the work they had done, and to return the jewels to the Sultan and to the Grand Vizier. They undid in a few hours what they had accomplished in a month, and retired, leaving Aladdin alone in the hall. He took the lamp, which he carried about with him, rubbed it, and the Genie appeared. "Genie," said Aladdin, "I order thee to complete the four-and-twentieth window." And immediately the window became perfect like the others.

Scarcely was the window completed before the Sultan arrived to question Aladdin as to why the jewellers and goldsmiths had desisted from their work. Aladdin received him at the door, and conducted him directly to the hall, where he was amazed to see the window perfect like the rest. "My son," exclaimed the Sultan, embracing him, "what a man thou art to do all this in the twinkling of an eye! Verily, the more I know thee the more I admire thee!" And the Sultan returned to his palace content.

After this Aladdin lived in great state. He visited mosques, attended prayers, and returned the visits of the principal lords of the Court. Every time he went out he caused two slaves, who walked by the side of his horse, to throw handfuls of money among the people as he passed through the streets and the squares; and no one came to his palace gates to ask alms but returned satisfied with his liberality, which gained him the love and blessings of the people.

Aladdin had conducted himself in this manner for several years when the African magician, who had undesignedly been the instrument of Aladdin's prosperity, became curious to know whether he had perished in the subterranean garden. He employed his magic arts to discover the truth, and he found that Aladdin, instead of having perished miserably in the cave, had made his escape, and was living splendidly, and that he was in possession of the wonderful lamp, and had married a princess. The magician no sooner learned this than his face became inflamed with anger, and he cried out in a rage, "This miserable tailor's son has discovered the secret and the virtue of the lamp! I will, however, prevent his enjoying it long!"

The next morning he mounted a horse, set forward, and never stopped until he arrived at the capital of China, where he alighted, and took up his residence at an inn. The next day his first object was to inquire what people said of Aladdin, and, taking a walk through the town, he heard them talking of the wonderful palace and of Aladdin's marriage to the Princess. He went instantly and viewed the palace from all sides, and he doubted not but that Aladdin had made use of the lamp to build it, for none but Genii, the slaves of the lamp, could have performed such wonders. Piqued to the quick at Aladdin's happiness and splendour, he returned to the inn where he lodged.

As soon as he entered his chamber he ascertained by the means of his magic arts that Aladdin was absent on the hunt, and that the lamp was in the palace. He then went to a copper-smith's and bought a dozen copper lamps. These he placed in a basket, which he bought for the purpose, and with the basket on his arm went directly to Aladdin's palace. As he approached he began crying, "Who will change old lamps for new ones? Who will change old lamps for new ones?" And all who passed by thought him a madman or a fool to offer to change new lamps for old.

Now the Princess Badroulboudour, who was in the hall with the four-and-twenty windows, heard a man crying, "Who will change old lamps for new ones?" and, remembering the old lamp which Aladdin had laid upon a shelf before he went to the chase, the Princess, who knew not the value of the lamp, commanded a eunuch to take it and make the exchange. The eunuch did so, and the African magician, as soon as he saw the lamp, snatched it eagerly from his hand, and gave him a new one in its place.

The magician then hastened away until he reached a lonely spot in the country, when he pulled the lamp out of his bosom and rubbed it. At that summons the Genie appeared, and said, "What wouldst thou have? I am ready to obey thee as thy slave, and the slave of all those who hold that lamp in their hands, I and the other slaves of the lamp!" "I command thee," replied the magician, "to transport me immediately, and the palace which thou and the other slaves of the lamp have built in this city, with all the people in it, to Africa." The Genie disappeared, and immediately the magician, and the palace, and all its inhabitants, were lifted up and transported from the capital of China and set down in Africa.

As soon as the Sultan arose the next morning he went, according to his custom, to the window to contemplate and admire Aladdin's palace. When he looked that way instead of a palace he saw an empty space. He thought that he was mistaken, and looked again in front, to the right and left, and beheld only empty space where formerly had stood the palace. His amazement was so great that he remained for some time turning his eyes towards the spot, and at last convinced that no palace stood opposite his own he returned to his apartment and ordered his Grand Vizier to be sent for with expedition.

The Grand Vizier came with much precipitation. "Tell me," said the Sultan, "what has become of Aladdin's palace." "His palace!" exclaimed the Vizier. "Is it not in its usual place?" "Go to my window," answered the Sultan, "and tell me if thou canst see it." The Grand Vizier went to the window, where he was struck with no less amazement than the Sultan had been. When he was well assured that there was not the least appearance of the palace he returned to the Sultan. "Well," said the Sultan, "hast thou seen Aladdin's palace?" "Alas," answered the Grand Vizier, "it has vanished completely! I have always thought that the edifice, which was the object of thy admiration, with all its immense riches, was only the work of magic and a magician."

At these words the Sultan flew into a passion. "Where is that impostor, that wicked wretch," cried he, "that I may have his head taken off immediately? Go thou, bring him to me loaded with chains!" The Grand Vizier hastened to obey these orders, and commanded a detachment of horse to meet

Aladdin returning from the chase, and to arrest him and bring him before the Sultan.

The detachment pursued their orders, and about five or six leagues from the city met Aladdin returning from the chase. Without explanation they arrested him, and fastened a heavy chain about his neck, and one around his body, so that both his arms were pinioned to his sides. In this state they carried him before the Sultan, who ordered him to be put to death immediately. But a multitude of people had followed Aladdin as he was led in chains through the city, and they threatened a riot if any harm should befall him. The Sultan, terrified at this menace, ordered the executioner to put up his scimitar, to unbind Aladdin, and at the same time commanded the porters to declare unto the people that the Sultan had pardoned him, and that they might retire.

When Aladdin found himself at liberty he turned towards the Sultan, and said, "I know not what I have done to lose thy favour. Wilt thou not tell me what crime I have committed?" "Your crime, perfidious wretch!" answered the Sultan. "Dost thou not know it? Where is thy palace? What has become of the Princess my daughter?" Aladdin looked from the window, and, perceiving the empty spot where his palace had stood, was thrown into such confusion and amazement that he could not return one word of answer. At length, breaking the silence, he said, "I know not whither my palace has vanished. Neither can I tell thee where it may be. Grant me but forty days in which to make inquiry, and if at the end of that time I have not the success I wish I will offer my head at the foot of thy throne, to be disposed of at thy pleasure." "Go," said the Sultan. "I give thee the forty days thou askest for, but if thou dost not find my daughter thou shalt not escape my wrath. I will find thee out in whatsoever part of the world thou mayest conceal thyself, and I will cause thy head to be struck off!"

Aladdin went out of the Sultan's presence in great humiliation, and filled with confusion. For three days he wandered about the city making inquiries, but all in vain: he could find no trace of the vanished palace. At last he wandered into the country, and at the approach of night came to the banks of a river, where he sat down to rest. Clasping his hands in despair, he accidentally rubbed the ring which the African magician had placed upon his finger before he went down into the subterranean abode to fetch the precious lamp. Immediately the same Genie appeared whom he had seen in the cave where the magician had left him. "What wouldest thou have?" said the Genie. "I am ready to obey thee as thy slave, and the slave of all those who have that ring on their fingers, I and the other slaves of the ring!"

Aladdin, agreeably surprised at an apparition he so little expected, replied, "Save my life, Genie, by showing me the place where the palace I caused to be built now stands, or immediately transport it back where it first stood." "What thou commandest is not in my power," answered the Genie. "I am only the slave of the ring. Thou must address thyself to the slave of the lamp." "If that be the case," replied Aladdin, "I command thee by the power of the ring to transport me to the spot where my palace stands, in what part of the world soever it may be, and set me down under the window of the Princess Badroulboudour."

These words were no sooner out of his mouth than the Genie transported him into Africa, to the middle of a large plain, where his palace stood, and, placing him exactly under the window of the Princess Badroulboudour's apartment, left him. The next morning when the Princess looked out of her window she perceived Aladdin sitting beneath it. Scarcely believing her eyes, she opened the window and motioned to him to come up. Aladdin hastened to her apartment, and it is impossible to express the joy of both at seeing each other after so cruel a separation.

After embracing and shedding tears of joy they sat down,

and Aladdin said, "I beg of thee, Princess, both for thine own sake and the Sultan thy father's and mine, tell me what became of an old lamp which I left upon a shelf in my robing-room when I departed for the chase?" "Alas, dear husband," answered the Princess, "I was afraid our misfortune might be owing to that lamp, and what grieves me most is that I have been the cause of it!" "Princess," replied Aladdin, "do not blame thyself, but tell me what has happened, and into whose hands it has fallen."

The Princess then related how she had changed the old lamp for a new, and how the next morning she had found herself in an unknown country, which she was told was Africa by the traitor who had transported her hither by his magic arts. She also told how the wicked magician visited her daily, forcing upon her his unwelcome attentions, and how he daily tried to persuade her to take him for a husband in the place of Aladdin. "And," added the Princess, "he carries the wonderful lamp carefully wrapped in his bosom, and this I can assure thee of, because he pulled it out before me and showed it to me in triumph."

"Princess," said Aladdin, "this magician is a most perfidious wretch, and I have here the means to punish him, and to deliver thee from both thine enemy and mine. To accomplish this thou must obey my directions most carefully. When the African magician comes to-night place this powder in his cup of wine, offer him the cup, and he will esteem it so great a favour that he will not refuse, but will eagerly quaff it off. No sooner will he have drunk than thou wilt see him fall backwards." After the Princess had agreed to the measures proposed by Aladdin he took his leave, and spent the rest of the day in the neighbourhood of the palace till it was night and he might safely return by a private door.

When the evening arrived the magician came at the usual hour, and as soon as he was seated the Princess handed him a cup of wine, in which the powder had been dissolved. The magician reclined his head back to show his eagerness, drank the wine to the very last drop, turned his eyes in his head, and fell to the floor dead. At a signal from the Princess Aladdin entered the hall, and he requested her to retire immediately to her own apartment.

When the Princess, her women and eunuchs, were gone out of the hall Aladdin shut the door, and, going to the magician, opened his vest, took out the lamp, which was carefully wrapped up, and unfolded and rubbed it, whereupon the Genie immediately appeared. "Genie," said Aladdin, "transport this palace instantly to China, to the place from whence it was brought hither." The Genie bowed his head in token of obedience, and disappeared. Immediately the palace was lifted up and transported to China.

The morning of the return of Aladdin's palace the Sultan stood at his window absorbed in grief. He cast his eyes towards the spot where the palace had once stood, and which he now expected to find vacant, but to his surprise and amazement there stood Aladdin's palace in all its former grandeur. He immediately ordered a horse to be saddled and bridled and brought to him without delay, which he mounted that instant, thinking that he could not make haste enough to reach the palace.

Aladdin received the Sultan at the foot of the great staircase, helped him to dismount, and led him into the Princess's apartment. The happy father embraced her with his face bathed in tears of joy, and the Princess related to him all that had happened to her from the time the palace was transported to Africa to the death of the African magician.

Aladdin ordered the magician's body to be removed, and in the meantime the Sultan commanded the drums, trumpets, cymbals, and other instruments of music to announce his joy to the public, and a festival of ten days to be proclaimed for the return of the Princess and Aladdin.

THE SLEEPING BEAUTY

THERE was once a King and Queen who were very sorrowful because they had no children. When at last, after long waiting, a daughter was born the King showed his delight by giving a christening feast, the like of which had never been known before. He invited all the fairies in the land—there were seven altogether—to become the little princess's godmothers, hoping that each one would bestow a gift upon her.

After the christening all the guests returned to the palace, where a grand feast was prepared. Before each fairy was placed a splendid cover, with a spoon and knife and fork of pure gold studded with diamonds and rubies. As they were all sitting down at the table a very old fairy came into the hall. She had not been invited, because for more than fifty years she had not been heard of.

The King ordered a cover to be placed for her, but he could not give her one of gold, as he had the others, for he had had only seven made. The old fairy thought herself slighted, and muttered some angry threats that were overheard by one of the young fairies who chanced to sit beside her.

Thinking that some harm might be done to the pretty babe, the young fairy hid herself behind the curtains in the hall. She did this so that all the others might speak first. Then if any evil gift were bestowed upon the child she might be able to counteract it.

The six fairies now began to make their gifts to the princess. She was to grow up the fairest person in the world. She was to have a temper as sweet as that of an angel. She was to be graceful and gracious in every way. She was to sing like a nightingale and to dance like a leaf fluttering in the breeze, and she was to be able to play upon all kinds of musical instruments with perfection.

Then came the turn of the old fairy. Shaking her head spitefully, she uttered the wish that when the baby grew up she might prick her finger with a spindle and die of the wound.

At this terrible prophecy all the guests shuddered, and some of them began to weep. The parents, who till then had been so happy, were now almost beside themselves with grief. Just then the young fairy appeared from behind the curtains, and said in a cheerful tone, "Your Majesties may comfort yourselves; the princess shall not die. I have not the power to change entirely the ill-fortune just wished her by my ancient sister. The princess must indeed pierce her finger with a spindle, though she will not die, but sink instead into a deep sleep that will last a hundred years. At the end of that time a King's son shall come and awaken her."

As soon as these words were spoken all the fairies vanished.

The King, in the hope of warding off the evil, issued a command forbidding all persons to spin, or even to have spinning-wheels in their houses, on pain of instant death.

But it was in vain.

One day, when she was just fifteen years of age, the princess was left by her parents in one of the castles. Wandering about idly she came to a room at the top of a tower, where she found a very old woman—so deaf that she had never heard of the King's command—busy with her wheel.

"What are you doing, my good woman?" asked the princess.

"I'm spinning, my pretty child," was the answer.

"Ah, how charming! How do you do it? Do let me try."

She had no sooner taken the spindle than, being hasty and a little awkward, she pierced her finger with the point. Though it was but a small wound, she immediately fainted and fell to the floor. The poor old woman, thoroughly frightened, called for help, and there soon came ladies-in-waiting, who tried their best to restore the young princess. They threw water upon her face, loosened her clothing, smacked the palms of her hands, and bathed her temples; but all their efforts were in vain. There she lay, as beautiful as an angel, with the colour still lingering in her lips and cheeks, but her eyes were tightly closed.

When the King and Queen saw her thus they knew that all regrets were idle. This was the fulfilment of the cruel fairy's wish. But they also knew that the princess would not sleep for ever, though it was not likely that they would behold her awakening. So they determined to let her sleep in peace. They sent away all the physicians and attendants, and laid her upon a bed in the finest apartment of the palace, where she slept and continued to look like an angel.

While this was happening the good young fairy who had saved the life of the princess by changing her sleep of death into this sleep of a hundred years was twelve thousand leagues away, in the kingdom of Matakin. As soon as she heard the news she left the kingdom immediately, and arrived at the palace about an hour after in a chariot drawn by dragons. The King was rather startled by the sight, but nevertheless he went to the door and handed the fairy out of her chariot.

She sympathized with his Majesty, and approved of all that he had done. Then, being a fairy of great common sense and foresight, she thought that the princess, awakening after a long sleep of one hundred years in this ancient castle, might find it irksome and awkward to find herself all alone. Accordingly, without asking anyone's permission, she touched with her magic wand everybody and everything in the palace—except the King and Queen. Governesses, kitchen-maids, pages, footmen, the horses in the stables and the grooms that attended them, all received the magic touch. Even the princess's little spaniel, who had laid himself beside his mis-

tress, fell asleep in a moment. The very spits before the
kitchen-fire ceased turning, the fire went out, and everything
became as silent as in the dead of night.

The King and Queen, having kissed their daughter, went
sorrowfully from the castle, and gave orders that no one
should come near it. The command was unnecessary, for in
a quarter of an hour there grew up round the castle a wood
of thorny briars so thick and close that neither beasts nor
men could get through it. All that could be seen of the
building was the top of the high tower where the lovely
princess slept.

Many things happen in a hundred years. The King, who
never had a second child, died, and his throne passed to another family. The story of the poor princess was quite forgotten, and one day the son of the reigning King when out
hunting asked what wood this was and what tower it was
that appeared over the tops of the trees. Nobody could give
him an answer, until an old peasant was found who remembered hearing his grandfather tell his father that in this tower
was a beautiful princess who was doomed to sleep there for
one hundred years until awakened by the King's son, her
destined bridegroom.

When the young prince heard this he determined to find
out the truth for himself. He straightway leapt from his
horse and began to force his way through the thick wood.
This seemed as if it would be most difficult, but to his astonishment the stout branches all gave way, the ugly thorns
sheathed themselves so as not to hurt him, and the brambles
buried themselves in the ground to let him pass. But they
closed again behind him, so that he alone was able to pass
that way.

The first thing he saw was enough to fill the heart of the
bravest man with dread. On the ground before him were
the bodies of men and horses. They appeared to be dead, but
the rosy faces of the men and the goblets beside them, half

filled with wine, showed that they had gone to sleep while in the act of drinking. Then the prince entered a large court paved with marble, where there stood rows of guards presenting arms, but quite motionless, as if they had been carved out of stone. After that he passed through room after room, where ladies and gentlemen, all dressed in the clothes that were worn a hundred years before, were soundly sleeping. Some were sitting, and some were standing. In the corners pages were lurking, the ladies of honour were stooping over their embroidery frames, or appeared to be listening very attentively to the gentlemen of the Court, but all were as silent and as motionless as statues. What was most strange was that their clothes appeared as fresh and new as ever. There was not a speck of dust upon the furniture, and not a spider's web to be seen anywhere, though neither duster nor broom had been used for a hundred years.

At last the prince came to an inner chamber, where was the fairest sight his eyes had ever beheld. In an embroidered bed a young girl of surpassing beauty lay asleep. She looked as if she had only just closed her eyes. Trembling and filled with admiration, the prince approached the bed and knelt beside it. Some say he kissed her, but as nobody saw it and she never told we can never be quite sure. Be that as it may, the end of the enchantment had come, and the princess awakened immediately. Looking at him very tenderly, she said, in a drowsy tone, "Is that you, my prince? I have waited for you very long."

Charmed with these words, and still more with the manner in which they were uttered, the prince answered that he loved her more than his life. Nevertheless he was more embarrassed than she was, for she had had plenty of time to dream of him during her long sleep of a hundred years, whereas he had never heard of her before. For a long time they sat talking together, and still they had not said half enough. The only interruption came from the princess's spaniel, who had

"Is that you, my prince? I have waited for you very long"

also awakened and was very jealous because his mistress did not notice him as much as she had formerly.

Meanwhile all the attendants had had their enchantment broken, and as they were not in love they were ready to die of hunger after their fast of a hundred years. A lady of honour ventured to intimate that dinner was served, and, the prince giving the princess his arm, they at once proceeded to the great hall. There was no need for the princess to wait to dress for dinner, as she was already magnificently attired, though in a style that was somewhat out of date. The prince was polite enough not to tell her of this, nor to remind her that she was dressed exactly like his grandmother, whose portrait hung upon the palace walls.

During dinner the musicians gave a concert, and, considering that they had not touched their instruments for a hundred years, they played extremely well. They ended with a wedding march, for that very evening the marriage of the prince and princess was celebrated, and though the bride was nearly one hundred years older than the bridegroom nobody would ever have imagined it.

After a few days they left the castle and the enchanted wood, and immediately both of these vanished, never again to be beheld by mortal eyes. The princess was restored to her ancestral kingdom, but her history was kept secret. During a hundred years people had become so much wiser that they would not have believed the story if they had been told. So nothing was explained, and nobody presumed to ask any questions about her, for a prince could marry whom he pleased.

THE BARMECIDE'S FEAST

THIS is the story that was told to the Caliph Mostanser Billah by the barber of Bagdad about Schacabac, the Hare-lipped, who was the barber's sixth brother.

Though at one time, he said, my brother Schacabac was industrious and successful in his business, at length he was reduced by reverse of fortune to the necessity of begging his bread. In this occupation he acquitted himself with great address, his chief aim being to procure admission into the houses of the great by bribing the officers and domestics, and then, when he had once managed to get admitted to them, he failed not to excite their compassion.

One day he passed by a very magnificent building, through the door of which he could see a spacious court, wherein were a vast number of servants. He went up to one of them and inquired to whom the house belonged. "My good man," answered the servant, "where can you come from, that you ask such a question? Anyone you met would tell you it belonged to a Barmecide." My brother, who well knew the liberal and generous disposition of the Barmecides, addressed himself to the door-keepers, for there were more than one, and begged them to bestow some charity upon him. "Come in," answered they, "no one prevents you, and speak to our master—he will send you back well satisfied."

My brother did not need much persuasion, and entered the palace. He passed through a handsome vestibule, which led to a fine garden, the walks of which were formed of tiles of many colours very pleasing to the eye; and at last he entered a painted hall, richly furnished in azure and gold, where he saw a venerable old man with a long white beard, seated on a sofa in the most distinguished place. This proved to be the

Barmecide himself, who bade him welcome, and asked him
what he wished. When my brother informed him of his
poverty the Barmecide exclaimed, with every gesture of
pity, "Is it possible that in Bagdad such a man as you should
be so distressed? I cannot suffer this to be!" My brother
then told him that he had eaten nothing that day.

"How!" cried the Barmecide. "Is it true that at this late
hour you have not yet broken your fast? Alas, poor man,
you will die of hunger! Here, boy," he added, raising his
voice, "bring us instantly a basin of water, that we may wash
our hands."

Although no boy appeared, and my brother could see
neither basin nor water, the Barmecide began to rub his hands,
as if some one held the water for him; and as he did so he said
to my brother, "Come hither, and wash with me." Schacabac by this supposed that the Barmecide loved his jest, and as
he was himself of the same humour and knew the submission
the rich expected from the poor, he imitated all the movements of his host.

"Come," said the Barmecide, "now bring us something
to eat, and do not keep us waiting." When he had said this,
although nothing had been brought, he pretended to help
himself from a dish, and to carry food to his mouth and
chew it, while he called out to my brother, "Eat, I entreat
you, my guest. You are heartily welcome. Eat, I beg of
you: you seem, for a hungry man, to have but a poor
appetite."

"Pardon me, my lord," replied Schacabac, who was imi-
tating the motions of his host very accurately. "You see I
lose no time, and understand my business very well."

"What think you of this bread?" said the Barmecide.
"Don't you find it excellent?"

"In truth, my lord," answered my brother, who saw
neither bread nor meat, "I never tasted anything more white
and delicate."

"Eat your fill, then," said the Barmecide. "I assure you the slave who made this excellent bread cost me five hundred pieces of gold."

He continued to praise the female slave who was his baker, and to boast of his bread, which my brother devoured only in imagination. Presently he said, "Boy, bring us another dish. Come, my friend," he continued to my brother, though no boy appeared, "taste this fresh dish, and tell me if you have ever eaten boiled mutton and barley better dressed than this."

"Oh, it is admirable," answered my brother, "and you see that I help myself very plentifully."

"I am rejoiced to see you," said the Barmecide; "and I beg you not to suffer any of these dishes to be removed, since you find them so much to your taste."

He presently called for a goose with sweet sauce, dressed with vinegar, honey, raisins, peas, and figs. And after that for many rich dishes of different kinds, of which my brother, who felt completely famished, continued to pretend to eat in turn. At last, in reply to his persuasions, my brother protested that in truth he could not eat any more.

"Then let the dessert be served" said the Barmecide, and he went on to press on my brother all the most delightful fruits and sweetmeats, which were, of course, as imaginary as the earlier dishes had been.

"O my master," at last exclaimed Schacabac, whose jaws were aching with moving with nothing to chew, "I assure you I am so full that I cannot eat a morsel more."

"Then," cried the Barmecide, "after a man has eaten so heartily he should drink a little! You have no objection to good wine?"

"My master," replied my brother, "I pray you to forgive me. I never drink wine, because it is forbidden me."

"You are too scrupulous," said the Barmecide. "Come, come, do as I do!" And at last, after much pressing,

Schacabac gave way, and pretended to take the glass that the Barmecide appeared to hold out to him. He held it up, and admired its bright colour, put it to his nose to enjoy its aroma, and then, making a most profound reverence to the Barmecide, he drank it off, pretending that it gave him the most exquisite pleasure.

The Barmecide proceeded to pour out one kind after another of this invisible wine, drinking and filling my brother's cup, until at last Schacabac pretended that the wine had got into his head, and feigned intoxication. He raised his hand and gave the Barmecide such a violent blow that he knocked him down. He was going to strike him a second time, but the Barmecide, holding up his arm to ward off the blow, called out, "Are you mad?"

My brother then pretended to recollect himself, and said, "O my master, you had the goodness to receive your slave into your house, and to make a great feast for him; you should have been satisfied with making him eat; but you compelled him to drink wine. I told you how unused I was to it, and I can only say now that I am very sorry, and humbly ask your pardon."

When Schacabac had finished this speech the Barmecide, instead of being angry, burst into a violent fit of laughter. "For a long time," said he, "I have sought a person of your disposition. I not only pardon the blow you have given me, but from this moment I look upon you as one of my friends, and desire you to make my house your home. You have had the good sense to accommodate yourself to my humour, and the patience to carry on the jest to the end; but we will now eat in reality." So saying he clapped his hands, and this time several slaves appeared, whom he commanded to set out the table and serve the dinner. He was quickly obeyed, and my brother was now in reality regaled with all the dishes he had before partaken of in imagination. As soon as the table was cleared wine was brought; and a number of beautiful and richly adorned female slaves appeared, and began to sing and dance to the sound of instruments.

Schacabac had in the end every reason to be satisfied with the kindness and hospitality of the Barmecide, who took a great fancy to him, and treated him as a familiar friend, giving him, moreover, a handsome dress from his own wardrobe.

TOADS AND DIAMONDS

THERE was once upon a time a widow who had two daughters. The elder was so much like her both in appearance and in nature that whoever looked upon the daughter saw the mother. They were both so disagreeable and proud that there was no living with them.

The younger, who was the very picture of her father for courtesy and sweetness of temper, was also one of the most beautiful maidens ever seen. As people naturally love their own likeness, this mother even doted upon her elder daughter, and at the same time showed the greatest dislike for the younger, whom she kept at work continually and forced to eat in the kitchen.

Among other things, this poor child was made twice a day to fetch water from a spring above a mile and a half from the house, and bring home a pitcher full of it. One day as she was at the fountain there came to her a poor woman, who begged of her to let her drink.

"Ay, with all my heart, Goody," said this pretty little girl; and at once she rinsed the pitcher and took up some water at the clearest place of the fountain and gave it to her, holding up the pitcher all the while, that she might drink the easier.

The good woman, having drunk, said to her, "Thou art so very pretty, my dear, and so good and mannerly, that I cannot help giving thee a gift." For this was a fairy, who had taken the form of a poor country-woman to see how far the civility and good manners of this pretty maiden would go. "I will give thee this gift," said the fairy, "that at every word thou speakest there shall come from thy mouth either a flower or a precious jewel."

When the little maiden came home her mother scolded her for staying so long at the fountain.

"I beg thee to pardon me, Mother," said the poor girl, "for not making more haste." And as she spoke there came out of her mouth two lovely roses, two pearls, and two diamonds.

"What can this be?" said her mother, in amazement. "I really do believe that pearls and diamonds are falling from the girl's mouth! My dear! How can this be?"

Now this was the very first time she had called her "my dear."

Then the little maiden told her what had happened at the fountain in the forest, and all the time she spoke numbers of diamonds and pearls kept on dropping from her mouth.

"This is wonderful!" cried her mother. "I must send thy sister there also. Fanny, Fanny, come here! Look what drops from thy sister's mouth when she speaks! Dear, wouldst not thou be glad to have the same gift bestowed on thee too? Thou hast nothing else to do but go and draw water from the fountain, and when a poor old woman appears and asks thee for a drink to give it to her very civilly."

"Oh," said this ill-bred minx, "it would be a very fine sight indeed to see me go draw water!"

"Go you shall, hussy," said her mother, "and this minute!"

And she had to go, grumbling all the way, taking with her the best silver tankard in the house.

She no sooner reached the fountain than she saw coming out of the wood a lady splendidly dressed, who came up to her and asked to drink. This, you must know, was the very fairy who had appeared to her sister, but had now taken the form and dress of a beautiful princess, in order to see how far this girl's rudeness would go.

"Am I come hither, pray," said the proud, saucy slut, "to serve thee with water? Dost thou think my fine silver tankard was brought for that? However, if thou hast a fancy thou canst fill it thyself and drink."

"Thou art not over and above mannerly," said the fairy, without showing that she was at all angry. "Well, then, since thou hast so little breeding and art so disobliging the gift I will bestow on thee is that at every word thou speakest there shall spring from thy mouth a snake or a toad." At this she vanished, and the girl went off home.

So soon as her mother saw her coming she cried out, "Well, my child?"

"Well, Mother?" answered the pert little hussy, and out of her mouth there jumped two vipers and two toads.

"Mercy!" cried her mother. "What is this I see? Oh, it's that wretch your sister who has caused all this! But she shall pay for it!" And immediately seizing a stick, she ran to beat her. Hearing her angry words, the poor child fled from the house and hid herself among the trees in the forest.

At that moment the King's son, who was on his way home from hunting, rode by the spot where she was hiding, and, seeing her among the bushes and how beautiful she was, he asked her what she did there alone, and why she was crying.

"Alas, sir," she answered, "my mother has driven me out of doors."

And as she spoke the King's son, who had already fallen in love with her beauty, saw the pearls and the diamonds that dropped from her mouth. He desired her to tell him the whole story, and when he had heard it he lifted her on to his horse and took her with him to the palace of the King his father, and there he married her.

LITTLE RED RIDING-HOOD

ONCE upon a time there lived in a certain village a little
country girl, the prettiest creature was ever seen. Her
mother was excessively fond of her; and her grandmother
doted on her much more. This good woman got made for
her a red riding-hood, which became the girl so extremely
well that everybody called her Little Red Riding-hood.

One day her mother, having made some girdle-cakes, said
to her, "Go, my dear, and see how thy grandmamma does,
for I hear she has been very ill. Carry her a girdle-cake and
this little pot of butter."

Little Red Riding-hood set out immediately to go to her
grandmother, who lived in another village. As she was
going through the wood she met with Gaffer Wolf, who
had a very great mind to eat her up, but he durst not, because
of some faggot-makers hard by in the forest.

He asked her whither she was going. The poor child, who did not know that it was dangerous to stay and hear a wolf talk, said to him, "I am going to see my grandmamma, and carry her a girdle-cake and a little pot of butter from my mamma."

"Does she live far off?" said the wolf.

"Oh, ay," answered Little Red Riding-hood, "it is beyond that mill you see there, at the first house in the village."

"Well," said the wolf, "and I'll go and see her too. I'll go this way, and you go that, and we shall see who will be there soonest."

The wolf began to run as fast as he could, taking the nearest way; and the little girl went by that farthest about, diverting herself in gathering nuts, running after butterflies, and making nosegays of such little flowers as she met with. The wolf was not long before he got to the old woman's house: he knocked at the door—*tap, tap.*

"Who's there?"

"Your grandchild Little Red Riding-hood," replied the wolf, counterfeiting her voice, "who has brought you a girdle-cake and a little pot of butter sent you by Mamma."

The good grandmother, who was in bed, because she found herself somewhat ill, cried out, "Pull the peg, and the bolt will fall."

The wolf pulled the peg, and the door opened, and then presently he fell upon the good woman, and ate her up in a moment, for it was above three days that he had not touched a bit. He then shut the door, and went into the grandmother's bed, expecting Little Red Riding-hood, who came some time afterwards, and knocked at the door—*tap, tap.*

"Who's there?"

Little Red Riding-hood, hearing the big voice of the wolf, was at first afraid; but, believing her grandmother had got a cold and was hoarse, answered, "'Tis your grandchild

Little Red Riding-hood, who has brought you a girdle-cake and a little pot of butter Mamma sends you."

The wolf cried out to her, softening his voice as much as he could, "Pull the peg, and the bolt will fall."

Little Red Riding-hood pulled the peg, and the door opened. The wolf, seeing her come in, said to her, hiding himself under the bedclothes, "Put the cake and the little pot of butter upon the bread-bin and come and lie down with me."

Little Red Riding-hood undressed herself, and went into bed, where, being greatly amazed to see how her grandmother looked in her nightclothes, she said to her, "Grandmamma, what great arms you have got!"

"That is the better to hug thee, my dear."

"Grandmamma, what great legs you have got!"

"That is to run the better, my child."

"Grandmamma, what great ears you have got!"

"That is to hear the better, my child."

"Grandmamma, what great eyes you have got!"

"It is to see the better, my child."

"Grandmamma, what great teeth you have got!"

"That is to eat thee up."

And, saying these words, this wicked wolf fell upon poor Little Red Riding-hood and ate her all up.

THE THREE BEARS

ONCE upon a time there were Three Bears, who lived together in a house of their own in a wood. One of them
was a Little, Small, Wee Bear; and one was a Middle-sized
Bear; and the other was a Great, Huge Bear. They had each
a pot for their porridge: a little pot for the Little, Small, Wee
Bear; and a middle-sized pot for the Middle Bear; and a
great pot for the Great, Huge Bear. And they had each a
chair to sit in: a little chair for the Little, Small, Wee Bear;
and a middle-sized chair for the Middle Bear; and a great
chair for the Great, Huge Bear. And they had each a bed to
sleep in: a little bed for the Little, Small, Wee Bear; and a
middle-sized bed for the Middle Bear; and a great bed for
the Great, Huge Bear.

One day after they had made the porridge for their breakfast and poured it into their porridge-pots they walked out
into the wood while the porridge was cooling, that they
might not burn their mouths by beginning too soon to eat
it. And while they were walking a little old Woman came
to the house. She could not have been a good, honest old
Woman, for first she looked in at the window, and then she
peeped in at the keyhole; and, seeing nobody in the house,
she lifted the latch. The door was not fastened, because the
Bears were good Bears, who did nobody any harm and never
suspected that anybody would harm them. So the little old
Woman opened the door and went in, and well pleased she
was when she saw the porridge on the table. If she had been
a good little old Woman she would have waited till the
Bears came home, and then, perhaps, they would have asked
her to breakfast, for they were good Bears—a little rough or
so, as the manner of Bears is, but for all that very good-

natured and hospitable. But she was an impudent, bad old Woman, and set about helping herself.

So first she tasted the porridge of the Great, Huge Bear, and that was too hot for her; and she said a bad word about that. And then she tasted the porridge of the Middle Bear, and that was too cold for her; and she said a bad word about that too. And then she went to the porridge of the Little, Small, Wee Bear, and tasted that; and that was neither too hot nor too cold, but just right; and she liked it so well that she ate it all up. But the naughty old Woman said a bad word about the little porridge-pot, because it did not hold enough for her.

Then the little old Woman sat down in the chair of the Great, Huge Bear, and that was too hard for her. And then she sat down in the chair of the Middle Bear, and that was too soft for her. And then she sat down in the chair of the Little, Small, Wee Bear, and that was neither too hard nor too soft, but just right. So she seated herself in it, and there she sat till the bottom of the chair came out, and down she came, plump upon the ground. And the naughty old Woman said a wicked word about that too.

Then the little old Woman went upstairs into the bed-chamber in which the Three Bears slept. And first she lay down upon the bed of the Great, Huge Bear, but that was too high at the head for her. And next she lay down upon the bed of the Middle Bear, and that was too high at the foot for her. And then she lay down upon the bed of the Little, Small, Wee Bear, and that was neither too high at the head nor at the foot, but just right. So she covered herself up comfortably and lay there till she fell fast asleep.

By this time the Three Bears thought their porridge would be cool enough, so they came home to breakfast. Now, the little old Woman had left the spoon of the Great, Huge Bear standing in his porridge.

"SOMEBODY HAS BEEN AT MY PORRIDGE!" said

"Somebody has been sitting in my chair, and has sat the bottom out of it!" said the Little, Small, Wee Bear

the Great, Huge Bear, in his great, rough, gruff voice. And when the Middle Bear looked at his he saw that the spoon was standing in it too. They were wooden spoons; if they had been silver ones the naughty old Woman would have put them in her pocket.

"SOMEBODY HAS BEEN AT MY PORRIDGE!" said the Middle Bear, in his middle voice.

Then the Little, Small, Wee Bear looked at his, and there was the spoon in the porridge-pot, but the porridge was all gone.

"*Somebody has been at my porridge, and has eaten it all up!*" said the Little, Small, Wee Bear, in his little, small, wee voice.

Upon this the Three Bears, seeing that some one had entered their house and eaten up the Little, Small, Wee Bear's breakfast, began to look about them. Now, the little old Woman had not put the hard cushion straight when she rose from the chair of the Great, Huge Bear.

"SOMEBODY HAS BEEN SITTING IN MY CHAIR!" said the Great, Huge Bear, in his great, rough, gruff voice.

And the little old Woman had squatted down the soft cushion of the Middle Bear.

"SOMEBODY HAS BEEN SITTING IN MY CHAIR!" said the Middle Bear, in his middle voice.

And you know what the little old Woman had done to the third chair.

"*Somebody has been sitting in my chair, and has sat the bottom out of it!*" said the Little, Small, Wee Bear, in his little, small, wee voice.

Then the Three Bears thought it necessary that they should make further search; so they went upstairs into their bed-chamber. Now, the little old Woman had pulled the pillow of the Great, Huge Bear out of its place.

"SOMEBODY HAS BEEN LYING IN MY BED!" said the Great, Huge Bear, in his great, rough, gruff voice.

And the little old Woman had pulled the bolster of the Middle Bear out of its place.

"SOMEBODY HAS BEEN LYING IN MY BED!" said the Middle Bear, in his middle voice.

And when the Little, Small, Wee Bear came to look at his bed there was the bolster in its right place, and the pillow in its place upon the bolster; and upon the pillow was the little old Woman's ugly, dirty head—which was not in its place, for she had no business there.

"*Somebody has been lying in my bed—and here she is!*" said the Little, Small, Wee Bear, in his little, small, wee voice.

The little old Woman had heard in her sleep the great, rough, gruff voice of the Great, Huge Bear; but she was so fast asleep that it was no more to her than the roaring of wind or the rumbling of thunder. And she had heard the middle voice of the Middle Bear, but it was only as if she had heard some one speaking in a dream. But when she heard the little, small, wee voice of the Little, Small, Wee Bear it was so sharp and so shrill that it awakened her at once. Up she started; and when she saw the Three Bears on one side of the bed she tumbled herself out of the other and ran to the window. Now, the window was open, because the Bears, like good, tidy bears, as they were, always opened their bed-chamber window when they got up in the morning. Out the little old Woman jumped; and whether she broke her neck in the fall, or ran into the wood and was lost there, or found her way out of the wood and was taken up by the constable and sent to the House of Correction for a vagrant, as she was, I cannot tell. But the Three Bears never saw anything more of her.

WHAT THE OLD MAN DOES
IS ALWAYS RIGHT

I WILL tell you the story which I heard when I was a little boy. Every time I thought of the story it seemed to me to become more and more charming, for it is with stories as it is with many people—they become better and better the older they grow; and that is so delightful.

You have been in the country, of course. Well, then, you must have seen a very old farmhouse with a thatched roof, and mosses and weeds growing wild upon it. There is a stork's nest on the ridge of the roof, for we can't do without the stork. The walls of the house are aslant, and the windows low, and only one of the latter is made so that it will open.

The baking-oven sticks out of the wall like a little fat body. The elder-tree hangs over the paling, and beneath its branches, at the foot of the paling, is a little pond with a duck and some ducklings under a knotted old willow-tree. There is a yard dog too, who barks at every passer-by.

Well, there was just such a farmhouse out in the country, and in it dwelt an old couple—a peasant and his wife. Small as was their property, there was one of their possessions that they could do without—a horse, which managed to live on the grass it found in the ditch by the side of the highroad. The old peasant rode it to town, and often his neighbours borrowed it, and rendered the old couple some service in return for the loan. But still they thought it would be best if they sold the horse or exchanged it for something that might be more useful to them. But what was it to be?

"You'll know that best, old man," said the wife. "It is fair-day to-day; so ride to town and get rid of the horse for money, or make a good exchange—whatever you do will be right to me. Ride off to the fair."

And she tied his neckerchief for him, for she could do that better than he could; and she tied it in a double bow, and made him look quite smart. Then she brushed his hat round and round with the palm of her hand and gave him a kiss. So he rode away upon the horse that was to be sold or exchanged for something else. Yes, the old man knew what he was about.

The sun shone hot, and there was not a cloud in the sky. The road was very dusty, for many people who were all bound for the fair were driving, or riding, or walking upon it. There was no shade anywhere from the burning sun.

Among the rest a man was going along driving a cow to the fair. The cow was as pretty as a cow could be.

"She gives good milk, I'm sure," thought the peasant. "That would be a very good exchange—the cow for the horse.

"Hallo, you there with the cow!" he said. "Let's have a word together. I fancy a horse costs more than a cow, but I don't mind that; a cow would be more useful to me. If you like we'll exchange."

"To be sure I will," said the man with the cow. And so they exchanged.

So that was settled, and the peasant might just as well have

turned back, for he had done the business he came to do, but as he had once made up his mind to go to the fair he thought he'd go all the same, if only to have a look at it; and so he went on to the town with his cow.

Leading the cow, he strode on briskly, and after a short time he overtook a man who was driving a sheep. It was a fine fat sheep, well covered with wool.

"I should like to have that," said our peasant to himself. "It would find plenty of grass by our fence, and in winter we could have it in the room with us. Perhaps it would be more practical to have a sheep instead of a cow. Shall we change?"

The man with the sheep was quite ready, and the exchange

was made. So our peasant went on along the highroad with
his sheep.

Soon he saw another man, who came into the road from a
field, carrying a big goose under his arm.

"That's a heavy bird you have there. It has plenty of
feathers and plenty of fat, and would look well tied by a
string in our pond at home. That would be something for

my old woman to save up her scraps for. How often she
has said, 'If only we had a goose!' Now, perhaps, she can
have one; and, if possible, it shall be hers. Shall we exchange? I'll give you my sheep for your goose, and say
'Thank you' into the bargain."

The other man had no objection, and so they exchanged,
and our peasant got the goose.

By this time he was very near the town. The crowd on
the highroad became greater and greater; there was quite
a crush of men and cattle. They walked in the road and
close by the palings, and at the toll-gate they even went into
the toll-keeper's potato-field, where his only hen was strut-
ting about with a string to her leg, lest she should take fright

at the crowd and run away and get lost. She had short feathers on her tail, and winked with one eye, and looked very cunning. "Cluck, cluck!" said the hen. What she meant by it I cannot tell you; but directly our good man saw her he thought, "That's the finest hen I've ever seen in my life! Why, she's finer than our parson's brood hen. Upon my word, I should like to have that hen. A fowl can always

find a grain or two; she can almost keep herself. I think it would be a good exchange if I could get that for my goose.

"Shall we exchange?" he asked the toll-keeper.

"Exchange!" said the man. "Well, that wouldn't be a bad thing."

And so they exchanged, and the toll-keeper got the goose and the peasant got the hen.

Now he had done a good deal of business on his way to town, and he was hot and tired. He must have a drop of brandy and a bit to eat, and soon he was in front of the inn.

He was just about to go in when the ostler came out, and

they met in the doorway. The ostler was carrying a sackful of something on his back.

"What have you there?" said the peasant.

"Rotten apples," answered the ostler. "A whole sackful of them—enough to feed the pigs with."

"Why, that's terrible waste! I wish my old woman at home could see that lot. Last year the old tree by the turf-

stack only bore a single apple, and we kept it in the cupboard till it was quite rotten and spoiled. 'It's something, anyhow,' my old woman said; but here she could see any quantity—a whole sackful. Yes, I should be glad to show her that."

"What will you give me for the sackful?" asked the ostler.

"What'll I give? I'll give you my hen in exchange."

And so he gave him the hen and got the apples, which he carried into the bar parlour. He stood the sack carefully by the stove, and then went to the table. But the stove was hot; he had not thought of that. There were many strangers in the room—horse-dealers, drovers, and two Englishmen, and the two Englishmen were so rich that their pockets were bursting with gold, and they were making bets too, just as they are always supposed to.

Hiss-s-s! hiss-s-s! What was that by the stove? The apples were beginning to roast!

"What's that?"

"Why, do you know——" said our peasant.

And he told the whole story of the horse that he had changed for a cow, and all the rest of it, right down to the apples.

"Well, your old woman will give it you well when you get home!" said the Englishman. "There'll be a pretty row!"

"What? She'll give me what?" said the peasant. "She will kiss me, and say, 'What the old man does is always right.'"

"Shall we have a bet?" said the Englishman. "We'll wager gold by the ton—a hundred pounds to the hundred-weight!"

"A bushel will be enough," said the peasant. "I can only set the bushel of apples against it; and I'll throw in myself and my old woman into the bargain—and that's piling up the measure, I should say."

"Done!"

And so the bet was made. The innkeeper's cart was brought out, and the Englishman got in, and the peasant got in, and

the rotten apples, and away they went, and soon they reached the peasant's little farm.

"Good evening, old woman!"

"Good evening, old man!"

"Well, I've made the exchange!"

"Yes, you know what you're about," said the woman, and she put her arms round him, paying no attention to the strangers, nor did she notice the sack.

"I got a cow in exchange for the horse," said he.

"Heaven be thanked!" said she. "What lovely milk we shall have now, and butter and cheese on the table! That was a most capital exchange!"

"Yes, but I changed the cow for a sheep."

"Why, that's better still!" said the old woman. "You always think of everything. We have just grass enough for a sheep. Ewe's milk and cheese, and woollen stockings, and even woollen jackets too! The cow cannot give those, and her hairs will only come off. How you think of everything!"

"But I gave away the sheep for a goose."

"Then this year we shall really have roast goose to eat, my dear old man. You are always thinking of something to give me pleasure. How lovely that is! We can let the goose walk about with a string to her leg, and she'll grow fatter still before Michaelmas."

"But then I exchanged the goose for a hen," said the man.

"A hen? That *was* a good exchange!" replied the woman. "The hen will lay eggs and hatch them, and we shall have chickens; we shall have a whole poultry-yard! Oh, that's just what I was wishing for."

"Yes, but then I exchanged the hen for a sack of rotten apples."

"Well! Now I must really kiss you for that," exclaimed the wife. "My dear, good husband! Now I'll tell you something. Do you know, you had hardly left me this morning before I began thinking how I could give you something very nice this evening. I thought it should be pancakes with savoury herbs. I had eggs, and bacon too; but I wanted herbs. So I went over to the schoolmaster's—they have herbs there, I know—but his wife is a mean woman, though she looks so sweet. I begged her to lend me a handful of herbs. 'Lend!' she answered. 'Nothing at all grows in our garden, not even a rotten apple. I could not even lend you a rotten apple.' But now I can lend *her* ten—a whole sackful even. That I'm very glad of; that makes me laugh!" And with that she gave him a good smacking kiss.

"I like that!" said both the Englishmen together. "Always going downhill, and always happy; that's easily worth the money."

So they paid a bushel of gold to the peasant, who had not been cuffed but kissed.

Yes, it always pays when the wife always sees and says that her husband is the wisest, and that whatever he does is right.

You see, that's my story. I heard it when I was a child, and now you've heard it too, and know that "What the old man does is always right."

CINDERELLA

THERE was once an honest gentleman who took for his second wife the proudest and most disagreeable lady in the whole country. She had two daughters exactly like herself. He himself had one little girl, who resembled her dead mother, the best woman in all the world. Scarcely had the second marriage taken place before the stepmother became jealous of the good qualities of the little girl, who was so great a contrast to her own two daughters. She gave her all the hard work of the house, compelling her to wash the floors and staircases, to dust the bedrooms, and clean the grates. While her sisters occupied carpeted chambers hung with mirrors, where they could see themselves from head to foot, this poor little girl was sent to sleep in an attic, on an old straw mattress, with only one chair and not a looking-glass in the room.

She suffered all in silence, not daring to complain to her father, who was entirely ruled by his new wife. When her daily work was done she used to sit down in the chimney-corner among the ashes, from which the two sisters gave her the nickname of 'Cinderella.' But Cinderella, however shabbily clad, was handsomer than they were, with all their fine clothes.

It happened that the King's son gave a series of balls, to which were invited all the rank and fashion of the city, and among the rest the two elder sisters. They were very proud and happy, and occupied their whole time in deciding what they should wear. This was a source of new trouble to Cinderella, whose duty it was to get up their fine linen and laces, and who never could please them, however much she tried. They talked of nothing but their clothes.

"I," said the elder, "shall wear my velvet gown and my trimmings of English lace."

"And I," added the younger, "will have but my ordinary silk petticoat, but I shall adorn it with an upper skirt of flowered brocade, and shall put on my diamond tiara, which is a great deal finer than anything of yours."

Here the elder sister grew angry, and the dispute began to run so high that Cinderella, who was known to have excellent taste, was called upon to decide between them. She gave them the best advice she could, and gently and submissively offered to dress them herself, and especially to arrange their hair, an accomplishment in which she excelled many a noted coiffeur. The important evening came, and she exercised all her skill in adorning the two young ladies. While she was combing out the elder's hair this ill-natured girl said sharply, "Cinderella, do you not wish you were going to the ball?"

"Ah, madam"—they obliged her always to say madam— "you are only mocking me; it is not my fortune to have any such pleasure."

"You are right; people would only laugh to see a little cinder-wench at a ball."

After this any other girl would have dressed the hair all awry, but Cinderella was good, and made it perfectly even and smooth.

The sisters had scarcely eaten for two days, and had broken a dozen stay-laces a day in trying to make themselves slender; but to-night they broke a dozen more, and lost their tempers over and over again before they had completed their toilet. When at last the happy moment arrived Cinderella followed them to the coach, and after it had whirled them away she sat down by the kitchen fire and cried.

Immediately her godmother, who was a fairy, appeared beside her. "What are you crying for, my little maid?"

"Oh, I wish—I wish——" Her sobs stopped her.

"You wish to go to the ball; isn't it so?"

Cinderella nodded.

"Well, then, be a good girl, and you shall go. First run into the garden and fetch me the largest pumpkin you can find."

Cinderella did not understand what this had to do with her going to the ball, but, being obedient and obliging, she went.

Her godmother took the pumpkin, and, having scooped out all its inside, struck it with her wand. It then became a splendid gilt coach, lined with rose-coloured satin.

"Now fetch me the mouse-trap out of the pantry, my dear."

Cinderella brought it; it contained six of the fattest, sleekest mice.

The fairy lifted up the wire door, and as each mouse

ran out she struck it and changed it into a beautiful black horse.

"But what shall I do for your coachman, Cinderella?"

Cinderella suggested that she had seen a large black rat in the rat-trap, and he might do for want of better.

"You are right. Go and look again for him."

He was found, and the fairy made him into a most respectable coachman, with the finest whiskers imaginable. She afterwards took six lizards from behind the pumpkin frame and changed them into six footmen, all in splendid livery, who immediately jumped up behind the carriage, as if they had been footmen all their days.

"Well, Cinderella, now you can go to the ball."

"What, in these clothes?" said Cinderella piteously, looking down on her ragged frock.

Her godmother laughed, and touched her also with the wand, at which her wretched, threadbare jacket became stiff with gold and sparkling with jewels, her woollen petticoat lengthened into a gown of sweeping satin, from underneath which peeped out her little feet, covered with silk stockings and the prettiest glass slippers in the world.

"Now, Cinderella, you may go; but remember, if you stay one instant after midnight your carriage will become a pumpkin, your coachman a rat, your horses mice, and your footmen lizards, while you yourself will be the little cinder-wench you were an hour ago."

Cinderella promised without fear, her heart was so full of joy.

Arrived at the palace, the King's son, whom some one, probably the fairy, had told to await the coming of an uninvited princess whom nobody knew, was standing at the entrance, ready to receive her. He offered her his hand, and led her with the utmost courtesy through the assembled guests, who stood aside to let her pass, whispering to one another, "Oh, how beautiful she is!" It might have turned

"Now, Cinderella, you may go; but remember . . ."

the head of anyone but poor Cinderella, who was so used to being despised, but she took it all as if it were something happening in a dream.

Her triumph was complete; even the old King said to the Queen that never since her Majesty's young days had he seen so charming a person. All the Court ladies scanned her eagerly, clothes and all, and determined to have theirs made next day of exactly the same pattern. The King's son himself led her out to dance, and she danced so gracefully that he admired her more and more. Indeed, at supper, which was fortunately early, his admiration quite took away his appetite. Cinderella herself sought out her sisters, placed herself beside them, and offered them all sorts of civil attentions. These, coming as they supposed from a stranger, and so magnificent a lady, almost overwhelmed them with delight.

While she was talking with them she heard the clock strike a quarter to twelve, and, making a courteous *adieu* to the royal family, she re-entered her carriage, escorted gallantly by the King's son, and arrived in safety at her own door. There she found her godmother, who smiled approval, and of whom she begged permission to go to a second ball the following night, to which the Queen had invited her.

While she was talking the two sisters were heard knocking at the gate, and the fairy godmother vanished, leaving Cinderella sitting in the chimney-corner, rubbing her eyes and pretending to be very sleepy.

"Ah," cried the eldest sister spitefully, "it has been the most delightful ball, and there was present the most beautiful princess I ever saw, who was so exceedingly polite to us both."

"Was she?" said Cinderella indifferently. "And who might she be?"

"Nobody knows, though everybody would give their eyes to know, especially the King's son."

"Indeed!" replied Cinderella, a little more interested. "I should like to see her." Then she turned to the elder sister and said, "Miss Javotte, will you not let me go to-morrow, and lend me your yellow gown that you wear on Sundays?"

"What, lend my yellow gown to a cinder-wench! I am not so mad as that!" At which refusal Cinderella did not complain, for if her sister really had lent her the gown she would have been considerably embarrassed.

The next night came, and the two young ladies, richly dressed in different toilettes, went to the ball. Cinderella, more splendidly attired and more beautiful than ever, followed them shortly after. "Now, remember twelve o'clock," was her godmother's parting speech; and she thought she certainly should. But the prince's attentions to her were greater even than on the first evening, and in the delight of listening to his pleasant conversation time slipped by unperceived. While she was sitting beside him in a lovely alcove and looking at the moon from under a bower of orange-blossom she heard a clock strike the first stroke of twelve. She started up, and fled away as lightly as a deer.

Amazed, the prince followed, but could not catch her. Indeed, he missed his lovely princess altogether, and only saw running out of the palace doors a little dirty lass whom he had never beheld before, and of whom he certainly would never have taken the least notice. Cinderella arrived at home breathless and weary, ragged and cold, without carriage or footmen or coachman; the only remnant of her past magnificence being one of her little glass slippers; the other she had dropped in the ballroom as she ran away.

When the two sisters returned they were full of this strange adventure: how the beautiful lady had appeared at the ball more beautiful than ever, and enchanted every one who looked at her; and how as the clock was striking twelve she had suddenly risen up and fled through the ballroom, disappearing no one knew how or where, and dropping one of her glass slippers behind her in her flight.

The King's son had remained inconsolable until he chanced

to pick up the little glass slipper, which he carried away in his pocket and was seen to take out continually, and look at affectionately, with the air of a man very much in love; in fact, from his behaviour during the remainder of the evening all the Court and the royal family were sure that he was desperately in love with the wearer of the little glass slipper.

Cinderella listened in silence, turning her face to the kitchen fire, and perhaps it was that which made her look so rosy; but nobody ever noticed or admired her at home; so it did not signify, and next morning she went to her weary work again just as before.

A few days after the whole city was attracted by the sight of a herald going round with a little glass slipper in his hand, publishing, with a flourish of trumpets, that the King's son ordered this to be fitted on the foot of every lady in the kingdom, and that he wished to marry the lady whom it fitted best, or to whom it and the fellow-slipper belonged. Princesses, duchesses, countesses, and simple gentlewomen all tried it on, but, being a fairy slipper, it fitted nobody; and, besides, nobody could produce its fellow-slipper, which lay all the time safely in the pocket of Cinderella's old woollen gown.

At last the herald came to the house of the two sisters, and though they well knew neither of themselves was the beautiful lady they made every attempt to get their clumsy feet into the glass slipper, but in vain.

"Let me try it on," said Cinderella from the chimney-corner.

"What, you?" cried the others, bursting into shouts or laughter; but Cinderella only smiled and held out her hand.

Her sisters could not prevent her, since the command was that every maiden in the city should try on the slipper, in order that no chance might be left untried, for the prince was nearly breaking his heart; and his father and mother were afraid that, though a prince, he would actually die for love of the beautiful unknown lady.

So the herald bade Cinderella sit down on a three-legged stool in the kitchen, and he himself put the slipper on her pretty little foot. It fitted exactly. She then drew from her pocket the fellow-slipper, which she also put on, and stood up. With the touch of the magic shoes all her dress was changed likewise. No longer was she the poor, despised cinder-wench, but the beautiful lady whom the King's son loved.

Her sisters recognized her at once. Filled with astonishment, mingled with no little alarm, they threw themselves at her feet, begging her pardon for all their former unkindness. She raised and embraced them, telling them she forgave them with all her heart, and only hoped they would love her always. Then she departed with the herald to the King's palace, and told her whole story to his Majesty and the royal family. They were not in the least surprised, for everybody believed in fairies, and everybody longed to have a fairy godmother.

As for the young prince, he found her more lovely and lovable than ever, and insisted upon marrying her immediately. Cinderella never went home again, but she sent for her two sisters to the palace, and married them shortly after to two rich gentlemen of the Court.

PUSS IN BOOTS

A MILLER who was dying divided all his property between his three children. This was a very simple matter, as he had nothing to leave but his mill, his ass, and his cat; so he made no will, and called in no lawyer, for he would probably have taken a large slice out of these poor possessions. The eldest son took the mill, the second the ass, while the third was obliged to content himself with the cat, at which he grumbled very much. "My brothers," said he, "by putting their property together may gain an honest livelihood, but there is nothing left for me except to die of hunger; unless, indeed, I were to kill my cat and eat him, and make a coat out of his skin, which would be very scanty clothing."

The cat, who heard the young man talking to himself, looked at him with a grave and wise air, and said, "Master, I think you had better not kill me. I shall be much more useful to you alive."

"How so?" asked his master.

"You have but to give me a sack and a pair of boots such as gentlemen wear when they go shooting, and you will find you are not so ill off as you suppose."

Now, though the young miller did not put much faith in the cat's words, he thought it rather surprising that a cat should speak at all. And he had before now seen him show so much cleverness in catching rats and mice that it seemed well to trust him a little further, especially as, poor young fellow, he had nobody else to trust.

When the cat got his boots he drew them on with a grand air. Then, slinging his sack over his shoulder and drawing the cords of it round his neck, he marched bravely to a rabbit-warren hard by, with which he was well acquainted.

Putting some bran and lettuces into his bag, and stretching himself out beside it as if he were dead, he waited for some fine, fat young rabbit to peer into the sack to eat the food that was inside. This happened very shortly, for there are plenty of foolish young rabbits in every warren; and when one of them, who really was a splendid fat fellow, put his head inside, Master Puss drew the cords immediately, and took him and killed him without mercy. Then, very proud of his

prey, he marched direct up to the palace, and begged to speak with the King. He was desired to ascend to the apartment of his Majesty, where, making a low bow, he said, "Sire, here is a magnificent rabbit from the warren of my lord the Marquis of Carabas, which he has desired me to offer humbly to your Majesty."

"Tell your master," replied the King, "that I accept his present, and am very much obliged to him."

Another time Puss went and hid himself and his sack in a wheat-field, and there caught two splendid fat partridges in the same manner as he had done the rabbit. When he presented them to the King, with a similar message as before, his Majesty was so pleased that he ordered the cat to be taken down into the kitchen and given something to eat and drink.

One day, hearing that the King was intending to take a drive by the river with his daughter, the most beautiful princess in the world, Puss said to his master, "Sir, if you would only follow my advice your fortune is made. You have only to go and bathe in the river at a place which I shall show you, and leave all the rest to me. Only remember that you are no longer yourself, but my lord the Marquis of Carabas."

The miller's son agreed, not that he had any faith in the cat's promise, but because he no longer cared what happened.

While he was bathing the King and all the Court passed by, and were startled to hear loud cries of "Help! Help! My lord the Marquis of Carabas is drowning!" The King put his head out of the carriage, and saw nobody but the cat who had at different times brought him so many presents of game; however, he ordered his guards to go quickly to the help of my lord the Marquis of Carabas. While they were pulling the unfortunate marquis out of the water the cat came up bowing to the side of the King's carriage, and told a long and pitiful story about some thieves, who, while his master was bathing, had come and carried away all his clothes, so that it would be impossible for him to appear before his Majesty and the illustrious princess.

"Oh, we will soon remedy that," answered the King kindly, and immediately ordered one of the first officers of the household to ride back to the palace with all speed and bring back the most elegant supply of clothes for the young gentleman, who kept in the background until they arrived. Then, being handsome and well made, his new clothes became him so well that he looked as if he had been a marquis all his days, and advanced with an air of respectful ease to offer his thanks to his Majesty.

The King received him courteously, and the princess admired him very much. Indeed, so charming did he appear to her that she persuaded her father to invite him into the carriage with them, which, you may be sure, the young man did not refuse. The cat, delighted at the success of his scheme, went away as fast as he could, and ran so swiftly that he kept a long way ahead of the royal carriage. He went on and on

till he came to some peasants who were mowing in a meadow. "Good people," said he, in a very firm voice, "the King is coming past here shortly, and if you do not say that the field you are mowing belongs to my lord the Marquis of Carabas you shall all be chopped as small as mincemeat."

So when the King drove by and asked whose meadow it was where there was such a splendid crop of hay, the mowers all answered in trembling tones that it belonged to my lord the Marquis of Carabas.

"You have very fine land, marquis," said his Majesty to the miller's son.

"Yes, sire," he answered. "It is not a bad meadow, take it altogether."

Then the cat came to a wheat-field, where the reapers were reaping with all their might. He bounced in upon them: "The King is coming past to-day, and if you do not tell him that this wheat belongs to my lord the Marquis of Carabas I will have you every one chopped as small as mincemeat."

The reapers, very much alarmed, did as they were told, and the King congratulated the marquis upon possessing such beautiful fields, laden with such an abundant harvest.

They drove on, the cat always running before and saying the same thing to everybody he met—that they were to declare the whole country belonged to his master; so that even the King was astonished at the vast estate of my lord the Marquis of Carabas.

But now the cat arrived at a great castle where dwelt an ogre, to whom belonged all the land through which the King had been passing. He was a cruel tyrant, and his tenants and servants were terribly afraid of him. This accounted for their being so ready to say whatever they were told to say by the cat, who had taken pains to find out all about the ogre. So, putting on the boldest face he could assume, Puss marched up to the castle with his boots on, and asked to see the owner of it, saying that he was on his travels, but did not wish to pass so near the castle of such a noble gentleman without paying his respects to him. When the ogre heard this message he went to the door, received the cat as civilly as an ogre can, and begged him to walk in and repose himself.

"Thank you, sir," said the cat; "but first I hope you will satisfy a traveller's curiosity. I have heard in far countries of your many remarkable qualities, and especially how you have

the power to change yourself into any sort of beast you choose
—a lion, for instance, or an elephant."

"That is quite true," replied the ogre. "And lest you should
doubt it I will immediately become a lion."

He did so; and the cat was so frightened that he sprang up
to the roof of the castle and hid himself in the gutter—a proceeding rather inconvenient, on account of his boots, which
were not exactly fitted to walk with upon tiles. At length,
perceiving that the ogre had resumed his original form, he
came down again stealthily, and confessed that he had been
very much frightened.

"But, sir," said he, "it may be easy enough for such a big
gentleman as you to change himself into a large animal; I do
not suppose you can become a small one—a rat or mouse, for
instance. I have heard that you can; still, for my part, I
consider it quite impossible."

"Impossible?" cried the other indignantly. "You shall
see!" And immediately the cat saw the ogre no longer, but
a little mouse running along on the floor.

This was exactly what he wanted; and he did the most
natural thing a cat could do in the circumstances—he sprang
upon the mouse and gobbled it up in a trice. So there was
an end of the ogre.

By this time the King had arrived opposite the castle, and
was seized with a strong desire to enter it. The cat, hearing
the noise of the carriage-wheels, ran forward in a great hurry,
and, standing at the gate, said in a loud voice, "Welcome,
sire, to the castle of my lord the Marquis of Carabas."

"What," cried his Majesty, very much surprised, "does
the castle also belong to you? Truly, marquis, you have kept
your secret well up to the last minute. I have never seen anything finer than this courtyard and these battlements. Indeed,
I have nothing like them in the whole of my dominions."

The marquis, without speaking, helped the princess to
descend, and, standing aside, that the King might enter first—

for he had already acquired all the manners of a Court—followed his Majesty to the great hall, where a magnificent collation had been spread for the ogre and some of his friends. Without more delay they all sat down to feast.

The King, charmed with the good qualities of the Marquis of Carabas—and likewise his wine, of which he had drunk six or seven cups—said, bowing across the table at which the princess and the miller's son were talking very confidentially together, "It rests with you, marquis, whether you will not become my son-in-law."

" I shall be only too happy," said the Marquis, very readily, and the princess's eyes declared the same.

So they were married the very next day, and took possession of the ogre's castle, and of everything that had belonged to him.

As for the cat, he became at once a grand personage, and had never more any need to run after mice, except for his own amusement.

ALI BABA

THERE lived in ancient times in Persia two brothers, one named Cassim, the other Ali Baba. Their father left them scarcely anything, but he divided the little property he had equally between them.

Cassim married a wife, who soon after became an heiress to a large sum and a warehouse full of rich goods, so that he all at once became one of the wealthiest and most considerable merchants, and lived at his ease.

Ali Baba, on the other hand, who had married a woman as poor as himself, lived in a very wretched habitation, and maintained his wife and children by cutting wood, which he carried to town upon his three asses, and there sold.

One day when Ali Baba was in the forest and had cut wood enough to load his asses he saw at a distance a great cloud of dust, and soon he perceived a troop of horsemen coming towards him. Fearing that they might be thieves, he climbed into a large tree, whose branches were so thick that he was completely hidden, while he himself could see all that passed without being discovered. The tree stood at the base of a steep rock, at the foot of which the horsemen dismounted.

Ali Baba counted forty of them, and from their looks was assured that they were thieves. Nor was he mistaken, for they were a band of robbers, who, without doing any harm to the neighbourhood, robbed at a distance. Every man unbridled and tethered his horse, and hung about his neck a bag of corn. Then each of them took a wallet from his horse, which from its weight seemed to Ali Baba to be full of gold and silver One who seemed to be the captain of the band came under the tree in which Ali Baba was concealed, and, making his way through the shrubs, stood before the rock,

and pronounced distinctly these words: "Open Sesame."
As soon as he had uttered these words a door opened in the
rock, and after he had made all his band enter before him the
captain followed, and the door shut again of itself.

The robbers stayed some time within the rock, and Ali Baba,
who feared that one of them might come out and catch him
if he should endeavour to make his escape, was obliged to
sit patiently in the tree. At last the door opened again, and
the forty robbers came out. The captain came first, and stood
to see the others all pass by him; then he pronounced these
words: "Shut Sesame," and instantly the door of the rock
closed again as it was before. Every man bridled his horse,
fastened his wallet, and mounted, and when the captain saw
them ready he put himself at their head, and they returned
by the way they had come.

Ali Baba did not immediately quit his tree, but followed
the band of robbers with his eyes as far as he could see them.
He then descended, and, remembering the words the robber
captain had used to cause the door to open and shut, he was
filled with curiosity to try if his pronouncing them would
have the same effect. Accordingly he went among the shrubs,
and, perceiving the door concealed behind them, stood before
it, and said, "Open Sesame." The door instantly flew wide
open.

Ali Baba was surprised to find a cavern well lighted and
spacious, in the form of a vault, which received the light
from an opening at the top of the rock. He saw rich bales
of silk stuff, brocade, and valuable carpeting piled upon one
another, gold and silver ingots in great heaps, and money in
bags. The sight of all these riches made him suppose that this
cave must have been occupied for ages by bands of robbers
who had succeeded one another.

Ali Baba immediately entered the cave, and as soon as he
did so the door shut of itself. This did not disturb him, because he knew the secret with which to open it again. He

paid no attention to the silver, but carried out much of the gold coin, which was in bags. He collected his asses, which had strayed away, and when he had loaded them with the bags laid wood over in such a manner that the bags could not be seen. When he had done this he stood before the door and pronounced the words "Shut Sesame," and the door closed after him. He then made the best of his way to town.

When Ali Baba reached home he drove his asses into a little yard, shut the gates very carefully, threw off the wood that covered the bags, and carried them into the house, and ranged them in order before his wife. He then emptied the bags, which raised such a heap of gold as dazzled her eyes, and when he had done this he told her the whole adventure from beginning to end, and, above all, charged her to keep it secret.

Ali Baba found the heap of gold so large that it was impossible to count so much in one night; he therefore sent his wife out to borrow a small measure in the neighbourhood. Away she ran to her brother-in-law Cassim, who lived near by, and asked his wife to lend her a measure for a little while. The sister-in-law did so, but as she knew Ali Baba's poverty she was curious to discover what sort of grain his wife wanted to measure, and she artfully put some suet in the bottom of the measure.

Ali Baba's wife went home, and measured the heap of gold, and carried the measure back again to her sister-in-law, but without noticing that a piece had stuck to the bottom. As soon as she was gone Cassim's wife examined the measure, and was inexpressibly surprised to find a piece of gold stuck to it. Envy immediately possessed her breast. "What!" said she. "Has Ali Baba gold so plentiful as to measure it? Where has that poor wretch got all his wealth?" Cassim, her husband, was not at home, and she waited for his return with great impatience.

When Cassim came home his wife said to him, "Cassim,

I know that thou thinkest thyself rich, but thou art mistaken.
Ali Baba is infinitely richer than thou. He does not count
his money, but measures it!" Cassim desired her to explain
the riddle, which she did by telling him of the stratagem she
had used to make the discovery, and she showed him the
piece of money, which was so old that they could not tell in
what prince's reign it had been coined.

Cassim, instead of being pleased, conceived a base envy of
his brother's prosperity. He could not sleep all that night,
and in the morning went to him before sunrise. "Ali Baba,"
said he, showing him the piece of money which his wife had
given him, "thou pretendest to be miserably poor, and yet
thou measurest gold! How many of these pieces hast thou?
My wife found this at the bottom of the measure thou
borrowedest yesterday."

Ali Baba, perceiving that Cassim and his wife knew all,
told his brother, without showing the least surprise or trouble,
by what chance he had discovered this retreat of thieves. He
told him also in what place it was, and offered him part of
his treasure to keep the secret. "I expect as much," replied
Cassim haughtily, "but I must know exactly where this
treasure is, and how I may visit it myself when I choose;
otherwise I will go and inform the Cadi that thou hast this
gold. Thou wilt then lose all thou hast, and I shall have a
share for my information."

Ali Baba, more out of good nature than because he was
frightened by the insulting menaces of his unnatural brother,
told him all he desired, and taught him the very words he
was to use to gain admission into the cave. Cassim, who
wanted no more of Ali Baba, left him, and immediately set
out for the forest with ten mules bearing great chests, which
he designed to fill with treasure. He followed the road which
Ali Baba had pointed out to him, and it was not long before
he reached the rock and found out the place by the tree and
by the other marks which his brother had described.

When he discovered the entrance to the cave he pronounced the words "Open Sesame." The door opened immediately, and when he had entered closed upon him. In examining the cave he found much more riches than he had imagined. He was so covetous and greedy of wealth that he could have spent the whole day feasting his eyes upon so much treasure if the thought that he had come to carry away some had not hindered him.

He laid as many bags of gold as he could carry at the door of the cavern, but his thoughts were so full of the great riches he should possess that he could not think of the words to make the door open, but, instead of Sesame, said, "Open Barley," and was much amazed to find that the door remained fast shut. He named several sorts of grains, but still the door would not open, and the more he endeavoured to remember the word 'Sesame' the more his memory was confounded. He threw down the bags he had loaded himself with, and walked distractedly up and down the cave, without the least regard to the riches that were around him.

About noon the robbers chanced to visit their cave, and at some distance saw Cassim's mules straggling about with great chests upon their backs. Alarmed at this, the robbers galloped at full speed to the cave. They dismounted, and while some of them searched about the rock the captain and the rest went directly to the door, with their naked scimitars in their hands, and, pronouncing the proper words, it opened. Cassim, seeing the door open, rushed towards it in order to escape, but the robbers with their scimitars soon deprived him of his life.

The first care of the robbers after this was to examine the cave. They found all the bags which Cassim had brought to the door to be ready to load his mules, and they carried them again to their places, without missing what Ali Baba had taken before. Then, holding a council, they deliberated on the occurrence. They could not imagine how Cassim had gained entrance into the cave, for they were all persuaded that nobody knew their secret, little thinking that Ali Baba had watched them. It was a matter of the greatest importance to them to secure their riches. They agreed, therefore, to cut Cassim's body into four quarters, to hang two on one side and two on the other, within the door of the cave, in order to terrify any person who should attempt to enter. They had no sooner taken this resolution than they put it into execution. They then left the place, closed the door, mounted their horses, and departed to attack any caravans they might meet.

In the meantime Cassim's wife was very uneasy when darkness approached and her husband had not returned. She spent the night in tears, and when morning came she ran to Ali Baba in alarm. He did not wait for his sister-in-law to desire him to see what had become of Cassim, but departed immediately with his three asses, begging her first to moderate her anxiety.

He went to the forest, and when he came near the rock was seriously alarmed at finding some blood spilt near the door, but when he pronounced the words "Open Sesame" and the door opened he was struck with horror at the dismal sight of his brother's quarters. He entered the cave, took down the remains, and, having loaded one of his asses with them, covered them over with wood. The other two asses he loaded with bags of gold, covering them with wood also as before, then, bidding the door shut, he left the cave. When he came home he drove the two asses loaded with gold into his little yard, and left the care of unloading them to his wife, while he led the other to his sister-in-law's house.

Ali Baba knocked at the door, which was opened by Morgiana, an intelligent slave, whom Ali Baba knew to be faithful and resourceful in the most difficult undertakings. When he came into the court he unloaded the ass, and, taking Morgiana aside, said to her, "The first thing I ask of thee is inviolable secrecy, which thou wilt find is necessary both for thy mistress's sake and mine. Thy master's body is contained in these two bundles, and our business is to bury him as though he had died a natural death. Go tell thy mistress that I wish to speak to her, and mind what I have said to thee."

Morgiana went to her mistress, and Ali Baba followed her. Ali Baba then detailed the incidents of his journey and of Cassim's death. He endeavoured to comfort the widow, and said to her, "I offer to add the treasures which Allah hath sent to me to what thou hast, and marry thee, assuring thee that my wife will not be jealous, and that we shall be happy together. If this proposal is agreeable to thee I think that thou mayest leave the management of Cassim's funeral to Morgiana, the faithful slave, and I will contribute all that lies in my power to thy consolation."

What could Cassim's widow do better than accept this proposal? She therefore dried her tears, which had begun to flow abundantly, and showed Ali Baba that she approved of his proposal. He then left the widow, recommended Morgiana to care for her master's body, and returned home with his ass.

The next morning, soon after day appeared, Morgiana, knowing an old cobbler who opened his stall early, went to him and, bidding him good-morrow, put a piece of gold into his hand. "Well," said Baba Mustapha, which was his name, "what must I do for it? I am ready!"

"Baba Mustapha," said Morgiana, "thou must take thy sewing materials and come with me, and I will blindfold thee until thou comest to a certain place."

Baba Mustapha hesitated a little at these words, but after some persuasion he went with Morgiana, who, when she had bound his eyes with a handkerchief, led him to her deceased master's house, and never unbandaged his eyes until he had entered the room where she had put the quarters. "Baba Mustapha," said she, "make haste and sew these quarters together, and when thou hast done so I will give thee another piece of gold."

After Baba Mustapha had finished his task Morgiana blind-folded him, gave him another piece of gold, and, recommending secrecy, led him to his shop and unbandaged his eyes. She then returned home and prepared Cassim's body for the

funeral, which was held the next day with the usual pomp and ceremony.

Let us now leave Ali Baba to enjoy the beginning of his fortune and return to the forty thieves. They came again to their retreat in the forest, but great was their surprise to find Cassim's body taken away, with some of their bags of gold. "We certainly are discovered," said the captain, "and if we do not speedily apply some remedy shall gradually lose all the riches which our ancestors and ourselves have been many years amassing with so much pain and danger. It is evident that the thief whom we surprised has an accomplice, and now that one of the villains has been caught we must discover the other. One of you who is bold, artful, and enterprising must go into the town disguised as a traveller. He will thus be able to ascertain whether any man has lately died a strange death. But in case this messenger return to us with a false report I ask you all if ye do not think that he should suffer death?" All the robbers found the captain's proposal so advisable that they unanimously approved of it. Thereupon one of the robbers started up and requested to be sent into the town. He received great commendation from the captain and his comrades, disguised himself, and, taking his leave of the band, went into the town just before daybreak. He walked up and down until accidentally he came to Baba Mustapha's stall, which was always open before any of the other shops.

Baba Mustapha was seated with an awl in his hand. The robber saluted him, and, perceiving that he was old, said, "Honest man, thou beginnest work very early. Is it possible that one of thine age can see so well?"

"Certainly," said Baba Mustapha, "thou must be a stranger, and do not know me. I have extraordinary eyes, and thou wilt not doubt it when I tell thee that I sewed a dead body together in a place where I had not so much light as I have now."

The robber was overjoyed at this information, and proceeded to question Baba Mustapha, until he learned all that had occurred. He then pulled out a piece of gold, and, putting it into the cobbler's hand, said to him, "I can assure thee that I will never divulge thy secret. All that I ask of thee is to show me the house where thou stitchedest up the dead body. Come, let me blind thine eyes at the same place where the slave girl bound them. We will walk on together, and perhaps thou mayest go direct to the house where occurred thy mysterious adventure. As everybody ought to be paid for his trouble, here is a second piece of gold for thee." So saying he put another piece of gold in Baba Mustapha's hand.

The two pieces of gold were a great temptation to the cobbler. He looked at them a long time without saying a word, thinking what he should do, but at last he pulled out his purse and put them into it. He then rose up, to the great joy of the robber, and said, "I do not assure thee that I shall be able to remember the way, but since thou desirest it I will try what I can do."

The robber, who had his handkerchief ready, tied it over

Baba Mustapha's eyes and walked by him until he stopped, partly leading him and partly guided by him. "I think," said Baba Mustapha, "that I went no farther," and he had now stopped before Cassim's house, where Ali Baba lived. The robber, before he pulled off the bandage from the cobbler's eyes, marked the door with a piece of chalk, which he had ready in his hand, and, finding that he could discover nothing more from Baba Mustapha, he thanked him for the trouble he had taken, and let him go back to his stall. After this the robber rejoined his band in the forest, and triumphantly related his good fortune.

A little after the robber and Baba Mustapha had departed Morgiana went out of Ali Baba's house upon an errand, and upon her return, seeing the mark that the robber had made, stopped to observe it. "What can be the meaning of this mark?" said she to herself. "Somebody means my master no good!" Accordingly she fetched a piece of chalk and marked two or three doors on each side in the same manner, without saying a word to her master or mistress.

Meanwhile the robber captain had armed his men, and he said to them, "Comrades, we have no time to lose. Let us set off well armed, but without its appearing who we are. That it may not excite suspicion let only one or two go into the town together, and attain our rendezvous, which shall be the great square. In the meantime I will go with our comrade who brought us the good news and find the house, that we may decide what had best be done."

This speech and plan were approved of by all, and soon they were ready. They filed off in parties of two each, and got into the town without being in the least suspected. The robber who had visited the town in the morning led the captain into the street where he had marked Ali Baba's residence, and when they came to the first of the houses, which Morgiana had marked, he pointed it out. But the captain observed that the next door was marked in the same manner.

The robber was so confounded that he knew not what explanation to make, but was still more puzzled when he saw five or six houses similarly marked.

The captain, finding that their expedition had failed, went directly to the place of rendezvous, and told the members of the band that all was lost, and that they must return to their cave. He himself set them the example, and they all returned secretly as they had come. When they were gathered together the captain told his comrades what had occurred, and the robber spy was declared by all to be worthy of death. The spy condemned himself, acknowledging that he ought to have taken more precaution, and he received with courage the stroke from him who was appointed to cut off his head.

But as the safety of the band required that an injury should not go unpunished another robber offered to go into the town and see what he could discover. His offer being accepted, he went, and, finding Baba Mustapha, gave him a gold piece, and, being shown Ali Baba's house, marked it in an inconspicuous place with red chalk. Not long after Morgiana, whose eye nothing could escape, went out, and, seeing the red chalk, marked the other neighbours' houses in the same place and manner.

The second robber spy, on his return to the cave, reported his adventure, and the captain and all the band were overjoyed at the thought of immediate success. They went into the town with the same precautions as before, but when the robber and his captain came to the street they found a number of houses marked alike with red chalk. At this the captain was enraged, and retired with his band to the cave, where the robber spy was condemned to death, and was immediately beheaded.

The captain, having lost two brave fellows of his band, and being afraid lest he should lose more, resolved to take upon himself the important commission. Accordingly he went and addressed himself to Baba Mustapha, who did him

the same service he had done for the other robbers. The captain did not mark the house with chalk, but examined it so carefully that it was impossible for him to mistake it. Well satisfied with his attempt, he returned to the forest, and when he came to the cave, where the band awaited him, said, "Now, comrades, nothing can prevent our full revenge, as I am certain of the house." He then ordered the members of the band to go into the villages round about and buy nineteen mules and thirty-eight large leathern jars, one full of oil and the others empty.

In two or three days' time the robbers had purchased the mules and the jars. The captain, after putting one of his men into each jar, rubbed the outside of the vessels with oil. Things thus being prepared, when the nineteen mules were loaded with the thirty-seven robbers in jars and the jar of oil the captain, as their driver, set out with them, and reached the town by the dusk of the evening, as he had intended. He led the mules through the streets, until he came to Ali Baba's house, at whose door he stopped. Ali Baba was sitting there after supper to take a little fresh air, and the captain addressed him and said, "I have brought some oil a great distance to sell at to-morrow's market, and it is now so late that I do not know where to lodge. If I should not be troublesome to thee do me the favour to let me pass the night in thy house." Though Ali Baba had seen the robber captain in the forest, and had heard him speak, it was impossible to know him in the disguise of an oil-merchant. He told him that he should be welcome, and immediately opened his gates for the mules to pass through into the yard. At the same time he called a slave, and ordered him to fodder the mules. He then went to Morgiana, to bid her prepare a good supper for his guest.

Supper was served, after which the robber captain withdrew to the yard, under pretence of looking after his mules. Beginning at the first jar, and so on to the last, he said to each man, "As soon as I throw some stones out of my chamber window cut the jar open with the knife thou hast for that purpose, and come out, and I will immediately join thee." After this he returned to the house, and Morgiana, taking a light, conducted him to his chamber, where she left him.

Now, Morgiana, returning to her kitchen, found that there was no oil in the house, and as her lamp went out she did not know what to do, but, presently bethinking herself of the oil jars, she went into the yard. When she came nigh to the first jar the robber within said softly, "Is it time?" Though the robber spoke low Morgiana heard him distinctly, for the captain, when he unloaded the mules, had taken the lids off the jars to give air to his men, who were ill at ease and needed room to breathe.

Morgiana was naturally surprised at finding a man in a jar instead of the oil she wanted, but she immediately comprehended the danger to Ali Baba and his family, and the necessity of applying a speedy remedy without noise. Collecting herself, without showing the least emotion, she answered, "Not yet, but presently." She went in this manner to all the jars, giving the same answer, until she came to the jar of oil.

By this means Morgiana found that her master, Ali Baba, who thought that he was entertaining an oil-merchant, had really admitted thirty-eight robbers into his house, including the pretended oil-merchant, who was their captain. She made what haste she could to fill her oil pot, and returned to her kitchen, and as soon as she lighted her lamp she took a great kettle, went again to the oil jar, filled the kettle, set it upon a large wood-fire, and as soon as it boiled went and poured enough into every jar to scald and destroy the robber within. She then returned to her kitchen, put out the light, and resolved that she would not go to rest until she had observed what might happen through a window which opened into the yard.

She had not waited long before the captain of the robbers gave the appointed signal, by throwing little stones, several of which hit the jars. He then listened, and, not hearing or perceiving any movement among his companions, became uneasy and descended softly into the yard. Going to the first jar, he smelt the boiled oil, which sent forth a steam, and, examining the jars one after the other, he found all of his band dead, and by the oil that he missed out of the last jar guessed the means and manner of their death. Hence he suspected that his plot to murder Ali Baba and plunder the house was discovered. Enraged to despair at having failed in his design, he forced the lock of a door that led from the yard to the garden, and, climbing over the wall, he made his escape. Morgiana, satisfied and pleased to have succeeded so well in saving her master and his family, went to bed.

The next morning Morgiana took Ali Baba aside and communicated to him the events of the preceding night. Astonished beyond measure, Ali Baba examined all the jars, in each of which was a dead robber. He stood for some time motionless, now looking at the jars and now at Morgiana, without saying a word, so great was his surprise. At last, when he had recovered himself, he said, "I will not die without rewarding thee as thou deservest! I owe my life to thee, and as the first token of my gratitude I give thee thy liberty from this moment, and later I will complete thy recompense! I am persuaded with thee that the forty robbers had laid snares for my destruction. Allah, by thy means, hath delivered me from their wicked designs, and I hope he will continue to do so, and that he will deliver the world from their persecution and from their cursed race. All we now have to do is to bury the bodies of these pests of mankind."

Ali Baba's garden was very long, and there he and his slaves dug a pit in which they buried the robbers, and levelled the ground again. After which Ali Baba returned to his house and hid the jars and weapons; the mules he sold in the market. While Ali Baba was thus employed the captain of the forty robbers returned to the forest and entered the cave. He there sat down and determined how he could revenge himself upon Ali Baba.

When he awoke early next morning he disguised himself as a merchant, and, going into the town, took a lodging at an inn. He gradually conveyed from the cavern to the inn a great many rich stuffs and fine linens. He then took a shop opposite to Cassim's warehouse, which Ali Baba's son had occupied since the death of his uncle. Within a few days the pretended merchant had cultivated a friendship with the son, caressed him in the most engaging manner, made him small presents, and asked him to dine and sup with him.

Ali Baba's son did not choose to lie under such obligations to the pretended merchant without making the like return; he therefore acquainted his father with his desire to return these favours. Ali Baba, with great pleasure, took the entertainment upon himself, and invited his son to bring his friend to supper; he then gave orders to Morgiana to prepare a fine repast.

The pretended merchant accompanied the son to Ali Baba's house, and after the usual salutations said, "I beg of thee not to take it amiss that I do not remain for supper, for I eat nothing that has salt in it; therefore judge how I should feel at thy table!"

"If that be all," replied Ali Baba, "it ought not to deprive me of thy company at supper, for I promise thee that no salt shall be put in any meat or bread served this night. Therefore thou must do me the favour to remain."

Ali Baba then went into the kitchen, and commanded Morgiana to put no salt in the meat that was dressed that night. Morgiana, who was always ready to obey her master, was much dissatisfied at this peculiar order. "Who is this strange man," she asked, "who eats no salt in his meat? Does he not know that the eating of salt by host and guests cements for ever the bond of friendship?"

"Do not be angry, Morgiana," said Ali Baba. "He is an honest man; therefore do as I bid."

Morgiana obeyed, though with reluctance, and was filled with curiosity to see this man who would eat no salt with his host. To this end she helped Ali Baba to carry up the dishes, and, looking at the pretended merchant, she knew him at first sight, notwithstanding his disguise, to be the captain of the forty robbers, and, examining him carefully, she perceived that he had a dagger under his garment.

Thus having penetrated the wicked design of the pretended merchant, Morgiana left the hall, and, retiring to her own chamber, dressed herself as a dancer, and girded her waist with a silver girdle, to which there hung a poniard. When she had thus clad herself she said to a slave, "Take thy tabour, and let us go and divert our master and his son's guest." The slave took his tabour, and played all the way into the hall before Morgiana, who immediately began to dance in such a manner as would have created admiration in any company.

After she had danced several dances with equal grace she

drew the poniard, and, holding it in her hand, began a dance of light movements and surprising leaps. Sometimes she presented the poniard to one breast, then to another, and oftentimes seemed to strike her own. At length Morgiana presented the poniard to the breast of the pretended merchant, and with a courage worthy of herself plunged it into his heart.

Ali Baba and his son, shocked at this action, cried out aloud. "Unhappy wretch!" exclaimed Ali Baba. "What hast thou done to ruin me and my family!"

"It was to preserve, not to ruin thee," answered Morgiana, opening the pretended merchant's garment and showing the dagger. "See what an enemy thou hast entertained! Look well at him, and thou wilt find both the false oil-merchant and the captain of the band of forty robbers. Remember, too, that he would eat no salt with thee, and wouldst thou have more to persuade thee of his wicked design?"

Ali Baba, overcome with gratitude, embraced Morgiana, and said, "Morgiana, I gave thee thy liberty, and now I will marry thee to my son, who will consider himself fortunate to wed the preserver of his family." Ali Baba then turned and questioned his son, who, far from showing any dislike, readily consented to the marriage, not only because he wished to obey his father, but because it was agreeable to his inclinations. A few days after Ali Baba celebrated the nuptials of his son and Morgiana with great solemnity, a sumptuous feast, and the customary dancing.

Afterwards Ali Baba took his son to the cave, taught him its secret, which they handed down to their posterity, who ever after, using their good fortune with moderation, lived in great honour and splendour.

THE EMPEROR'S NEW CLOTHES

MANY years ago there lived an emperor who thought so much of new clothes that he spent all his money in order that he might be very fine. He did not care for his soldiers, nor for going to the play; or driving in the park, except to show his new clothes. He had a coat for every hour of the day, and just as they say of a king, "He is in the council-room," so they always said of him, "The Emperor is in his dressing-room."

The great city where he lived was very gay; and every day many strangers came there. One day there came two swindlers; they gave out that they were weavers, and said they could weave the finest cloth to be imagined. Their colours and patterns, they said, were not only exceptionally beautiful, but the clothes made of their material possessed the wonderful quality of being invisible to any man who was unfit for his office or hopelessly stupid.

"Those must be wonderful clothes," said the Emperor. "If I wore such clothes I should be able to find out which men in my empire were unfit for their places, and I could tell the clever from the stupid. Yes, I must have this cloth woven for me without delay." And he gave a lot of money to the two swindlers in advance, so that they should set to work at once. They set up two looms, and pretended to be very hard at work, but they had nothing whatever on the looms. They asked for the finest silk and the most precious gold; this they put in their own bags, and worked at the empty looms till late into the night.

"I should very much like to know how they are getting on with the cloth," thought the Emperor. But he felt rather uneasy when he remembered that he who was not fit for his office could not see it. He believed, of course, that he had nothing to fear for himself, yet he thought he would send somebody else first to see how matters **stood.** Everybody in the town knew what a wonderful property the stuff possessed, and all were anxious to see how bad or stupid their neighbours were.

"I will send my honest old Minister to the weavers," thought the Emperor. "He can judge best how the stuff looks, for he is intelligent, and nobody understands his office better than he."

So the good old Minister went into the room where the two swindlers sat working at the empty looms. "Heaven preserve us!" he thought, and opened his eyes wide. "I cannot see anything at all," but he did not say so. Both swindlers bade him be so good as to come near, and asked him if he did not admire the exquisite pattern and the beautiful colours. They pointed to the empty looms, and the poor old Minister opened his eyes wider, but he could see nothing, for there was nothing to be seen. "Good Lord!" he thought, "can I be so stupid? I should never have thought so, and nobody must know it! Is it possible that I am not fit for my office? No, no, I cannot say that I was unable to see the cloth."

"Well, have you got nothing to say?" said one, as he wove.

"Oh, it is very pretty—quite enchanting!" said the old Minister, peering through his spectacles. "What a pattern, and what colours! I shall tell the Emperor that I am very much pleased with it."

"Well, we are glad of that," said both the weavers, and they named the colours to him and explained the curious pattern. The old Minister listened attentively, that he might relate to the Emperor what they said; and he did so.

Now the swindlers asked for more money, more silk and gold, which they required for weaving. They kept it all for themselves, and not a thread came near the loom, but they continued, as hitherto, to work at the empty looms.

Soon afterwards the Emperor sent another honest courtier to the weavers to see how they were getting on, and if the cloth was nearly finished. Like the old Minister, he looked and looked, but could see nothing, as there was nothing to be seen.

"Is it not a beautiful piece of cloth?" said the two swindlers, showing and explaining the magnificent pattern, which, however, was not there at all.

"I am not stupid," thought the man. "Is it therefore my good appointment for which I am not fit? It is ludicrous, but I must not let anyone know it"; and he praised the cloth, which he did not see, and expressed his pleasure at the beautiful colours and the fine pattern. "Yes, it is quite enchanting," said he to the Emperor.

Everybody in the whole town was talking about the splendid cloth. At last the Emperor wished to see it himself while it was still on the loom. With a whole company of chosen men, including the two honest councillors who had already been there, he went to the two clever swindlers, who were now weaving as hard as they could, but without using any thread.

"Is it not *magnifique*?" said both the honest statesmen. "Will your Majesty see what a pattern and what colours?" And they pointed to the empty looms, for they imagined the others could see the cloth.

"What is this?" thought the Emperor. "I do not see anything at all. This is terrible! Am I stupid? Am I unfit to be emperor? That would indeed be the most dreadful thing that could happen to me."

"Yes, it is very fine," said the Emperor. "It has our highest approval"; and, nodding contentedly, he gazed at the empty loom, for he did not like to say that he could see nothing. All his attendants who were with him looked and looked, and, although they could not see anything more than the others, they said, like the Emperor, "It is very fine." And all advised him to wear the new magnificent clothes at a great procession which was soon to take place. "It is *magnifique*! beautiful, excellent!" went from mouth to mouth, and everybody seemed to be delighted. The Emperor gave each of the swindlers the cross of the order of knighthood and the title of Imperial Court Weavers.

All through the night before the procession was due to take place the swindlers were up, and had more than sixteen candles burning. People could see that they were busy getting the Emperor's new clothes ready. They pretended to take the cloth from the loom, they snipped the air with big scissors, they sewed with needles without thread, and said at last, "Now the Emperor's new clothes are ready!"

The Emperor, with all his noblest courtiers, then came in; and both the swindlers held up one arm as if they held something, and said, "See, here are the trousers! Here is the coat! Here is the cloak!" and so on. "They are all as light as a cobweb! They make one feel as if one had nothing on at all, but that is just the beauty of it."

"Yes!" said all the courtiers; but they could not see anything, for there was nothing to be seen.

"Will it please your Majesty graciously to take off your clothes?" said the swindlers. "Then we may help your Majesty into the new clothes before the large looking-glass!"

The Emperor took off all his clothes, and the swindlers pretended to put the new clothes upon him, one piece after another; and the Emperor looked at himself in the glass from every side.

"Oh, how well they look! How well they fit!" said all. "What a pattern! What colours! That is a splendid dress!"

"They are waiting outside with the canopy which is to be borne over your Majesty in the procession," said the chief master of the ceremonies.

"Yes, I am quite ready," said the Emperor. "Does not my suit fit me marvellously?" And he turned once more

to the looking-glass, that people should think he admired his garments.

The chamberlains, who were to carry the train, fumbled with their hands on the ground, as if they were lifting up a train. Then they pretended to hold something up in their hands; they dare not let people know that they could not see anything.

And so the Emperor marched in the procession under the beautiful canopy, and all who saw him in the street and out of the windows exclaimed, "How marvellous the Emperor's new suit is! What a long train he has! How well it fits him!" Nobody would let others know that he saw nothing, for then he would have been unfit for his office or too stupid. None of the Emperor's clothes had ever been such a success.

"But he has nothing on at all," said a little child. "Good heavens! Hear what the little innocent says!" said the father, and then each whispered to the other what the child said. "He has nothing on—a little child says he has nothing on at all!" "He has nothing on at all!" cried all the people at last. And the Emperor too was feeling very worried, for it seemed to him that they were right, but he thought to himself, "All the same, I must keep the procession going now." And he held himself stiffer than ever, and the chamberlains walked on and held up the train which was not there at all.

HANSEL AND GRETHEL

ONCE upon a time there dwelt near a large wood a poor woodcutter, with his wife and two children by his former marriage, a little boy called Hansel and a girl named Grethel. He had little enough to break or bite; and once, when there was a great famine in the land, he could not procure even his daily bread; and as he lay thinking in his bed one evening, rolling about for trouble, he sighed, and said to his wife, " What will become of us? How can we feed our children, when we have no more than we can eat ourselves?"

"Know, then, my husband," answered she, " we will lead them away quite early in the morning into the thickest part of the wood, and there make them a fire, and give them each a little piece of bread; then we will go to our work, and leave them alone, so they will not find the way home again, and we shall be freed from them."

"No, wife," replied he, "that I can never do. How can you bring your heart to leave my children all alone in the wood, for the wild beasts will soon come and tear them to pieces?"

"Oh, you simpleton!" said she. "Then we must all four die of hunger: you had better plane the coffins for us."

But she left him no peace till he consented, saying, " Ah, but I shall regret the poor children."

The two children, however, had not gone to sleep for very hunger, and so they overheard what the stepmother said to their father. Grethel wept bitterly, and said to Hansel, " What will become of us?"

"Be quiet, Grethel," said he. "Do not cry—I will soon help you."

And as soon as their parents had fallen asleep he got up, put on his coat, and, unbarring the back-door, slipped out. The moon shone brightly, and the white pebbles which lay before the door seemed like silver pieces, they glittered so brightly. Hansel stooped down, and put as many into his pocket as it would hold; and then going back he said to Grethel, "Be comforted, dear sister, and sleep in peace; God will not forsake us." So saying he went to bed again.

The next morning before the sun arose the wife went and awoke the two children. "Get up, you lazy things: we are going into the forest to chop wood." Then she gave them each a piece of bread, saying, "There is something for your dinner. Do not eat it before the time, for you will get nothing else."

Grethel took the bread in her apron, for Hansel's pocket was full of pebbles; and so they all set out upon their way. When they had gone a little distance Hansel stood still, and peeped back at the house; and this he repeated several times, till his father said, "Hansel, what are you peeping at, and why do you lag behind? Take care, and remember your legs."

"Ah, Father," said Hansel, "I am looking at my white cat sitting upon the roof of the house, trying to say good-bye."

"You simpleton!" said the wife. "That is not a cat; it is only the sun shining on the white chimney." But in reality Hansel was not looking at a cat; but every time he stopped he dropped a pebble out of his pocket upon the path.

When they came to the middle of the wood the father told the children to collect wood, and he would make them a fire, so that they should not be cold. So Hansel and Grethel gathered together quite a little mountain of twigs. Then they set fire to them; and as the flame burnt up high the wife said, "Now, you children, lie down near the fire and rest yourselves, while we go into the forest and chop wood. "When we are ready I will come and call you."

Hansel and Grethel sat down by the fire, and when it was noon each ate the piece of bread; and because they could hear the blows of an axe they thought their father was near; but it was not an axe, but a branch which he had bound to a withered tree, so as to be blown to and fro by the wind. They waited so long that at last their eyes closed from weariness, and they fell fast asleep. When they awoke it was quite dark, and Grethel began to cry, "How shall we get out of the wood?"

Hansel tried to comfort her by saying, "Wait a little while till the moon rises, and then we will quickly find the way."

The moon soon shone forth, and Hansel, taking his sister's hand, followed the pebbles, which glittered like new-coined silver pieces and showed them the path. All night long they walked on, and as day broke they came to their father's house. They knocked at the door, and when the wife opened it and saw Hansel and Grethel she exclaimed, "You wicked children! Why did you sleep so long in the wood? We thought you were never coming home again." But their father was very glad, for it had grieved his heart to leave them all alone.

Not long afterwards there was again great scarcity in every corner of the land; and one night the children overheard their mother saying to their father, "Everything is again consumed; we have only half a loaf left, and then the song is ended: the children must be sent away. We will take them deeper into the wood, so that they may not find the way out again: it is the only means of escape for us."

But her husband felt heavy at heart, and thought, "It were better to share the last crust with the children." His wife, however, would listen to nothing that he said, and scolded and reproached him without end.

He who says *A* must say *B* too; and he who consents the first time must also the second.

The children, however, had heard the conversation as they lay awake, and as soon as the old people went to sleep Hansel got up, intending to pick up some pebbles as before; but the wife had locked the door, so that he could not get out. Nevertheless he comforted Grethel, saying, "Do not cry; sleep in quiet; the good God will not forsake us."

Early in the morning the stepmother came and pulled them out of bed, and gave them each a slice of bread, which was still smaller than the former piece. On the way Hansel broke his in his pocket, and, stooping every now and then, dropped a crumb upon the path.

"Hansel, why do you stop and look about?" said the father. "Keep in the path."

"I am looking at my little dove," answered Hansel, "nodding a good-bye to me."

"Simpleton!" said the wife. "That is no dove, but only the sun shining on the chimney." But Hansel kept still dropping crumbs as he went along.

The mother led the children deep into the wood, where they had never been before, and there making an immense fire she said to them, "Sit down here and rest, and when you feel tired you can sleep for a little while. We are going into the forest to hew wood, and in the evening, when we are ready, we will come and fetch you."

When noon came Grethel shared her bread with Hansel, who had strewn his on the path. Then they went to sleep; but the evening arrived, and no one came to visit the poor children, and in the dark night they awoke, and Hansel comforted his sister by saying, "Only wait, Grethel, till the moon comes out; then we shall see the crumbs of bread which I have dropped, and they will show us the way home."

The moon shone and they got up, but they could not see any crumbs, for the thousands of birds which had been flying about in the woods and fields had picked them all up. Hansel kept saying to Grethel, "We will soon find the way"; but they did not, and they walked the whole night long and the next day, but still they did not come out of the wood; and

they got so hungry, for they had nothing to eat but the berries
which they found upon the bushes. Soon they got so tired
that they could not drag themselves along, so they lay down
under a tree and went to sleep.

It was now the third morning since they had left their
father's house, and they still walked on; but they only got
deeper and deeper into the wood, and Hansel saw that if
help did not come very soon they would die of hunger. As
soon as it was noon they saw a beautiful snow-white bird
sitting upon a bough, which sang so sweetly that they stood
still and listened to it. It soon left off, and spreading its wings
flew off; and they followed it until it arrived at a cottage,
upon the roof of which it perched; and when they went
close up to it they saw that the cottage was made of bread
and cakes, and the window-panes were of clear sugar.

"We will go in there," said Hansel, "and have a glorious
feast. I will eat a piece of the roof, and you can eat the
window. Will they not be sweet?"

So Hansel reached up and broke a piece off the roof, in
order to see how it tasted; while Grethel stepped up to the
window and began to bite it. Then a sweet voice called out
in the room, "*Tip-tap, tip-tap*, who raps at my door?" and
the children answered, "The wind, the wind, the child of
heaven"; and they went on eating without interruption.

Hansel thought the roof tasted very nice, and so he tore
off a great piece, while Grethel broke a large round pane out
of the window, and sat down quite contentedly. Just then
the door opened, and a very old woman walking upon
crutches came out. Hansel and Grethel were so frightened
that they let fall what they had in their hands; but the old
woman, nodding her head, said, "Ah, you dear children,
what has brought you here? Come in and stop with me, and
no harm shall befall you." So saying she took them both by
the hand, and led them into her cottage. A good meal of
milk and pancakes, with sugar, apples, and nuts, was spread

on the table, and in the back-room were two nice little beds, covered with white, where Hansel and Grethel laid themselves down and thought themselves in heaven.

The old woman behaved very kindly to them, but in reality she was a wicked witch who waylaid children, and built the bread-house in order to entice them in; but as soon as they were in her power she killed them, cooked and ate them, and made a great festival of the day. Witches have red eyes, and cannot see very far; but they have a fine sense of smelling, like wild beasts, so that they know when children approach them.

When Hansel and Grethel came near the witch's house she laughed wickedly, saying, "Here come two who shall not escape me." And early in the morning before they awoke she went up to them, and saw how lovingly they lay sleeping, with their chubby red cheeks; and she mumbled to herself, "That will be a good bite." Then she took up Hansel with her rough hand, and shut him up in a little cage with a lattice-door; and although he screamed loudly it was of no use. Grethel came next, and, shaking her till she awoke, she said, "Get up, you lazy thing, and fetch some water to cook something good for your brother, who must remain in that stall and get fat. When he is fat enough I shall eat him." Grethel began to cry, but it was all useless, for the old witch made her do as she wished. So a nice meal was cooked for Hansel, but Grethel got nothing else but a crab's claw.

Every morning the old witch came to the cage and said, "Hansel, stretch out your finger, that I may feel whether you are getting fat." But Hansel used to stretch out a bone, and the old woman, having very bad sight, thought it was his finger, and wondered very much that he did not get more fat.

When four weeks had passed and Hansel still kept quite lean she lost all her patience, and would not wait any longer. "Grethel," she called out in a passion, "get some water

quickly! Be Hansel fat or lean, this morning I will kill and cook him."

Oh, how the poor little sister grieved as she was forced to fetch the water, and fast the tears ran down her cheeks! "Dear, good God, help us now!" she exclaimed. "Had we only been eaten by the wild beasts in the wood, then we should have died together." But the old witch called out, "Leave off that noise: it will not help you a bit."

So early in the morning Grethel was forced to go out and fill the kettle and make a fire. "First we will bake, however," said the old woman. "I have already heated the oven and kneaded the dough." So saying, she pushed poor Grethel up to the oven, out of which the flames were burning fiercely. "Creep in," said the witch, "and see if it is hot enough, and then we will put in the bread." But she intended when Grethel got in to shut up the oven and let her bake, so that she might eat her as well as Hansel.

Grethel perceived what her thoughts were, and said, "I do not know how to do it. How shall I get in?"

"You stupid goose!" said she. "The opening is big enough. See, I could even get in myself!" And she got up, and put her head into the oven.

Then Grethel gave her a push, so that she fell right in, and then shutting the iron door she bolted it. Oh, how horribly she howled! But Grethel ran away, and left the ungodly witch to burn to ashes.

Now she ran to Hansel, and, opening his door, called out, "Hansel, we are saved; the old witch is dead!" So he sprang out, like a bird out of his cage when the door is opened; and they were so glad that they fell upon each other's neck, and kissed each other over and over again.

And now, as there was nothing to fear, they went into the witch's house, where in every corner were caskets full of pearls and precious stones. "These are better than pebbles," said Hansel, putting as many into his pocket as it would hold;

while Grethel thought, "I will take some home too," and filled her apron full.

"We must be off now," said Hansel, "and get out of this enchanted forest"; but when they had walked for two hours they came to a large piece of water. "We cannot get over," said Hansel. "I can see no bridge at all."

"And there is no boat either," said Grethel, "but there swims a white duck. I will ask her to help us over." And she sang:

> "Little Duck, good little Duck,
>   Grethel and Hansel, here we stand,
>   There is neither stile nor bridge;
>   Take us on your back to land."

So the Duck came to them, and Hansel sat himself on, and bade his sister sit behind him.

"No," answered Grethel, "that will be too much for the Duck; she shall take us over one at a time."

This the good little bird did, and when both were happily arrived on the other side and had gone a little way they came to a well-known wood, which they knew the better every step they went, and at last they perceived their father's house. Then they began to run, and, bursting into the house, they fell on their father's neck. He had not had one happy hour since he had left the children in the forest; and his wife was dead. Grethel shook her apron, and the pearls and precious stones rolled out upon the floor, and Hansel threw down one handful after the other out of his pocket. Then all their sorrows were ended, and they lived together in great happiness.

My tale is done. There runs a mouse: whoever catches her may make a great, great cap out of her fur.

RIP VAN WINKLE

WHOEVER has made a voyage up the Hudson must remember the Kaatskill mountains. They are a dismembered branch of the great Appalachian family, and are seen away to the west of the river, swelling up to a noble height, and lording it over the surrounding country. Every change of season, every change of weather, indeed, every hour of the day, produces some change in the magical hues and shapes of these mountains, and they are regarded by all the good wives, far and near, as perfect barometers. When the weather is fair and settled, they are clothed in blue and purple, and print their bold outlines on the clear evening sky; but sometimes, when the rest of the landscape is cloudless, they will gather a hood of grey vapours about their summits, which, in the last rays of the setting sun, will glow and light up like a crown of glory

At the foot of these fairy mountains the voyager may have descried the light smoke curling up from a village, whose shingle-roofs gleam among the trees, just where the blue tints of the upland melt away into the fresh green of the nearer landscape. It is a little village, of great antiquity, having been founded by some of the Dutch colonists in the early times of the province, just about the beginning of the government of the good Peter Stuyvesant (may he rest in peace!), and there were some of the houses of the original settlers standing within a few years, built of small yellow bricks brought from Holland, having latticed windows and gable fronts, surmounted with weathercocks.

In that same village, and in one of these very houses (which, to tell the precise truth, was sadly time-worn and weather-beaten), there lived, many years since, while the country was yet a province of Great Britain, a simple, good-natured fellow, of the name of Rip Van Winkle. He was a descendant of the Van Winkles who figured so gallantly in the chivalrous days of Peter Stuyvesant, and accompanied him to the siege of Fort Christina. He inherited, however, but little of the martial character of his ancestors. I have observed that he was a simple, good-natured man; he was, moreover, a kind neighbour, and an obedient, hen-pecked husband. Indeed, to the latter circumstance might be owing that meekness of spirit which gained him such universal popularity; for those men are most apt to be obsequious and conciliating abroad who are under the discipline of shrews at home. Their tempers, doubtless, are rendered pliant and malleable in the fiery furnace of domestic tribulation; and a curtain-lecture is worth all the sermons in the world for teaching the virtues of patience and long-suffering. A termagant wife may, therefore, in some respects, be considered a tolerable blessing; and if so, Rip Van Winkle was thrice blessed.

Certain it is that he was a great favourite among all the good wives of the village, who, as usual with the amiable sex, took his part in all family squabbles; and never failed, whenever they talked those matters over in their evening gossipings, to lay all the blame on Dame Van Winkle. The children of the village, too, would shout with joy whenever he approached. He assisted at their sports, made their playthings, taught them to fly kites and shoot marbles, and told them long stories of ghosts, witches, and Indians. Whenever he went dodging about the village, he was surrounded by a troop of them, hanging on his skirts, clambering on his back, and playing a thousand tricks on him with impunity; and not a dog would bark at him throughout the neighbourhood.

The great error in Rip's composition was an insuperable

aversion to all kinds of profitable labour. It could not be from the want of assiduity or perseverance; for he would sit on a wet rock, with a rod as long and heavy as a Tartar's lance, and fish all day without a murmur, even though he should not be encouraged to a single nibble. He would carry a fowling-piece on his shoulder for hours together, trudging through woods and swamps, and up hill and down dale, to shoot a few squirrels or wild pigeons. He would never refuse to assist a neighbour in even the roughest toil, and was a foremost man at all country frolics for husking Indian corn, or building stone fences; the women of the village, too, used to employ him to run their errands, and to do such little odd jobs as their less obliging husbands would not do for them. In a word, Rip was ready to attend to anybody's business but his own; but as to doing family duty, and keeping his farm in order, he found it impossible.

In fact, he declared it was of no use to work on his farm; it was the most pestilent little piece of ground in the whole country; everything about it went wrong, and would go wrong, in spite of him. His fences were continually falling to pieces; his cow would either go astray, or get among the cabbages; weeds were sure to grow quicker in his fields than anywhere else; the rain always made a point of setting in just as he had some out-door work to do; so that though his patrimonial estate had dwindled away under his management, acre by acre, until there was little more left than a mere patch of Indian corn and potatoes, yet it was the worst-conditioned farm in the neighbourhood.

His children, too, were as ragged and wild as if they belonged to nobody. His son Rip, an urchin begotten in his own likeness, promised to inherit the habits, with the old clothes, of his father. He was generally seen trooping like a colt at his mother's heels, equipped in a pair of his father's cast-off galligaskins, which he had much ado to hold up with one hand, as a fine lady does her train in bad weather.

Rip Van Winkle, however, was one of those happy mortals, of foolish, well-oiled dispositions, who take the world easy, eat white bread or brown, whichever can be got with least thought or trouble, and would rather starve on a penny than work for a pound. If left to himself, he would have whistled life away in perfect contentment; but his wife kept continually dinning in his ears about his idleness, his carelessness, and the ruin he was bringing on his family. Morning, noon, and night her tongue was incessantly going, and everything he said or did was sure to produce a torrent of household eloquence. Rip had but one way of replying to all lectures of the kind, and that, by frequent use, had grown into a habit. He shrugged his shoulders, shook his head, cast up his eyes, but said nothing. This, however, always provoked a fresh volley from his wife; so that he was fain to draw off his forces, and take to the outside of the house—the only side which, in truth, belongs to a hen-pecked husband.

Rip's sole domestic adherent was his dog Wolf, who was as much hen-pecked as his master; for Dame Van Winkle regarded them as companions in idleness, and even looked upon Wolf with an evil eye, as the cause of his master's going so often astray. True it is, in all points of spirit befitting an honourable dog, he was as courageous an animal as ever scoured the woods; but what courage can withstand the ever-during and all-besetting terrors of a woman's tongue? The moment Wolf entered the house his crest fell, his tail dropped to the ground, or curled between his legs, he sneaked about with a gallows air, casting many a sidelong glance at Dame Van Winkle, and at the least flourish of a broomstick or ladle he would fly to the door with yelping precipitation.

Times grew worse and worse with Rip Van Winkle as years of matrimony rolled on; a tart temper never mellows with age, and a sharp tongue is the only edged tool that grows keener with constant use. For a long while he used to console himself, when driven from home, by frequenting a kind of perpetual club of the sages, philosophers, and other idle personages of the village, which held its sessions on a bench before a small inn, designated by a rubicund portrait of His Majesty George the Third. Here they used to sit in the shade through a long, lazy summer's day, talking listlessly over village gossip, or telling endless sleepy stories about nothing. But it would have been worth any statesman's money to have heard the profound discussions that sometimes took place when by chance an old newspaper fell into their hands from some passing traveller. How solemnly they would listen to the contents, as drawled out by Derrick Van Bummel, the schoolmaster, a dapper learned little man, who was not to be daunted by the most gigantic word in the dictionary; and how sagely they would deliberate upon public events some months after they had taken place.

The opinions of this junto were completely controlled by Nicholas Vedder, a patriarch of the village, and landlord or the inn, at the door of which he took his seat from morning till night, just moving sufficiently to avoid the sun and keep in the shade of a large tree; so that the neighbours could tell the hour by his movements as accurately as by a sundial. It is true he was rarely heard to speak, but smoked his pipe incessantly. His adherents, however (for every great man has his adherents), perfectly understood him, and knew how to gather his opinions. When anything that was read or related displeased him, he was observed to smoke his pipe vehemently, and to send forth short, frequent, and angry puffs; but when pleased, he would inhale the smoke slowly and tranquilly, and emit it in light and placid clouds; and sometimes, taking the pipe from his mouth, and letting the fragrant vapour curl about his nose, would gravely nod his head in token of perfect approbation.

From even this stronghold the unlucky Rip was at length routed by his termagant wife, who would suddenly break in upon the tranquillity of the assemblage and call the members

all to naught; nor was that august personage Nicholas
Vedder himself sacred from the daring tongue of this terrible
virago, who charged him outright with encouraging her husband in habits of idleness.

Poor Rip was at last reduced almost to despair; and his only
alternative, to escape from the labour of the farm and clamour
of his wife, was to take gun in hand and stroll away into the
woods. Here he would sometimes seat himself at the foot of
a tree, and share the contents of his wallet with Wolf, with
whom he sympathized as a fellow-sufferer in persecution.
"Poor Wolf," he would say, "thy mistress leads thee a dog's
life of it; but never mind, my lad, whilst I live thou shalt
never want a friend to stand by thee!" Wolf would wag his
tail, look wistfully in his master's face; and if dogs can feel
pity, I verily believe he reciprocated the sentiment with all
his heart.

In a long ramble of the kind on a fine autumnal day Rip
had unconsciously scrambled to one of the highest parts of
the Kaatskill mountains. He was after his favourite sport of
squirrel-shooting, and the still solitudes had echoed and re-
echoed with the reports of his gun. Panting and fatigued,
he threw himself, late in the afternoon, on a green knoll,
covered with mountain herbage, that crowned the brow of
a precipice. From an opening between the trees he could
overlook all the lower country for many a mile of rich wood-
land. He saw at a distance the lordly Hudson, far, far below
him, moving on its silent but majestic course, with the reflec-
tion of a purple cloud, or the sail of a lagging bark, here and
there sleeping on its grassy bosom, and at last losing itself in
the blue highlands.

On the other side he looked down into a deep mountain
glen, wild, lonely, and shagged, the bottom filled with frag-
ments from the impending cliffs, and scarcely lighted by
the reflected rays of the setting sun. For some time Rip lay
musing on this scene; evening was gradually advancing; the

mountains began to throw their long blue shadows over the valleys; he saw that it would be dark long before he could reach the village, and he heaved a heavy sigh when he thought of encountering the terrors of Dame Van Winkle.

As he was about to descend, he heard a voice from a distance, hallooing, "Rip Van Winkle! Rip Van Winkle!" He 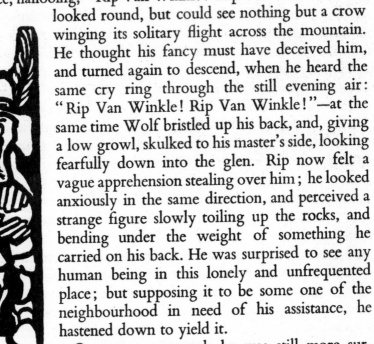looked round, but could see nothing but a crow winging its solitary flight across the mountain. He thought his fancy must have deceived him, and turned again to descend, when he heard the same cry ring through the still evening air: "Rip Van Winkle! Rip Van Winkle!"—at the same time Wolf bristled up his back, and, giving a low growl, skulked to his master's side, looking fearfully down into the glen. Rip now felt a vague apprehension stealing over him; he looked anxiously in the same direction, and perceived a strange figure slowly toiling up the rocks, and bending under the weight of something he carried on his back. He was surprised to see any human being in this lonely and unfrequented place; but supposing it to be some one of the neighbourhood in need of his assistance, he hastened down to yield it.

On nearer approach he was still more surprised at the singularity of the stranger's appearance. He was a short, square-built old fellow, with thick bushy hair and a grizzled beard. His dress was of the antique Dutch fashion—a cloth jerkin strapped round the waist, several pairs of breeches, the outer one of ample volume, decorated with rows of buttons down the sides, and bunches at the knees. He bore on his shoulder a stout keg, that seemed full of liquor, and made signs for Rip to approach and assist him with the load. Though rather shy and distrustful of this new acquaintance, Rip complied with his usual alacrity; and mutually relieving one another, they clambered up a narrow gully, apparently the dry bed of a mountain torrent. As they ascended, Rip every now and then heard long, rolling peals, like distant thunder, that seemed to issue out of a deep ravine, or rather cleft, between lofty rocks, towards which their rugged path conducted. He paused for an instant, but supposing it to be the muttering of one of those transient thunder-showers which often take place in mountain heights, he proceeded. Passing through the ravine, they came to a hollow like a small amphitheatre, surrounded by perpendicular precipices, over the brinks of which impending trees shot their branches, so that you only caught glimpses of the azure sky and the bright evening cloud. During the whole time Rip and his companion had laboured on in silence; for though the former marvelled greatly what could be the object of carrying a keg of liquor up this wild mountain, yet there was something strange and incomprehensible about the unknown, that inspired awe and checked familiarity.

On entering the amphitheatre new objects of wonder presented themselves. On a level spot in the centre was a company of odd-looking personages playing at ninepins. They were dressed in a quaint, outlandish fashion; some wore short doublets, others jerkins, with long knives in their belts, and most of them had enormous breeches, of similar style with that of the guide's. Their visages, too, were peculiar: one had a large beard, broad face, and small piggish eyes; the face of another seemed to consist entirely of nose, and was surmounted by a white sugar-loaf hat, set off with a red cock's tail. They all had beards, of various shapes and colours. There was one who seemed to be the commander. He was a stout old gentleman, with a weather-beaten countenance; he wore a laced doublet, broad belt and hanger, high-crowned hat and feather, red stockings, and high-heeled shoes, with roses in them. The whole group reminded Rip of the figures in an old Flemish painting, in the parlour of Dominie Van Shaick, the village parson, and which had been brought over from Holland at the time of the settlement.

What seemed particularly odd to Rip was that, though these folks were evidently amusing themselves, yet they maintained the gravest faces, the most mysterious silence, and were, withal, the most melancholy party of pleasure he had ever witnessed. Nothing interrupted the stillness of the scene but the noise of the balls, which, whenever they were rolled, echoed along the mountains like rumbling peals of thunder.

As Rip and his companion approached them, they suddenly desisted from their play, and stared at him with such fixed, statue-like gaze, and such strange, uncouth, lack-lustre countenances, that his heart turned within him, and his knees smote together. His companion now emptied the contents of the keg into large flagons, and made signs to him to wait upon the company. He obeyed with fear and trembling; they quaffed the liquor in profound silence, and then returned to their game.

By degrees Rip's awe and apprehension subsided. He even ventured, when no eye was fixed upon him, to taste the beverage, which he found had much of the flavour of excellent Hollands. He was naturally a thirsty soul, and was soon tempted to repeat the draught. One taste provoked another; and he reiterated his visits to the flagon so often that at length his senses were overpowered, his eyes swam in his head, his head gradually declined, and he fell into a deep sleep.

On waking, he found himself on the green knoll whence he had first seen the old man of the glen. He rubbed his eyes— it was a bright sunny morning. The birds were hopping and twittering among the bushes, and the eagle was wheeling aloft, and breasting the pure mountain breeze. "Surely," thought Rip, "I have not slept here all night." He recalled the occurrences before he fell asleep. The strange man with a keg of liquor—the mountain ravine—the wild retreat among

the rocks—the woe-begone party at ninepins—the flagon—
"Oh! that flagon! that wicked flagon!" thought Rip, "what
excuse shall I make to Dame Van Winkle?"

He looked round for his gun, but in place of the clean, well-
oiled fowling-piece he found an old firelock lying by him,
the barrel incrusted with rust, the lock falling off, and the
stock worm-eaten. He now suspected that the grave roisterers

of the mountain had put a trick upon him, and having dosed
him with liquor, had robbed him of his gun. Wolf, too, had
disappeared, but he might have strayed away after a squirrel
or partridge. He whistled after him, and shouted his name,
but all in vain; the echoes repeated his whistle and shout, but
no dog was to be seen.

He determined to revisit the scene of the last evening's
gambol, and if he met with any of the party, to demand his
dog and gun. As he rose to walk, he found himself stiff in
the joints, and wanting in his usual activity. "These mountain
beds do not agree with me," thought Rip, "and if this frolic
should lay me up with a fit of the rheumatism, I shall have a

blessed time with Dame Van Winkle." With some difficulty he got down into the glen: he found the gully up which he and his companion had ascended the preceding evening; but to his astonishment a mountain stream was now foaming down it, leaping from rock to rock, and filling the glen with babbling murmurs. He, however, made shift to scramble up its sides, working his toilsome way through thickets of birch, sassafras, and witch-hazel, and sometimes tripped up or entangled by the wild grape-vines that twisted their coils or tendrils from tree to tree, and spread a kind of network in his path.

At length he reached to where the ravine had opened through the cliffs to the amphitheatre; but no traces of such opening remained. The rocks presented a high, impenetrable wall, over which the torrent came tumbling in a sheet of feathery foam, and fell into a broad deep basin, black from the shadows of the surrounding forest. Here, then, poor Rip was brought to a stand. He again called and whistled after his dog; he was only answered by the cawing of a flock of idle crows, sporting high in air about a dry tree that overhung a sunny precipice; and who, secure in their elevation, seemed to look down and scoff at the poor man's perplexities. What was to be done? the morning was passing away, and Rip felt famished for want of his breakfast. He grieved to give up his dog and gun; he dreaded to meet his wife; but it would not do to starve among the mountains. He shook his head, shouldered the rusty firelock, and, with a heart full of trouble and anxiety, turned his steps homeward.

As he approached the village he met a number of people, but none whom he knew, which somewhat surprised him, for he had thought himself acquainted with every one in the country round. Their dress, too, was of a different fashion from that to which he was accustomed. They all stared at him with equal marks of surprise, and whenever they cast their eyes upon him invariably stroked their chins. The constant recurrence of this gesture induced Rip, involuntarily, to do the same, when, to his astonishment, he found his beard had grown a foot long!

He had now entered the skirts of the village. A troop of strange children ran at his heels, hooting after him, and pointing at his grey beard. The dogs, too, not one of which he recognized for an old acquaintance, barked at him as he passed. The very village was altered; it was larger and more populous. There were rows of houses which he had never seen before, and those which had been his familiar haunts had disappeared. Strange names were over the doors—strange faces at the windows—everything was strange. His mind now misgave him; he began to doubt whether both he and the world around him were not bewitched. Surely this was his native village, which he had left but the day before. There stood the Kaatskill mountains—there ran the silver Hudson at a distance—there was every hill and dale precisely as it had always been. Rip was sorely perplexed. "That flagon last night," thought he, "has addled my poor head sadly!"

It was with some difficulty that he found the way to his own house, which he approached with silent awe, expecting every moment to hear the shrill voice of Dame Van Winkle. He found the house gone to decay—the roof fallen in, the windows shattered, and the doors off the hinges. A half-starved dog that looked like Wolf was skulking about it. Rip called him by name, but the cur snarled, showed his teeth, and passed on. This was an unkind cut indeed. "My very dog," sighed poor Rip, "has forgotten me!"

He entered the house, which, to tell the truth, Dame Van Winkle had always kept in neat order. It was empty, forlorn, and apparently abandoned. This desolateness overcame all his connubial fears—he called loudly for his wife and children— the lonely chambers rang for a moment with his voice, and then all again was silence.

He now hurried forth, and hastened to his old resort, the

village inn—but it too was gone. A large rickety wooden building stood in its place, with great gaping windows, some of them broken and mended with old hats and petticoats, and over the door was painted, "The Union Hotel, by Jonathan Doolittle." Instead of the great tree that used to shelter the quiet little Dutch inn of yore, there now was reared a tall naked pole, with something on the top that looked like a red night-cap, and from it was fluttering a flag, on which was a singular assemblage of stars and stripes;—all this was strange and incomprehensible. He recognized on the sign, however, the ruby face of King George, under which he had smoked so many a peaceful pipe; but even this was singularly metamorphosed. The red coat was changed for one of blue and buff, a sword was held in the hand instead of a sceptre, the head was decorated with a cocked hat, and underneath was painted in large characters, GENERAL WASHINGTON.

There was, as usual, a crowd of folk about the door, but none that Rip recollected. The very character of the people seemed changed. There was a busy, bustling, disputatious tone about it, instead of the accustomed phlegm and drowsy tranquillity. He looked in vain for the sage Nicholas Vedder, with his broad face, double chin, and fair long pipe, uttering clouds of tobacco-smoke instead of idle speeches; or Van Bummel, the schoolmaster, doling forth the contents of an ancient newspaper. In place of these, a lean, bilious-looking fellow, with his pockets full of hand-bills, was haranguing vehemently about rights of citizens—elections—members of Congress—liberty—Bunker's Hill—heroes of seventy-six—and other words, which were a perfect Babylonish jargon to the bewildered Van Winkle.

The appearance of Rip, with his long, grizzled beard, his rusty fowling-piece, his uncouth dress, and an army of women and children at his heels, soon attracted the attention of the tavern politicians. They crowded round him, eyeing him from head to foot with great curiosity. The orator bustled up to him, and, drawing him partly aside, inquired "On which side he voted?" Rip stared in vacant stupidity. Another short but busy little fellow pulled him by the arm, and, rising on tiptoe, inquired in his ear, "Whether he was Federal or Democrat?" Rip was equally at a loss to comprehend the question; when a knowing, self-important old gentleman, in a sharp cocked hat, made his way through the crowd, putting them to the right and left with his elbows as he passed, and planting himself before Van Winkle, with one arm akimbo, the other resting on his cane, his keen eyes and sharp hat penetrating, as it were, into his very soul, demanded in an austere tone, "What brought him to the election with a gun on his shoulder, and a mob at his heels; and whether he meant to breed a riot in the village?" "Alas! gentlemen," cried Rip, somewhat dismayed, "I am a poor quiet man, a native of the place, and a loyal subject of the King, God bless him!"

Here a general shout burst from the bystanders—"A tory! a tory! a spy! a refugee! hustle him! away with him!" It was with great difficulty that the self-important man in the cocked hat restored order; and, having assumed a tenfold austerity of brow, demanded again of the unknown culprit what he came there for, and whom he was seeking? The poor man humbly assured him that he meant no harm, but merely came there in search of his neighbours, who used to keep about the tavern.

"Well—who are they?—name them."

Rip bethought himself a moment, and inquired, "Where's Nicholas Vedder?"

There was a silence for a little while, when an old man replied, in a thin, piping voice, "Nicholas Vedder! why, he is dead and gone these eighteen years! There was a wooden tombstone in the churchyard that used to tell all about him, but that's rotten and gone too."

"Where's Brom Dutcher?"

"Oh, he went off to the army in the beginning of the war;

some say he was killed at the storming of Stony Point—others say he was drowned in a squall at the foot of Antony's Nose. I don't know—he never came back again."

"Where's Van Bummel, the schoolmaster?"

"He went off to the wars too, was a great militia general, and is now in Congress."

Rip's heart died away at hearing of these sad changes in his home and friends, and finding himself thus alone in the world. Every answer puzzled him too, by treating of such enormous lapses of time, and of matters which he could not understand: war—Congress—Stony Point—he had no courage to ask after any more friends, but cried out in despair, "Does nobody here know Rip Van Winkle?"

"Oh, Rip Van Winkle!" exclaimed two or three, "oh, to be sure! that's Rip Van Winkle yonder, leaning against the tree."

Rip looked, and beheld a precise counterpart of himself as he went up the mountain; apparently as lazy, and certainly as ragged. The poor fellow was now completely confounded. He doubted his own identity, and whether he was himself or another man. In the midst of his bewilderment, the man in the cocked hat demanded who he was, and what was his name.

"God knows," exclaimed he, at his wits' end; "I'm not myself—I'm somebody else—that's me yonder—no—that's somebody else got into my shoes—I was myself last night, but I fell asleep on the mountain, and they've changed my gun, and everything's changed, and I'm changed, and I can't tell what's my name, or who I am!"

The bystanders began to look at each other, nod, wink significantly, and tap their fingers against their foreheads. There was a whisper, also, about securing the gun, and keeping the old fellow from doing mischief, at the very suggestion of which the self-important man in the cocked hat retired with some precipitation. At this critical moment a fresh, comely woman pressed through the throng to get a peep at the grey-bearded man. She had a chubby child in her arms, which, frightened at his looks, began to cry. "Hush, Rip," cried she, "hush, you little fool; the old man won't hurt you." The name of the child, the air of the mother, the tone of her voice, all awakened a train of recollections in his mind. "What is your name, my good woman?" asked he.

"Judith Gardenier."

"And your father's name?"

"Ah, poor man, Rip Van Winkle was his name, but it's twenty years since he went away from home with his gun, and never has been heard of since—his dog came home without him; but whether he shot himself, or was carried away by the Indians, nobody can tell. I was then but a little girl."

Rip had but one question more to ask; but he put it with a faltering voice:

"Where's your mother?"

"Oh, she too had died but a short time since; she broke a bloodvessel in a fit of passion at a New England pedlar."

There was a drop of comfort, at least, in this intelligence. The honest man could contain himself no longer. He caught his daughter and her child in his arms. "I am your father!" cried he. "Young Rip Van Winkle once—old Rip Van Winkle now!—Does nobody know poor Rip Van Winkle?"

All stood amazed, until an old woman, tottering out from among the crowd, put her hand to her brow, and peering under it in his face for a moment exclaimed, "Sure enough! it is Rip Van Winkle—it is himself! Welcome home again, neighbour. Why, where have you been these twenty long years?"

Rip's story was soon told, for the whole twenty years had been to him but as one night. The neighbours stared when they heard it; some were seen to wink at each other, and put their tongues in their cheeks: and the self-important man in the cocked hat, who, when the alarm was over, had returned to the field, screwed down the corners of his mouth, and shook his head—upon which there was a general shaking of the head throughout the assemblage.

It was determined, however, to take the opinion of old Peter Vanderdonk, who was seen slowly advancing up the road. He was a descendant of the historian of that name, who wrote one of the earliest accounts of the province. Peter was the most ancient inhabitant of the village, and well versed in all the wonderful events and traditions of the neighbourhood. He recollected Rip at once, and corroborated his story in the most satisfactory manner. He assured the company that it was a fact, handed down from his ancestor the historian, that the Kaatskill mountains had always been haunted by strange beings. That it was affirmed that the great Hendrick Hudson, the first discoverer of the river and country, kept a kind of vigil there every twenty years, with his crew of the Half-moon; being permitted in this way to revisit the scenes of his enterprise, and keep a guardian eye upon the river and the great city called by his name. That his father had once seen them in their old Dutch dresses playing at ninepins in a hollow of the mountain; and that he himself had heard, one summer afternoon, the sound of their balls like distant peals of thunder.

To make a long story short, the company broke up and returned to the more important concerns of the election. Rip's daughter took him home to live with her; she had a snug, well-furnished house, and a stout, cheery farmer for a husband, whom Rip recollected for one of the urchins that used to climb upon his back. As to Rip's son and heir, who was the ditto of himself, seen leaning against the tree, he was employed to work on the farm; but evinced an hereditary disposition to attend to anything else but his business.

Rip now resumed his old walks and habits; he soon found many of his former cronies, though all rather the worse for the wear and tear of time; and preferred making friends among the rising generation, with whom he soon grew into great favour.

Having nothing to do at home, and being arrived at that happy age when a man can be idle with impunity, he took his place once more on the bench at the inn-door, and was reverenced as one of the patriarchs of the village, and a chronicle of the old times "before the war." It was some time before he could get into the regular track of gossip, or could be made to comprehend the strange events that had taken place during his torpor. How that there had been a revolutionary war—that the country had thrown off the yoke of old England—and that, instead of being a subject of his Majesty George the Third, he was now a free citizen of the United States. Rip, in fact, was no politician ; the changes of states and empires made but little impression on him ; but there was one species of despotism under which he had long groaned, and that was—petticoat government. Happily that was at an end ; he had got his neck out of the yoke of matrimony, and could go in and out whenever he pleased, without dreading the tyranny of Dame Van Winkle. Whenever her name was mentioned, however, he shook his head, shrugged his shoulders, and cast up his eyes ; which might pass either for an expression of resignation to his fate, or joy at his deliverance.

He used to tell his story to every stranger that arrived at Mr Doolittle's hotel. He was observed, at first, to vary

on some points every time he told it, which was, doubtless, owing to his having so recently waked. It at last settled down precisely to the tale I have related, and not a man, woman, or child in the neighbourhood but knew it by heart. Some always pretended to doubt the

reality of it, and insisted that Rip had been out of his head, and that this was one point on which he always remained flighty. The old Dutch inhabitants, however, almost universally gave it full credit. Even to this day they never hear a thunderstorm of a summer afternoon about the Kaatskill but they say Hendrick Hudson and his crew are at their game of ninepins; and it is a common wish of all hen-pecked husbands in the neighbourhood, when life hangs heavy on their hands, that they might have a quieting draught out of Rip Van Winkle's flagon.